THE BOAT SHED

J.M. OZANNE

Published in 2021 by Hollingwood Design & Print Ltd

ISBN 978-1-5272-9447-9

If you wish to contact the author Julia Ozanne, please email:
juliaozanne@rocketmail.com

Cover and design by Hollingwood Design & Print Ltd
01422 646720
07771 965063
hello@hwdap.co.uk
www.hollingwooddesignandprint.co.uk

For Mac, James and Michael

My thanks to the following for giving me the love, support and encouragement during the difficult time writing this book:

To my family, especially my sons, James and Michael, my brother Michael and his wife Ruth, my sister Jane, brother-in-law Graham and their children.

To Margaret White, for the detailed edit of the first draft and keeping an eye on me.

To Kathy Hopewell, The Freewriter's Companion for her professional edit, comments and suggestions.

To all my friends and family far and wide. You know who you are.
And to Mac, my husband and companion in adventures, always with me in spirit.

"There is a tide in the affairs of men which, taken at the flood, leads on to fortune..."

Act IV, Scene 3 Julius Caesar

William Shakespeare, 1564-1616

CHAPTER 1

NOVEMBER 2014

I was a seventeen year-old schoolgirl when my dad died; seventeen years and two days to be precise. He was on his way home from Imperial College where he'd been lecturing and was robbed by a coke addict and then stabbed, horribly and brutally in the chest, all for a mobile phone and two hundred pounds to pay for the guy's next fix.

They caught the man running down Exhibition Road carrying the phone with dad's wallet stuffed into his back pocket and found the knife in a hedge not far from the tube station. There were witnesses, people who gave chase and bravely decked him and held him down and the CCTV footage showed the man screaming and fighting when the police arrived. After the tedious waiting for court reports and the inquest, he was sentenced to life but that was no consolation to us who were left behind in shock where the life sentence of grief really meant life, not just a token stretch at Her Majesty's Pleasure.

We were to be hosting a dinner at home that night for four of dad's colleagues and a visiting professor in astrophysics from Poland. Dad said she had more brains than the rest of them put together and had just published a paper on helping to discover a new nebula. She was eager to share her findings informally. Even by our standards of entertaining, this was a special night and called for special preparations.

Mother disappeared upstairs at five o'clock with her second gin while Milly and I set the dining table, polished glasses, attended to the food and lit the fire in the dining room. Milly nodded her seal of approval as she checked the settings, measuring the distances between the cutlery and tweaking the napkins. Nothing perturbed Milly. She'd arrived from Jamaica when I was a child, carrying a single suitcase, an armoury of recipes in her head and skills that wouldn't have disgraced a 5-star hotel. Mother was relieved when I preferred her company and the kitchen to the grand rooms upstairs and Milly became not only cook but my nurse and mentor.

"Learn to cook and wait on," she said when I'd hit the grown-up age of twelve, "and you'll never go hungry."

I shook my head, looking round at our designer kitchen sporting every electrical appliance you could think of and the cupboards and freezer stocked to the hilt.

"I don't think so," I said shaking my head, laughing, poverty and starvation outside my radar.

She wagged her figure at me. "Never know what's round the corner, girl. Just because you're clever in school and can get your tongue round all them fancy words, don't mean nothing."

Mother was sniffy about my new-found talents at the table but dad found it vaguely amusing when I practiced on them at weekend dinners, learning to balance the plates on my arm and pouring the wine just so. They indulged me, and I was glad of an excuse not to eat at the polished table groaning with long silences, mother drinking too much wine and dad itching to get back to his computer.

I was first allowed to wait on guests, first our family friend Uncle

Frank who had been around ever since I could remember. He had a thick luxuriant moustache that covered his top lip and grew down to join his beard around the sides of his mouth, bright blue eyes and a sense of mischief when we played board games and I was allowed to cheat. Then when I progressed to include some lecturers from the college, mother finally realised I was indeed useful and dad boasted that they had brought their 'shining star' up to be grounded and practical as well as clever and successful at school. They got all the credit of course; Milly was never mentioned. He boasted about my talents as I cleared plates and poured wine.

"She even edits the school magazine and writes articles for the website. Doesn't know her galaxies from her supernovas, but never mind."

I could always detect the disappointment in his voice. He wanted me to follow in his footsteps, immerse myself in the physics of refractive and reflective telescopes. I preferred words and was writing stories as soon as I could hold a pencil. They'd even named me, optimistically, after a constellation and its Greek namesake, Cassiopeia, albeit one with a dubious history. I just stuck to 'Cassie' or 'Cass' and people assumed I was called Cassandra.

It was too complicated to explain the story of Cassiopeia and I never much liked what she did for her daughter Andromeda, anyway. I mean, who goes around boasting about their beautiful daughter to the Queen of the Fishes who already has an ego the size of an ostrich egg? Stands to reason she was going to be jealous and take revenge. I loved the pictures in my old book of Greek mythology dad gave me for Christmas when I was eight, the black and white sketch of Andromeda chained to the rock and the sea monster waiting to devour her. On the next page, Perseus arrived like a scene from 'Mission; Impossible' and rescued her. Proper stories, dad used to say, tucked up beside me for bedtime reading.

I learned a lot about other mothers while I was waiting for Milly to fetch me from school in the afternoons. She was always late, bustling along with her wide hips swinging and the apron she wore showing under her coat, a stark contrast to the groups of well-groomed women with the sleek hair and polished nails, the Range Rovers and Mercedes parked nose to tail just up the road while they waited for their children. We walked.

While the other kids played around in groups until they were collected, I crept up to the fence at the edge of the playground and lurked like an animal in a cage with my face pressed against the cold bars, listening to fragments of conversation. Milly said eavesdropping was rude. I couldn't see why. They gossiped and competed with each other over their children's test marks, gymnastic medals, music exams and length times in the swimming pool.

Nobody boasted about me. Mother was either shopping at home time or at home preparing herself for evening dinners or the theatre. Even at the age of eight I think I recognised that these children were like trophies. I felt different to them, even then with my strange name and plaited hair down to my waist, straight and black like the famed long tresses of my namesake. Milly trimmed the split ends once a month with a pair of sharp scissors from the kitchen drawer. Mother disapproved but as long as I looked neat and tidy, comments about hairdressers and appointments were soon forgotten. Milly kept any creatures at bay with a nit comb kept in a plastic box, combing and conditioning until my head ached.

Protected from the world by money and security, teenage years passed in a gloriously uneventful way; Saturday shopping, meeting friends in coffee shops, holidays abroad. Dad began to be away a lot, Mother socialised and drank gin but it never impinged on my life.

Despite my so-called juvenile interest in becoming a journalist, fantasising about exciting features and seeing my name in print, it never related to the tough, uncompromising characteristics necessary to ask real questions of real people.

I carried my Saturday carrier bags with their designer logos past the homeless and the junkies and the down and outs without a thought. This was what happened to other people. Walk past, avoid, move on, crossover, don't go there. Even debate and discussion in media studies in school never seemed more than theoretical. I wasn't prepared when life took a horrible turn. How could I be?

The night dad died, we were waiting for him to come home. It was already seven o'clock. The guests had all arrived and mother and I took coats, attended to drinks and chatted away, glancing at the clock. I sat with the professor from Poland, marvelling at her perfect English. Mother apologised charmingly as seven thirty came and went and Milly put her head anxiously around the door, her dinner carefully timed for eight o'clock at the latest.

"He'll be here any minute now," she reassured our guests. The doorbell chimed cheerfully down the hall and into the front lounge.

"I'll go. He'll have forgotten his keys again," I said leaping up in relief, glancing across at mother, her eyebrows raised in mock despair. I headed down the hall, shadows and lights moving in the stained glass panel of the oak door.

The uniforms, the bemused guests uncertain whether to finish their drinks, glasses placed haphazardly on tables, coats and hats to be found, passing the dining room door as they left where the firelight flickered on crystal and the cut flowers and the immaculate place settings, police cars, blue lights and taxis outside. Then the awful silence. No, I was not prepared. Could anybody be?

I went to my room for a week and stayed there watching crap on the telly, just creeping down to the kitchen for food occasionally but couldn't bear Milly's warmth and questions of concern. School was a vague idea and friends stopped texting. I lived in a vacuum while mother prepared for the funeral in a tight-lipped haze of alcohol.

I sneaked into their bedroom one day and took one of his old jumpers out of the chest of drawers. It smelt of cigarette smoke and after shave and I put my cheek against it at night, the soft presence of my childhood daddy who read me stories so real it obliterated the recent one he seemed to have become, whose regular absence for work trips and indifference when he came home I conveniently forgot. Nobody cared about me. They left me alone. I didn't cry. I immersed myself in YouTube videos. It didn't seem real.

It was a month before they let him go. We were exhausted by then, so much to do, so many people to inform, obituaries and funeral arrangements. Mother drank steadily but never out of control. We only spoke to each other of practicalities, like suitable clothes and what flowers to order.

"Shall we have lilies, darling? Felicity will do them. What do you think, Cassie?" her words bright and brittle.

She'd put on her evening makeup as always before Uncle Frank arrived for supper and had hit the gin early, her lipstick smeared over her top lip and on the glass as she turned the pages in a copy of Cosmopolitan. I went into hate mode, irritated by his constant presence at mealtimes and his over-sympathetic manner. He'd put his arm round my shoulder one evening but I shrugged him off. I wasn't a little girl anymore but he didn't get it.

"I don't give a fuck and neither would dad," I said, about the flowers. "You might as well have dandelions. He liked dandelions. We used to blow the seed heads away and count the number of puffs like a clock. He said that's what the universe was all about – just like a puff of wind." I fled out of the room and slammed the door. That was the first time I got angry.

It was my first funeral. The crematorium was full, a sea of black impressions, of people I'd never met, who'd come from far and wide to pay their respects.

' ...sorry for your loss...sadly missed, a great man, contributions to science...' I became impervious to the condolences, horribly conscious of how mother would cope. Would she become embarrassingly drunk and stumble in the aisle, or at worst, fall over? As it was, she kept up a steady but respectable and discreet intake before the ceremony and no-one but Uncle Frank and myself would have noticed.

I was too overwhelmed by the whole thing to be openly upset; I kept that for later. Uncle Frank, to be fair, was brilliant. He was organised and supportive and we couldn't have managed without him. He even did the eulogy, simple and articulate, without the simpering platitudes dad would have hated. He'd been an astronomer after all and had the healthy belief of mankind just passing through space and time and not attributing too much importance to his place in any of it.

There was one moment, as people were taking their seats before the ceremony, when curiosity briefly overtook my emotions. We were sitting in the front row, but I turned around to look for familiar faces, staggered at the number of people, the seats filling up until there was standing room only. In the back row, tucked into the corner furthest away from the aisle and virtually hidden by an urn of Felicity's beautifully arranged lilies, a man with white hair and a white beard occupied more than his fair share of seat owing to the stick he grasped in his left hand and placed firmly away from him. He was bending forward a little as though the back to the upright seat would not accommodate his spine, his head jutting forward almost belligerently. The white hair on his hatless head and the frill of beard stood out starkly against the black of the congregation.

He lifted his head as though aware of my interest. Despite the rows of people in between us, he stared straight at me, holding my gaze until I had to turn back. I tapped my mother on the arm.

"Who's that man? Is he one of dad's friends? He looks very old."
She turned around, turned back quickly, a quick intake of breath.

"Good God," she said, her eyes now fixed firmly ahead, sitting very straight as though someone had stuck her with a cattle prod.

"What is it? Who is he?"
But the organist had stopped playing, the priest gave a short welcoming speech and we rose for the first hymn. Mother's choice, to keep everyone happy, she'd said, even if your father was a committed atheist. My breath caught in my throat when the coffin finally slid behind the curtain. I could not, would not cry.

We waited outside until the last of the condolences fogged the cold air, frozen feet in silly shoes. A convoy of taxis and cars left. A small select group of friends from the university had been invited to a local hotel. Uncle Frank had suggested a private affair, knowing mother would struggle with a bigger group. Family friends knew her well enough to make allowances if things got out of hand. I looked around in vain for the old man with the white hair. I finally collared mother on the last of the handshakes while we waited for Frank to fetch the car.

"So who was he?" I asked again.
She looked slightly vacant, as though she had detached herself from the reality of the whole thing.

"I'll tell you later," she'd said, turning her head briefly towards me.

"No, now mum, we've got a few minutes."
I needed to know, couldn't shake that targeted, piercing stare when he'd raised his head and looked directly into my eyes.

"That," she said, staring across the tended flower beds to the garden of remembrance, "was your father's great-uncle John." She shook her head. "I can't believe he came."

"I've never heard of a great-uncle John. I thought all dad's relatives were dead."

"That's because he was never mentioned. Your grandfather wouldn't talk about him and your father wouldn't either. There was a family tragedy. I don't know all the details."

I felt a cold grip on my stomach. As though all this wasn't enough, there were some bad things I didn't know about. Did I want to know? Most certainly I did. Anything to take my mind off the misery I couldn't yet face.

"Way back in the seventies," she continued, seeming almost glad to talk, "your grandfather, Owen, lived in a small town called Porthmadog in North Wales. His brother, your great-uncle John still lives there, the family going back to the nineteenth century when it was a thriving slate town.

The brothers owned a boatyard, built on one of the old slate wharves. They both lived in a village near there and had a good business renovating and building small boats. Owen, your grandfather, had been to sea as a merchant seaman in his younger days but came back to help John run the yard. John had two children and Owen had one, your father, who was about the same age as his brother's children."

"Did they fall out?"

"Worse. I don't know the details but John's two children drowned."

"Drowned? Both kids? That's dreadful."

She stamped her feet and tucked her hands under her armpits.

"God, I'm frozen. Anyway, he blamed his brother, Owen, your grandfather, for their deaths. There was a boating accident. He'd taken the two children out in a sailing dinghy. It was in all the newspapers. Of course, John never forgave him for what happened, even though it was an accident. How could he? They couldn't work together anymore and

John ostracised him completely. He'd lost both his children but his brother still had the one son, your father, who was about six at the time. Your grandfather left Wales and came to London, bringing his family with him. He worked as a tug skipper on the Thames. That's all I know."

The cars for the next funeral began to arrive, just to remind us, I thought briefly, that death escapes no-one.

"So dad was brought up with a second generation guilt trip? He never talked about it. But then Grandad was never very friendly, was he? He was always so stiff and formal when we went to visit. Imagine carrying all that guilt round with you."

I mused on the thought, like heavy iron manacles slaves wore round their ankles, locked into an inescapable horror, my memories of him softening and surprising me with a mixture of understanding and curiosity.

"I don't know why John came to the funeral," she said. "He must have known about your father's death from the papers. He'd know you'd be there, of course, to remind him of the children he'd lost and the grandchildren he might have had."

She craned her neck to look for the car. A cold mist had settled over the grounds in front of us. I was freezing.

"Anyway, you're the budding journalist so if you want to find out more, you'll do it, knowing you. Won't you?" Her voice was sharp. My nosiness had always annoyed her. But that was unfair. It was my family after all, for good or ill. Of course I wanted to know.

Uncle Frank brought the BMW up to the door of the crematorium and helped mother in, fixed her seat belt for her, unnecessarily I thought, and shut the door. I got into the back seat.

"God I need a drink," she said, "a proper one".

We drove out of the cemetery, Uncle Frank commenting how well it all went, so many people attending.

"Well done, Gracie," he said, patting her knee. Well meant, but patronising and I was surprised at my reaction. Was I criticising Uncle Frank, who'd been so brilliant? Mother didn't even notice. She swivelled in her seat suddenly so I could hear her over the purr of the engine.

"There was something else."

"What else?"

I leaned forward to catch her words.

"We went to visit him once."

I waited.

"We toured Wales once when you were a child. We left you with Milly. We drove to the Welsh border near Hereford and then through Mid Wales to Barmouth, up through Porthmadog and stayed on the Lleyn peninsula in a place called Abersoch."

"I know about that place," I said. "They have a wakeboarding festival there in the summer. Trish and I were thinking of going." I couldn't help the enthusiasm. Her look said everything.

"I mean, sometime," I said, suddenly aware of a life outside all this. But now was not the time to be talking about festivals and summer holidays.

"On the way home," she continued, "your father announced we'd take a detour and see if we could find out if John still lived near. We didn't have an address. Do you know how many Joneses there are in Wales? We found the Harbour Master who'd been there for years. It was easy then to find him still working the boatyard. Your father had an idea that perhaps he could heal the family rift, leapfrog the generations. We were only in our early thirties, full of enthusiasm and the belief that the sins of the fathers shouldn't be visited on the sons."

She turned back to face the front as the car drew up outside the Black Lion.

"What happened?"

I was desperate to know, the thirst for story-telling in me overriding the ordeal ahead.

She undid her seat belt as Frank came round to open the door.

"We found him alright. It was a chandlery and still a boatyard. There was stuff everywhere; timbers, old boats, ropes, lobster pots. He was bending over an old wooden dinghy, sanding the bottom and didn't hear us coming. Your father stood the other side until he saw us, switched off the sander and just stared, right into his eyes."

"And then?" I asked, remembering that gaze at the crematorium.

"He recognised your father of course, switched the sander back on and carried on working as though we didn't exist."

I sat back heavily against the seat.

"It was the worst experience of rejection I've ever experienced. Your father just stood there. Then we left. You could see there was no point. He was terribly upset. He was such a mild man, your father, wasn't he?"

I felt my throat tighten.

"He never talked about trying again. He'd done his best but I think he knew it was impossible. He never spoke of it again and he never told your grandfather we'd visited his brother."

I could see the old man's eyes again, the jutting chin with the white frill of beard and the belligerent angle of his head jutting forward in the pew, the hand grasping the stick firmly and shutting out those sitting next to him. The intensity of his gaze imprinted itself on my brain.

I thought that he must have been looking at me, knowing he was cheated. Maybe he was wondering what his children would have been like as teenagers and adults...and grandchildren. Would they have looked like me? Poor man. Poor dad for taking the brunt of it.

Then the tears came. I'd been so clever so far, so strong in supporting mother. Everybody said so. I couldn't go into the hotel, not like that. I forgave Uncle Frank his recent inappropriate attempts to be close and kind to me when he placed a box of tissues on my knee and handed me the car keys, understanding and practical.

"Lock up and come in when you're ready," he said.

I cried then for the loss, not just for my dad who simply didn't exist in the material world anymore but the tragedy of two little children dying, the blame shouldered by my stern grandfather and the misery of my great-uncle, old and childless.

Life went into meltdown. I started to look at my London life differently and see all the ills where once I shopped and drank lattes and giggled with my friends. I went back to school and completed a project on drug addiction and homelessness. My media studies teacher said at last there was some meat on the bones.

"You'll make a good journalist," she said. "At least you'll be working for the right reasons if you're going to do features. Just be careful you don't get too obsessed with the dark side. Anger will cloud your judgement. Don't make too many assumptions about people and their way of life. You won't always know where they're coming from."

"You mean like the cokehead killing my dad?"

"Precisely," she said, closing my folder and giving me a straight 'A'.

Mother waited for probate and then the summons to the solicitors. Shock-horror when we learned that dad had remortgaged the house several times. There were debts and loans. It was all in his name, as were all the financial transactions. He'd just wanted a quiet life with his head in another galaxy, discovering new stars and attending seminars in all parts of the world. Mother just spent money at home and dad paid off the cards without a word. I couldn't pretend to understand. Life had been so smooth. Milly had to leave, choking back sobs as she climbed into the taxi to drive to her next position, pressing an envelope with her address into my hand.

"Keep your wits about you, girl. You'll be alright. Keep in touch."
The house was sold in June. Mother drank more and took pills for depression. I buried myself in end of term exams and prepared to move schools. I didn't mind. I figured I had two choices; either go off the rails now or work hard and get out of it. I had a life to lead. I was angry about mother's predicament and angry and bemused with dad for the mess he'd left us in.

We moved out of London up to Suffolk in the July, to Bury St Edmunds where mother had lived at one time and had old friends. Mother bought a poxy terraced house with two bedrooms and an attic and a plastic front door opening straight onto the pavement, as far removed from our London house as you could imagine. The dining table I'd polished, set for dinners and learned my waitressing round, settee and chairs, dad's roll-top desk and the heavy bedroom furniture, had to go. The piano went to auction but then only dad had played it. There was a trust fund for me, an allowance to see me through university set up years ago when he hoped I'd be a budding scientist. I blessed him for that.

At the new house, there was a small back garden with a cherry tree and a wooden shed with a tin roof where I set up a desk. I connected a cable for electricity so I could work, looping it round the branches of the tree and feeding it through a badly fitting window. I couldn't bear to be in the house. I knew I had to work hard in my last year of ' A' levels, get my exams and leave home. I dreaded the thought of being stuck in the same house as my mother any longer than I had to. At least in London, I'd had the kitchen and Milly to comfort me and big spaces to get away up three flights of stairs to my bedroom with its sloping ceiling and views over the rooftops to the river and St Paul's.

I was streets ahead of my peers in my new school, loved the English and Media studies, although it was a bit tame compared to the stuff we did in London with brilliant teachers who never baulked at discussing controversial issues. I waltzed through easily, remembering my teacher's advice about obsession and judgements, with the certainty of good grades and a promise of a place at the LSE to study journalism, if I wanted it, the following September.

Uncle Frank came down on Saturdays or Sundays all through that winter and spring. He said it helped mother to have the continuity of people they'd known together. Yeah right. He just wanted a freebie for the weekend, I reckoned. My mother just seemed to absorb it with no sense of self-direction. I'd always known she and dad were happiest apart and living their own lives but I never thought she'd betray his memory so fast.

I made new acquaintances and had a lot of sleepovers. I spent Christmas and Easter with my friend Trish back in London, almost choking with envy at her big house and the lifestyle I'd left behind, Trish's flower business running side by side with her mum Felicity's interior design company. She'd always been arty, her talent for flower arranging and her impeccable makeup made me feel like a downtrodden bookworm.

"Maybe your mum will get better," Trish said. "Maybe it's delayed reaction. Maybe she just needs comfort, like your Uncle Frank. She's known him ages. She never was one for being on her own."

"Yeah, but he's not Mr Nice Guy anymore," I said. "He's a creep." I was steaming. I remembered when our mothers set up the business, an inspiring mixture of exclusive floristry and interior design for functions. It was brilliant until mother hit the bottle and dad was away so much there was nothing to hold her back. She backed out leaving Felicity to soldier on until Trish left school and joined her.

Spring came and went and the June finals loomed. I was studying in the shed with the door open one Saturday afternoon whilst Frank, I'd dropped the 'uncle' crap, and my mother, were out shopping. I was suddenly aware of his presence. He'd been standing behind me watching me work on the computer.

"You ought to get out more," he said, stroking his moustache. "Have a good time. Got a boyfriend yet?"

I swivelled round in my chair and stared at his paunchy gut that had crept up on him over the years then his face, red from the pub most likely.

"None of your business," I said. "I'm studying. Now if you don't mind..."

I turned back to the screen and ignored him, aware of my increasing irritability with his presence and not quite able to identify the reason why. He kept stroking his moustache as he talked to me. That annoyed me. He got too close. That disgusted me, but he'd been a family friend for as long as I could remember. I was far too polite but I wanted to tell him to fuck off 'cos I was working hard so I could get the hell out of this God forsaken place where nothing ever happens and I wasn't cooped up with a drunken mother and her creepy minder. He shrugged, must have read my mind, pushed himself away from the door post and left.

Where did these thoughts come from, all of a sudden? Must have been the pressure of work but I knew deep down it was grief, grief and anger that my dad was no longer around to look out for me, conveniently forgetting he'd hardly ever been there anyway. I'd have to look after myself. I'd planned time away from home in July and August before starting university in September, meeting Trish and friends from London, playing my way up through Wales via festivals to the Glass Butter Beach festival at Abersoch. The name took my fancy although I hadn't a clue about wakeboarding and swimming in the sea had never appealed but I hadn't forgotten it was near the town of Porthmadog.

After the brief encounter with the old man, my great-uncle, at dad's funeral, I was curious to see what part of the world my grandfather, Owen and his brother John came from and where my father had spent the early years of his childhood. The story of the drowned children and the circumstances surrounding it, the terrible rift and hostility between the brothers and dad's attempts at reconciliation had captured my imagination. I'd found dad's old tent and bed roll in the attic and laid out clothes to pack in the rucksack. There wasn't much room, but I had money from weekend and evenings working in fast-food joints and cafés so I could buy what I needed. I blessed Milly and her training and words of advice.

I went out with friends from school to celebrate the end of exams. After a Saturday night in Bury St Edmunds, a binge on cider and a bottle of Smirnoff, a couple of us climbed up the statue of St Edmund himself and had to be warned off by the police. It was a laugh and they were very good about it. I staggered home, desperately trying to sober up and lurched against the front door fumbling with the key. It opened and I fell into the hall onto my hands and knees, looking up at trouser legs and trying not to be sick.

He was waiting for me, good old Uncle Frank, legs planted firmly on the floor and steadying himself with one hand on the wall. He'd been drinking. I could see an empty Highland Park bottle on the coffee table behind him. I crawled backwards towards the front door and got to my feet. He blocked the way to the stairs. I made a dash to one side and slid along the wall passing close to him to reach the stairs and could smell the whisky on his breath.

"Good night," I said, hoping that was enough. I didn't want a lecture which was all I assumed he'd been waiting up for. It wasn't his place anyway.

He stepped forward, pressing me up against the wall before I could reach the bottom stair, so close his moustache brushed against my face, his hands on the wall either side of my shoulders. He breathed whisky in my face and pressed his stomach against me.

It must have been the accumulated dislike over the months and the skinful of vodka I'd had that made me angry. I brought my hands up and pushed him hard in the chest. It took him by surprise and he rocked back on his heels.

"Fuck off," I said, spitting the words out with as much venom as I could muster. I ducked down, slid under his arms and shot upstairs, locking the door to my room, heart pounding.

That's when I left.

CHAPTER 2

I brought my holiday plans forward. I couldn't stay in the house after that. I'd already planned to spend the next six weeks away, taking in as many parties and free festivals as I could and meeting Trish for the last one in North Wales before heading back home in September and preparing for uni in October.

Porthmadog was en route to Abersoch. I was planning to meet Trish who was driving up with her boyfriend Simon before heading to the festival. If I had time, I could at least just see where the boatyard was. Mother's warnings of rejection sounded in my head, but I needed to toughen up a bit if I was going to have a career being nosy. I wondered if hurts could be healed. It might be my turn to try but it was only a passing thought as I'd other things on my mind. Like having a good time.

I packed in the early hours, my head splitting with too much alcohol and my mouth like sandpaper. I'd strapped dad's old one-man tent to the bottom of the rucksack and rolled the foam mat and sleeping bag together, fixing them to the top. I tried it on. It was heavy and awkward and tugged at my hair. I took it off and swept my hair to one side, twisting it into a loose plait over my right shoulder and fixed it with a purple band. Not for the first time did I consider cutting it but only fleetingly. It had been with me a long time.

Basic wash things and some light clothes filled the rucksack and I'd stuffed an old road map into one pocket, thinking that phones with their apps are all very well, if you can charge them. Festivals and parties in the middle of nowhere might be a different story. I packed my phone, cash, bank card, tickets and my camera and crept down stairs at four-thirty avoiding the squeaky bottom step, not that mother would have heard from her gin-soaked sleep. As for dear, supportive, trustworthy Uncle Frank, the family friend, I shut him out of my head. She was welcome to the old bastard with his disgusting moustache and fat belly.

I took a carton of milk out of the fridge and fifty quid out of mother's purse which was lying on the kitchen table. I didn't need it but it seemed like an act of defiance, a violent objection to her blind faith in a man who had been dad's best friend, trusted with intimate inclusion into our family life. My own naïvety stunned me. But mother's unawareness of the change in his attitude towards me? Was it just indifference? Denial? Neglect? An elemental emotion wandered around on the fringes of my booze-soaked brain; the duty of the parent to protect their offspring. I left a note.

'Started my holiday early. Gone to stay with Trish,' I lied.

I shut the back door, breathed in the chill of dawn, stepped out onto the pavement and hefted the rucksack onto my back with the sleeping bag pushing into my neck and headed out of town to catch the bus. It was a long wait, the bus-shelter stinking from a pile of vomit in one corner. Welcome to Bury St. Edmunds, I thought, but I'd planned this first stage by bus to take me as far as Coventry. The bus trundled past Newmarket, the headquarters of flat racing, past fields dotted with expensive horse flesh and the roads beginning to fill up with cars and wagons for the day's racing. I rang Trish. I was mildly bored with the flat landscape and knew nothing about racing and horses except that they didn't have any choice in the day's sport.

"I'm on the road," I said. "I decided to leave home early. There's a party in Hay-on-Wye. I'm meeting some friends from school."

She must have caught the tone in my voice.

"It's not like you to change plans," she said. "You're always the one who sticks to routine. Not like muddly old me." She paused.

"Everything alright, Cass?"

Muddly but perceptive, that's Trish, picking up the mood you're in before you've hardly opened your mouth.

"Yeah, fine. I just had to get away. That's all."

"Okay," she said. "I gather there's a problem. Will you tell?"

"Not now. When I see you. Maybe. I'll be fine."

The bus lurched around a corner.

"Hay-on-Wye's bit of an awkward place to get to, isn't it? What about buses and stuff up through Wales? How are you going to get there?"

I heard suspicion in her voice. She didn't wait for me to answer.

"You're not going to hitch, are you?"

Oh, for God's sake, I thought, exasperated.

"And you're not my nanny, are you?" I retorted. "I'll be in touch. See you in a few weeks."

I hadn't meant to be sharp but I was tired and hung-over and suddenly sick of everyone, including well-meaning Trish. There was silence. I could feel the hurt down the phone.

"I've got buses and trains booked," I said, "and I'm meeting school friends with a car in Worcester. They reckon there's a load of people just travelling up through Wales, going from one party to another. There are families and couples as well. All ages. It's not like it used to be. Probably safer than Bury St. sodding Edmund's on a Saturday night. I'll be fine."

I injected some confidence and enthusiasm into my voice, even as I felt guilty about lying. It didn't sit comfortably, disguising the anxiety I felt about the reality. I'd never been truly away on my own before, making decisions and looking out for myself.

"I'll be in touch. See you in a few weeks. Sorry I snapped at you."

"You're forgiven. Just stay safe," she said, "promise?"

"I promise. Thanks for caring."

I shut the phone off with a sense of relief. I didn't need to talk to anyone, didn't even want to text or check emails. I just wanted to be on my own, to sort out my head, to have time to think and grieve properly about dad, try to understand what went wrong with mother and not hate her too much for what she had become, to mull over tragedies and old family secrets, trust in other people and all the screwed up messages trying to connect in my brain. I needed some space, a change of pace, a new perspective and to immerse myself in the immediacy of survival instead of ancient family dynamics.

It took a couple of days before I started to feel calmer. I crossed over the M1 and M6 corridors via back-roads and villages, getting off buses in the middle of nowhere to bunk down for the night behind hedges, eating burgers at cheap cafes and making sure no-one was interested in me.

They weren't. It was key holiday time and a lone backpacker didn't raise an eyebrow. I'd expected a sense of trepidation, if not fear, but felt increasingly, unaccountably safe in the middle of nowhere, putting up dad's tent under hedgerows at the edges of hay fields ripening in the sun. I began to feel the confidence I'd lost, doing something on my own, something I'd never done before. Was there an urban myth I'd grown up with? Keep safe, never be alone in isolated places, beware of strangers... But it felt just fine in the company of rustling mice and voles and once the high pitched yelp of a fox. No threat to me. I was surprisingly unafraid.

I sneaked into a small copse one night through a broken-down gate decorated with the dried-out corpses of moles, their snouts and claws like flattened cardboard, the orange binder twine round their necks contrasting with the dull black of their coats as a stark warning to other would-be diggers and wreckers of fields. There was a peeling sign nailed to the gatepost with the phone number for a 'Michael Flynn, Mole Catcher.' Was the hanging of the beasts proof to the landowner that Mr Flynn was doing his job? I shut the gate carefully, not wishing to dislodge the bodies, more curious than disgusted.

It was blissfully peaceful with no one to answer to, just the rustling of the trees and the call of wood pigeons mingling with the distant roar of traffic. I wasn't far away enough from the madding crowd just yet for total silence, the holiday makers hurtling from north to south and south to north in search of their holiday nirvana just as I remembered as a child with mum and dad.

I watched the countryside change through the rolling hills of Worcestershire and finally via Hereford across the border into Wales, getting off the bus in Hay and counting my already dwindling cash. It was time to find some friends.

The music and camping in a field outside Hay and then up through Mid Wales to Llangurig turned into balloon-filled parties with laughter, gentle good humour and friendliness fuelled by good old nitrous oxide and the sweet smell of cannabis in the air. I baulked at the occasional offer of the hard stuff. I didn't do acid or coke either, preferring to keep my brain cells intact.

"Just a sniff, love? It's clean."

If the dealers knew about my dad and his totally unnecessary death, would they have approached me? Probably I thought. It wouldn't mean much to them. Dealing and making money was one thing, what the buyer did with their purchases was their problem.

I was hitching a lift out of Hay when I met up with a couple on the road for the summer. It seemed safe enough with children on board, two little girls strapped into seats behind us. They squeezed me into the front seat of the battered red LDV which had been converted for sleeping, introduced themselves as Zoe and Dave and we headed north to family chatter and 'I Spy'.

On one side of the van there were two little box-beds made out of plywood with carved figureheads like Viking warships. Drawings and sketches covered the sides of the van. The children slept safely here while their parents slung hammocks outside from poles or convenient trees, like guard-dogs watching over their princesses.

There was no pink prissiness here, though. The little girls ran around barefoot with grubby faces and tangled blonde curls, confident and curious, articulate and courteous and fascinated by my long hair. I showed them how to braid their unruly locks into French plaits, my dark and now lanky tresses past their best and needing a wash.

My preconceived ideas about their alternative ways of living as hippies on the road were politely shattered when Zoe said they were working teachers. She taught art and Dave, technology.

We sat outside under the trees one afternoon, the cooking fire smouldering at our feet, children's voices floating up from a nearby stream and watched the wood-smoke curl up through the leaves.

"We bring the children away from home every summer, away from their phones and tablets and computer games," explained Zoe. " They live in a natural environment for six weeks, play with other like-minded children, meet different people, some very strange," she added, laughing, "make up their own games, eat everything that's given to them and sleep like logs."

"But they have to go home, back to school, back to reality?"

She shrugged.

"They just fall straight back into it. But the difference is in the way they deal with peer group issues and falling out with each other; you know, typical seven year old stuff. It's their thoughtful way of dealing with it. They seem able to take problems out of their context, analyse them and look at them objectively. Not common for children."

She was thoughtful for a moment.

"You don't know much about small children, do you? Although you're very natural with them," she added. "They love your story telling."

I shook my head.

"Small children were never part of my teenage life." I said. "I suppose you tend to disappear into a world of your own making when you're an only child, I've always disappeared into books. Saved me worrying about real life."

"Was it that bad?" she asked, concern on her face. "Real life, I mean?"

"Good God, no. I was a spoilt kid with a sheltered life in a respectable middle class part of London."

"So what are you escaping from, then?"

I had to stop and think, dad's death too raw to invite analysis, loyalty to my mother and some time away had diluted the anger that had been festering. I shrugged.

"Everyone seemed to be too busy to spend any time with me when I got to be a teenager. Maybe they didn't want to. The more I disappeared into my own head the less they thought I needed anything. Except for Milly, of course, who loved the novelty of teaching me to be a waitress. That was the best bit."

"You must have had friends though?"

"Yeah, coffee and shopping in groups but I was never as outgoing and fearless as your little ones. I was always worried about something, or what people thought of me."

"Ha, good old anxiety. It's a great disorganiser of behaviour. Our two are at the age when kids have fantastic beliefs about the world. They have fantasies, worry about things they can't rationalise. That's why we bring them to these places. There's nothing much hidden when you're close to the earth. We only protect them from obvious dangers and try to explain the rest; the drugs and the drink and the odd bods it produces."

"They seem so free," I said, watching them in the distance in a group of other kids. "Don't you worry about them getting older, out of your control? Drugs and stuff?"

"They'll make their own decisions," she said, throwing a log on the fire. "The only thing we can do is make sure they're well-informed. That's why we bring them out here every summer. There's not much they haven't seen with drugs and drink. They'll make up their own minds when they're older whether they want to be part of it or not."

There'd been plenty of substances to choose from at everywhere I'd been. I could have been flying on anything from coke to ecstasy but I had a very good and sound reason not to. I'd read up a lot after dad's death, things I didn't really know about, especially the increase in coke and crack available on the streets. It seemed to be no longer just the stuff of parties.

I looked at the two little girls at the edge of the wood and wondered how much information they would take in, and more importantly, use for their own good. They burst out of the trees, blonde curls flying, carrying matchboxes full of insects, all alive and kicking and needing to be identified and sketched and let loose. Zoe emptied the bugs into an old washing-up bowl and fetched a magnifying glass from the van. Time, that's what she gave them, I thought in a moment of overwhelming revelation and sadness. She gave them her time. I could have cried. I lay back on the grass in the warm sunshine, closed my eyes and listened to the sounds of the pigeons cooing in the trees and the crackling of the sticks on the fire.

It seemed idyllic at that moment, this fantasy lifestyle of freedom and community living. Not completely for Zoe and Dave though, their feet firmly planted in careers and mortgage and the trappings of a conventional life but keeping this summer idyll for their kids. For some of the others who lived this way full-time? I didn't know, wasn't sure and was damned if I was going to make assumptions either, having had my head bitten off several times. Was I learning after all? Would it make a story? I filed it all away for another time.

I watched the little girls picking out the insects carefully and drawing pictures, sharing the tweezers and consulting each other. Nobody whined and nobody moaned. I envied them. I didn't have siblings and was too clever at junior school to be comfortable as part of a group, spending time on my own to avoid any bullying. Milly was my saviour at home with her wonderful, warm, unconditional positive love. These parents were like her; warm people, full of cuddles and praise and time to explain everything. Lucky kids.

I told Zoe and Dave about dad's death one night when the children were asleep, the logs spitting and flickering on the fire and the bottle of vodka I'd picked up at the local shop loosening my tongue. We'd only discovered details of the man at the inquest and the reasons for his actions that night; a paranoid schizophrenic who'd failed to take his medication on parole from a psychiatric unit, the failed supervision of an over-stretched mental health team and a flood of top strength crack that had hit the streets.

I explained what had happened at the funeral and the appearance of the old man with the white hair, then what my mother had told me about my great-uncle John and my grandfather, blamed for the death of his brother's children and the unrelenting enmity between the two. I told them about dad's sad efforts to heal the rift and the total rejection that had upset him so much.

"I thought I could at least go and look for the boatyard. If I met him..."

Their faces were earnest in the firelight, focused on mine.

"Should I try again?" I asked them, complete strangers I'd only just met. I trusted their judgement, their compassion and understanding.

"Yes," Zoe said, emphatically, "and keep trying. He'll be hurting. All those years without his children?" looking back to the van and the sleeping girls. We finished the vodka in silence.

They dropped me in Machynlleth in a shower of rain, sharing hugs and tears in the car-park and drove off on their way to Aberystwyth, leaving me warm and somehow more substantial.

It was market day in Machynlleth, the wide main street lined with stalls selling everything from watchstraps to local cheese, fresh bread and Indian clothes, wind chimes and joss sticks that filled the street air with sounds and scents. Takeaway stalls oozed Thai noodles, roast lamb baguettes dripping with mint sauce and gravy, Welsh Black beefburgers on buns and vegan bean stews with crusty rolls. I'd had a week of beans and brown rice and nearly convinced myself I should be vegan.

I found a vegetarian cafe and bought a bowl of roasted pepper and tomato soup with fresh bread, mopping up the juices and feeling pious. I stuck out my legs and studied my feet cased in my faded Doc Martens with their silver stars and purple laces and began to feel like a seasoned New Age traveller, the Jesus sandals in my rucksack kept for dry days. I felt fit, eating differently, out in the fresh air and toned up with all the camping. I began to explore being part of something else, some sense of belonging to a new life, a new way of thinking, a new culture of vegan stews and tofu.

But it was transient. The aroma of bacon rolls, roast meat and cheese burgers wafted down the street, mingling with scented candles and patchouli from a nearby stall. My head itched and my hair was coarse and greasy. I wanted to have a bath, to shave my legs and armpits, tidy up my eyebrows and put on makeup. I was a city girl after all, playing at escapism, dipping into a world of mock ethnicity, fake spiritualism and the zeitgeist of a generation grasping at straws in a drug-induced haze. But that was unfair. I castigated myself, remembering my new friends and their approach to parenthood, their awareness of bringing their children closer to nature for at least a part of their lives. I took my bowl and plate back inside.

"Is there a leisure centre here with a swimming pool?" I asked. But I decided it could wait. I'd arranged to meet Trish in Porthmadog in a few days. I'd clean up there before the festival. I scrounged a lift to the outskirts of town, crossed over the river Dyfi and hit the A487 to Dolgellau, stopping just before a lay-by and stuck out my thumb.

But it was holiday time. Cars whizzed past me, back seats spilling over with children, dogs, tents battened down on roof racks and bicycles strapped on racks at the back. I couldn't blame them for not stopping but as the morning wore on, I started to panic I'd miss my deadline for the weekend and didn't want to spend money on a bus. I walked as far as Corris, the steep sided gorge darkening as the sun disappeared and dusk set in and found the cafe in the visitor centre before it closed for the night. I bought a bottle of water and two sausage rolls heated up reluctantly by the tired girl behind the counter and set off to find somewhere to pitch the tent away from the road and away from people.

It wasn't hard and I settled to sleep fitfully, alert to all the strange sounds, missing the company and comfort of Zoe and Dave, the chatter of the little girls and the protection of the group and amazed at myself for braving the nights in Middle England on my own. But it was different here, more elemental than the rolling fields with the distant hum of a motorway and the constant faint light from towns and cities. Here, it was dark, inky dark with just the rushing of water in the gorge and the low moan of wind in the pine forests around me.

I surfaced in the morning, tired and grubby, realisation of the date finally dawning on me. It was Thursday, 'A'-level results day and no signal on my phone. I imagined the frenetic activity at school, the sick feeling of dreaded anticipation and the hysteria or tears over the brown envelopes laid out on the long desks in the hall. It was too early to phone anyway and I felt no more than a frisson of excitement, a dull optimism of a predictable outcome. I could be forgiven for accusing myself of arrogance, but I knew I'd walked through the papers as easily and enjoyably as the coursework. If I didn't get straight 'A's I'd be surprised. I picked up a signal around lunchtime and spoke to my tutor. She was ecstatic.

"You've got A's in English and Psychology and an A* in Media Studies. Well done Cassie."

"That's brilliant," I said, "and thanks for your advice."

"What advice would that be?"

"The bit about making assumptions about people's lives," I said. I was cold and wet, absorbed her congratulations and enthusiasm with good grace and headed back onto the road. I'd celebrate with Trish and Simon at the weekend. I remembered to text my mother.

The weather turned cold and it rained; heavy persistent rain that fogged the forest around me and soaked my boots. I was tired and footsore, damp through to my skin, hungry and grouchy from eating junk food. I resolved to catch a bus to Porthmadog, never mind the cost. I waited in a bus shelter near the river in Dolgellau, the rain pouring down and my jeans wet below the knees where it dripped off my plastic poncho. It was two hours to the next bus.

"You looking for a lift, love?"

A silver Focus drew up, the passenger window winding down and the innocuous sound of Radio Two over the sound of the rain thundering on the roof of the bus shelter. I moved towards the car, despite myself and Trish's words of warning in my ear, and was met with a blast of warmth and a nice-enough face, grey suit and white shirt and an air of respectability. Risky, I knew, but I'd learned a lot in the last few weeks, partying with off-beats of all ages, would-be spiritualists waving wands of sage twigs to dispel evil and even being groped through a hammock one night. I was wary, but the temptation was too much. Milly's mantra rose up to the forefront of my consciousness. "Keep your wits about you, girl."

I lowered myself into the passenger seat and kept my rucksack firmly on my knees.

"Do you want to put that in the back?" he said.

"No you're alright, thanks," keeping a tight hold.

He leaned across me to reach for my seat belt.

"I got it," I said firmly, pulling it down and clicking it into place.

"Don't want to be stopped for that," he said.

"Right," I said, staring straight ahead as he pulled out into the road, over the bridge and turned onto the A470, past the turning to Barmouth and headed for Porthmadog.

The car gathered speed as the road widened, through the hamlet of Glanllwyd dotted with stone houses. Newly planted trees on estate grounds stood beside sawn-off bases of massive trees that had survived hundreds of years, the new saplings in wire cages for protection. The forest of Coed y Brenin opened out onto moorland falling away down to the lake at Trawsfynydd and the defunct nuclear power station, its concrete edifice rising out of the water, slate-grey, dotted with whitecaps and forbidding in the rain. They'd used the power station as a background to the film "The Last Knight," covering the concrete building with a fake castle. I preferred the film effects.

He drove smoothly, chatting away about his work as a salesman for farm supplies, powering through the bends with the confidence of one who drives for a living. I told him nothing about myself, replying in monosyllables without appearing to be being rude. I was out of my comfort zone and knew I wouldn't settle until I got out of the car. But it was better than walking; my jeans dried in the blast from the heater and my feet warmed up. I pulled the map from my pocket and checked the route.

"Can you drop me off at the station in Porthmadog? The Ffestiniog Railway station. I'm meeting friends."

He nodded, drove through the village of Penrhyndeudraeth, towards the entrance for Portmeirion, indicated suddenly and turned off to the right.

"Short cut," he said, "avoids the queues"

"Liar," I thought, all my senses now on high alert as we crossed a railway bridge, forked right again down a narrow lane. I'd already reached for the door handle when he pulled in by a gate leading into a field. I reached down with my left hand and unclipped my belt.

"Oy," he said, the charming voice gone. "Looks as though you could do with twenty quid."

He slapped a twenty pound note on the dashboard and nodded meaningfully towards his crotch, right hand on his flies and the left reaching for the door lock on the dash.

But I was already flinging the door open, bundling my rucksack onto the mud and tumbling after it.

"Stinking hippy bitch."

I slammed the door on his words. He spun the back wheels, showering me in mud and grit and accelerated away, leaving me on the gravel with my back against the stone gate post and my new-found confidence in pieces. I stood up, trembling, my hands shaking as I hefted the rucksack onto my back, turned and threw up over the gate.

CHAPTER 3

I walked the rest of the way to the engine sheds at the beginning of the railway embankment called the Cob, my stomach sore with retching and my hands still shaky from the encounter. The thought of a blow-job with a total stranger who'd offered to pay me and thought I was a hippy on the game had been too much on top of the sausage rolls and chocolate bars I'd eaten but the walking soothed me, the immediate sense of disgust receding as normality returned. I wondered what would have happened if I'd taken the twenty quid and legged it. Then I thought of the awful possibilities if he'd hit the button and locked me in. What if... what if...

Steep steps had been built from the road into the protective wall of the Cob. At the top, I stood at the side of the railway track taking in the breathtaking perspective over the mountains to my right and away out to sea to my left and drank the rest of my last bottle of water. I'd walked off the worst of the incident by now, angry with myself for letting it happen and knowing I'd had a narrow escape. So much for 'A' levels and related intelligence, I thought ruefully, sucking a mint to take the taste of puke out of my mouth. You can learn what you like in textbook psychology but learning to read people's motives obviously hadn't quite hit the mark yet. To be fair though, I was prepared for something, but hadn't expected that. Stinking hippy? I needed a makeover and a bath. I slipped my rucksack off and pulled out dad's old Ordnance Survey map and a small guide book I'd picked up in Machynlleth. I had time to spare now before meeting Trish and Simon. The sun was out, helping to put the day behind me.

I'd never really thought about views much. London was a vista of buildings with the odd park and green belt and Suffolk I hardly noticed with my head in exams. But this was a view that stopped me in my tracks, despite the pervy salesman and the promise of a cold lager at Spooners, the pub at the other end of the footpath and railway line where I'd arranged to meet Trish. I sat down cross-legged on the gravel and folded the map in half trying to make sense of it with an unpractised eye.

The road below me buzzed with cars heading for holiday destinations on the Lleyn peninsula, but beyond that the land stretched away inland to the foot of the mountains of Snowdonia whose names I couldn't pronounce, their peaks a pale misty blue. I traced a blue line on the map with my finger then looked up from the map to follow where the Glaslyn River broadened out, turned in a wide arc and ran parallel to the side of the road opposite me before disappearing through a series of lock-gates I'd read about in the guide book and into the harbour. A small herd of cows stood motionless at the edge of the Glaslyn, a still life in dun and black and white. The clearing skies let the sun through and picked out the purples and greys and muted greens of rock and ferns and heathers in the distance. After the oppressive forests of Corris and the heavy rain, I could feel my mind expanding, throwing off the unpleasant experience and the loneliness of the last few days.

In the guide book, I flipped through the history of the pile of rocks that made up the embankment built between 1808 and 1812. William

Madocks knew what he was doing alright, but all for different reasons. He could never have predicted the future after the demise of the slate industry and the railway transport from the slate mines, the trains now an attraction for thousands of steam enthusiasts from all over the world with their passion for small gauge railways. I wondered if he had been as wowed by the landscape as I was. I thought not, probably, up to his neck in slate and stone, wind and weather and the ever-present threat of the sea he was trying to keep out.

I turned and looked out towards the sea. The tide was way out, the salt marsh below me dry but broken up by ribbons of dark water, a pattern of deep, snaking gullies with mud and sand banks glistening in the sun and dotted white with grazing sheep. The sand stretched on forever to a line of glittering water far away on the horizon. I checked the map again, following the rivers Dywrd and Glaslyn with a grubby finger until they merged heading out to sea.

"That's Portmeirion over the back of that hill there."

A disembodied voice floated down from above me. I turned and stared at a pair of white ankle socks with a yellow stripe around the top and an adult version of Clark's sandals for children. The ankles rose to a pair of hairless legs and two knobbly knees. I forced my gaze further up; baggy shorts and a blue shirt tucked in to a leather belt, Ffestiniog Railway emblazoned in big letters on the pocket.

"It's where they filmed 'The Prisoner,' you know. You must have heard of it. Visiting are you, miss?"

I stood up, a head taller than the little man with the squeaky voice and a black Beanie on a round head with wisps of hair sticking out below the knitted rim. Pale blue eyes looked out of round, frameless glasses, his head cocked on one side like a sparrow. He carried on as though reading from a script.

"To my left, the wooded cliffs of that peninsula hide the famous village of Portmeirion. It's tucked around the other side and has been home to the sixties series of 'The Prisoner,' and still holds regular commemorative events and the V6 festival these days."

Pushing the guide book back into the rucksack, I hefted it on to my shoulder ready to go. I didn't need it while he was still talking, my own private tour guide and a creepy railway nerd to boot. My manners took a back step. I took an obligatory photograph out towards Portmeirion, thanked him in mid-sentence and backed away, heading towards the town.

"Hugh Phillips," he called. "I work on the railway in the summer. If you want a tour of the engine sheds...Well, enjoy your holiday."

Thanks but no thanks. I was beginning to wonder why I attracted such creeps in such a short space of time: my mother's lecherous family friend, the pervy salesman and now a guy who probably had a spooky career stuffing dead animals. I picked up the pace, waved to happy kids in the train window as it steamed past and chuckled to myself all the way to Spooners, the pub on the platform.

The path followed the rail track along the top of the embankment to the station where an immaculate steam train painted racing green with polished copper brightwork and a funnel pumping steam into the air waited, the coaches full of people smiling and waving and the driver leaning out of the cab. I waved back, focused on my next job before meeting Trish and made my way to the ticket office, used my precious credit card for emergencies only and booked trains all the way back to London. No more hitching for me. I could get a train back to Bury St Edmunds and home easily from there but I didn't feel like calling it home any more.

Trish and Simon were sitting inside Spooners, a cold lager and a packet of crisps ready for me on the table. She rushed over and hugged me.

"God, you look like a bloody hippy. And you stink."

This was normality and after two lagers I didn't care whether I stank or not.

"I'll go for a swim when we get there," I reassured her. We toasted the summer and drove to the festival in Llanbedrog in high spirits.

Despite the music, having a good time and laughing a lot, my great-uncle John sneaked into my head at every break in the festival, every quiet moment, even at night. Should I go and find him? Would I ever get an opportunity to try again? He was old. What if he died while I was debating the pros and cons of the right thing to do? How it would affect me? Would I regret not trying or become involved in something I didn't want? What would dad have said? I remembered the passionate outburst from Zoe and Dave and their advice. Try, they'd said, and keep trying. If you don't find out, you'll never know and might regret it. It's too late when he's gone. It all sounded a bit sanctimonious now in the cold light of day without the ambience of the dope and the wood-smoke.

Trish and I took some beers down to the beach on Saturday night, sore from a flip round the BMX track and a go at windsurfing. I'd never been keen on bikes. Didn't much like getting wet, either but at least I'd cleaned up a bit. I hadn't had a chance to tell her about our 'trustworthy' family friend, Uncle Frank, but now seemed a good time to explain.

"...so I don't really want to go home," I said, "before I have to in case he's still there. I'll hang on as long as I can up here, go home and pack and then come straight down to the start of term. Will you still have me to stay until I get a room somewhere or stay in halls? I haven't decided yet but the offer's there if I want to."

"Of course, goes without saying," she said. "Mum says you can have the room for as long as you want. If she knew about Frank, she'd be furious. It's a big house. We need to let the room so you might as well stay."

She understood.

"Anyway, I'm not coming back to London with you tomorrow. I'm staying on here at the festival until it closes. Just for Sunday night. I said I'd help out clearing up in the food tent and then..."

"Then what? Where will you stay? How are you going to get home? You won't hitch, will you?"

The familiar warning crept into her voice.

"Ah," I said, enjoying winding her up. "Secret weapon."

I unzipped my body belt and pulled out a wad of train tickets, waving them under her nose.

"All the way home; train, train and more train. It's not quite straight forward getting out of here. Bought them on Friday before I met up with you. The lady in the ticket office just organised it all. She was brilliant."

Trish would never know what prompted me to do it. I wasn't going to tell her about the pervy salesman and my close escape.

"I'm going to stay to the end of the week. Or longer. There's something I need to do."

We sat on the beach listening to snatches of music from the band on stage back at the festival, the thud of the bass guitar filtering through the rattle of stones as the waves broke at our feet. The sun dipped below the trees behind us and the bay darkened, the sea changing from warm invitation to a deep, petrol blue. It felt chill, suddenly, and unwelcoming, the few boats at anchor like cardboard cut-outs in the still water. I shivered.

"Cold?" Trish asked.

"No, not really. I was just thinking about facing my demons."

"You're going to find your great-uncle John, from the funeral, aren't you? Is he the demon?"

"No, it's not that. I'm not scared of an old man."

I'd chewed it over all day. Trish knew about the surprise visit at the funeral and I'd told her the family history about the drowning. I'd made up my mind to find him and accept the consequences, rejection or not. I'd got that far. But I'd just told her about Frank.

"I don't see why you're so upset," she said. "He's just a dirty old man who'd had too much to drink."

"It's not that. It's the betrayal. He'd been like a second father. I'd sat on his knee, been for walks and holidays with him, Christmas, all the stuff childhood memories are made of. Makes me feel a bit sick."

"Have you told your mum?"

I shook my head thinking of all the text messages I'd sent just to inform her I was alive, if nothing else. Her whisky-swilling lover wasn't exactly a subject for text message or phone calls. It would have to wait until I faced her. Or maybe never. Maybe I'd just forget I had a home.

"No. That'll have to wait. For now, I think I've decided to go ahead and try and meet my great-uncle John."

"You looked up the press coverage on the children, though, didn't you?"

"The inquest said accidental death by drowning. But my grandfather was an experienced sailor, a seasoned mariner. It doesn't make sense." My head was bursting with questions, gaze drawn to the open sea, dark and forbidding now. She laughed suddenly.

"You've changed since you've been on the road, haven't you? Since when have you been interested in family tragedies? It was all nails and designer clothes the last time I saw you."

"I'm not really but I learned a lot when I was on the road, different ways of looking at things and why people behave the way they do. Besides which, you know me. I love a good story and I've just got to find out."

Trish picked up some pebbles and lobbed them into the sea.

"Ever the budding journalist," she said. "And where are you going to stay?"

"Bit of luck. You know Helen from last night? Works in the food tent? Well, we got talking. I told her the story. She was a stranger so it didn't seem to matter and I'd had a bit to drink."
The music had died to a round of applause and shouts.

"I saw her again this morning. She hadn't let on she knew about my great-uncle, John Jones, Boat Builder of Porthmadog but she'd phoned her Nain to see if I could camp in her garden for a few days. She could tell me more about it, she said. Her Nain was born and brought up there and went to school with Uncle John. She said she'd be happy to talk to me. She didn't know there were any distant relatives. Can you believe it? Coincidence or what?"
Trish stared at me.

"Bloody hell," was all she said. "You really are becoming an opportunist. God help the world of journalism."
She wished me good luck when she left on Sunday, apprehension in her voice but spared me a lecture. She reminded me, unnecessarily, that term started in a few weeks.

"I'll be back. See you in London. I won't be staying at home any longer than I have to and only if that disgusting man's not there."

I left with Helen on Monday afternoon in the aftermath of the festival. I liked her, a no-nonsense practical girl a few years older than me, who cleared up the food tent and issued instructions like a military general. We drove out of the site avoiding the bin lorries and toilet trucks, her battered Astra bumping over the rutted tracks and Helen muttering apologies for the sand, plastic bottles and chocolate wrappers in the foot-well.

We drove through the town of Pwllheli and out onto the road to Porthmadog, passing the turn to Llanystumdwy and the home of Lloyd George, and took a turning over the railway line in Criccieth towards the sea, along the promenade and up past the castle. She chattered away non-stop about the local history. I was full of questions I hadn't had a chance to ask. She pulled in at the bottom of the hill by the RNLI Station.

"Time for a treat as a reward for hard work," she said as we walked back up the hill to an ice-cream parlour.

"Cadwaladers," she said. "Been here for years but it's a bit posher now. Best ice-cream in the world. Just plain with a Flake for me but there's masses of choice."

We sat on a bench overlooking the beach with the tide lapping at the wall below, savouring the sweet richness as it dripped and melted down the sides of the cones. I asked her which hotels she worked at outside the festival. Did she cook or wait on? She laughed and spluttered, dribbling ice-cream down her chin, wiping it unselfconsciously with the back of her hand, paused, wiped her hands on a tissue and sat back against the bench, still chuckling.

"What? Have I said something funny?" I asked.

She finished the last of her cone and wiped her fingers on her jeans.

"You know when we met on Friday? I thought you were a down and out waster, lost your way on drugs and stuff."

"Did you?" I was horrified.

"Then you told me you were off to the LSE in a few weeks to do a degree in journalism. Shook me a bit."

"So..." I waited.

"Well, I'm not a waitress. Third year medical student at St. Barts. I stay with Nain during the summer holidays and do a bit of bar work. Home is in London."

She grinned. "Both wrong, eh?"

"Touché," I said. "Never judge a book... How brilliant. What will you do when you've trained?"

She shrugged.

"Not sure yet. Either surgery or maybe pathology."

"No. That's creepy. Cutting up dead bodies? Like Silent Witness?" She picked up the horror in my voice.

"Well you can go off live people sometimes. At least the dead'll give up their secrets without arguing."

"Wow," I said slightly taken aback as the ice-cream ran down the back of my hand. "Cool."

"And you?" she asked.

"Features," I said, no hesitation there, "if I'm lucky or good enough. Jobs on a paper that does features are like hen's teeth. I'll probably have to freelance if I want to get anywhere. It's a way off yet, though. Even when I get my degree there's still post degree stuff you have to do working for a paper to be qualified."

The road swept uphill out of Criccieth opening out to the view below the road, a panorama of white surf and shingle beach curving around to a headland of dark rock jutting into the sea.

"That's Black Rock. Craig Ddu. There are caves on the other side. Looks different in a storm, I can tell you. The other side is my playground, the beach, hence the state of the car. It's a big enough beach to bawl your eyes out on and no-one to know. Miles of nothing in the winter except the gulls and oyster catchers. At low tide you can walk over the channel onto the North Bank. The tide can sneak in behind you and cut you off in the blink of an eye. I'll show you if you're here for a couple of days."

We turned right off the main street in Porthmadog, up the hill past a Catholic Church and turned off left to a village sign-posted to Borth-y-Gest.

The bay opened out in a curve bordered by a protective crescent of sea wall, the road lined with pretty houses decorated with colourful hanging baskets and plants in tubs. The tide was in and filled the bay, small boats dotted out towards the estuary where the sea flooded past the entrance between headlands. She turned into a drive and stopped facing a high stone wall with a garden gate set into it.

"Nain's place," she said, switching off the engine. "Bed and Breakfast and full up at the moment. Nain says you can put the tent up at the bottom of the garden. She does evening meals as well, so I thought we'd just go up the road to the cafe for a bite tonight and then you can meet her tomorrow properly for a chat when the guests have all gone out for the day."

I pitched the tent under some apple trees at the bottom of the garden, separated from a marshy stretch of land by a wire fence that did nothing to deter the midges that night. There was an outside loo in a stone building by the house. I felt safe and secure there in the garden with a full belly of scampi and chips and a natter with Helen over a swig of her favourite vodka in the tent before shutting the flaps and snuggling into my sleeping bag, head full of the ship-building past of this picturesque holiday place.

Helen was passionate about it, brought up on the history even though she lived in London now and regaled me with tales of shipwrecks and drowned pilots and the slate industry. I almost forgot why I'd chosen to be there for a brief moment. I still wasn't sure what to do about my great-uncle looming like a black cloud on the fringes of my consciousness. I'd told her how I felt.

"Nain'll help. She's part of this place. She went to school with your great-uncle and then came back from college to be the teacher in the same school. There's not much she doesn't know. She'll tell you what's best to do tomorrow. It'll all become clear. You'll see."

I went to sleep sensing a change in the weather with the sound of rain pattering on the canvas and the incessant moan of the sea on the bar.

She called me in the morning, flinging back the tent flap, the grass damp from the overnight rain.

"Nain says come in for breakfast."

I stank of sweat and my head itched.

"I'm not very clean," I said, embarrassed by the thought of being dirty in someone else's house.

I sat up clutching the sleeping bag around me. She was crouched down outside the tent.

"We can sort that. Nain's gone out. She says you can have a bath while I cook you breakfast. Anyway, she wants to talk to you when she comes back. The guests are all gone for the day."

I followed her through the door into the kitchen and through into the hall. The house was homely and comfortable, the kitchen warm and infused with the smell of breakfasts, bacon and eggs, toast and coffee, the dishwasher purring gently next to the sink. Tourist brochures littered the Welsh dresser in the hall and I sneaked a look at the living room for the guests with over-stuffed chairs and art prints of local beauty spots. A gas fire set into an old-fashioned fire surround of tiles on one wall was topped by a mantelpiece dotted with brass ornaments and a grandmother clock. It was about as traditional as it could be for a seaside bed and breakfast. Lucky Helen to have this to spend her holidays in.

"The bathroom's up the stairs on your right. Take your time. Nain won't be back for an hour or so. You'll find some stuff for your hair. There should be enough. Nain keeps it for the other children – my brother's kids. It only needs the one treatment."

I turned on the stair, puzzled.

"Head lice," she said. "I could see one or two wandering around your ears last night. Not surprised you were scratching. One even wandered over your parting, bit like crossing a motorway from one side to the other. You must have picked them up from those kids on the road you

told me about."
I freaked out then, sat on the stairs and cried, holding the long, unkempt plait away from me in disbelief, my beautiful tresses dad had been so proud of.
She stood below me on the stairs, threw her head back and laughed.

"You're alright. It's not life threatening," she said, patting me on the knee. "Go on, sort yourself out. Been there, done that. There's a nit comb on the shelf, bring it down and I'll winkle out any visitors left."

I stood naked in front of the bathroom mirror, steam from the glorious hot water fogging the glass, wiped it and studied my face. Grey eyes stared back at me, my eyebrows defined but straggly, dark shadows underneath threatening and puffy. It was a tight face, I decided, more careworn and tired than I remembered, as though it had forgotten to smile. It was a grown-up face. I'd pulled my hair over one shoulder and it hung in a loose scruffy rope down to my waist, divided on the top of my head by the parting in the middle of my scalp. The skin should have been white against the black of the hair. It was a dismal grey. It was filthy. I scratched behind one ear without thinking.

The bottle of the special shampoo stood on a glass shelf above the basin, razor, nailbrush and scissors and nit comb laid out neatly by the side. I lifted up my hair in front of me, the loose plait dull and frizzy, studied it briefly, picked up the scissors and hacked it through at the level of my shoulders. It fell on the floor and lay like a dead rat. I looked at it, expecting a wave of emotion or at least regret. Nothing. I plastered the lotion on my head, lay in the bath and soaked, shaved my legs and armpits and rose from the steam like Venus rising from the waves. I rooted around in the rucksack for the carrier bag with the best of my clean clothes, picked up the disgusting plait and held it at arm's length. I dropped it into the carrier bag and tied the handles, consigning the remnants of my childhood to the bin and went downstairs to the clatter of dishes and the smell of bacon. Helen's Nain was breaking eggs. She offered a cursory but warm handshake over the frying pan.

"Sit down, cariad.We'll talk after breakfast. Tea?"

"Nice haircut. Good idea," was all Helen said, studying my ragged bob. "I'll tidy it up for you later. I'm good with scissors. And knives, but preferably on bodies."

She grinned and buttered toast, brandishing the butter knife unnecessarily.

We sat outside the front door in a riot of pink and red geraniums, lobelia and ivy trailing from hanging baskets and real coffee in a blue pot served in willow-pattern cups and saucers. I felt like a paying guest, the sharp little woman with faded blue eyes studying me intently and listening to every word.

"He's a bitter and lonely old man, your great-uncle John," she said.

"Owen, your grandfather, was the elder and dominated him completely when we were children. Bullied him terribly, but in those days no-one took any notice. Character building they said. Toughens you up. John was a solitary child always on his own in the playground, while us girls skipped and played games in groups. Owen was charming, charismatic when he wanted to be, especially around adults. He always had a gang of friends but John used to hide in the corner on his own until the bell went for class."

"Not the most loving relationship, then?"

"No indeed."

She gazed out of the window, musing on times past. I kept quiet.

"He didn't like being in the water, you know, most unusual for a child round here. Never went swimming but loved boats. He said the sea was for being on and definitely not in. When we were older, he used to take himself off in his rowing boat or shut himself up in his father's shed making models."

“Not so strange he started a boatyard, then,” I said.

“It was the model-making to start with. He started to make replicas of the sailing ships that were built here. He’s got quite a collection, I believe. Then it developed into restoring wooden boats. He has a wooden rowing skiff, beautifully varnished. Even now at his age he rows out to the bar on the ebb and back in on the flood to make it easy. I sometimes wonder how he feels when he remembers his children. Perhaps it’s his way of laying ghosts to rest. It was such a terrible tragedy when his children died.”

She put her cup down, the liquid spilling a little into the saucer.

“I taught them, you see. I came back here to teach after college. Funny coming back to the school you went to as a child. They were both in my class. It’s a small school. I had children of mixed ages in the one class. Ivor was seven and Carys just eight. Both of them drowned, their bodies washed up on the beach in Samson’s Bay just under the Powder House. Owen swam ashore after clinging to the upturned dinghy for two hours. He’d lost the children in the current and they were swept back in on the next flood tide.”

“Why did he take them out there? Seems a bit strange to go without their father.”

“We’ll never know. It’s always dangerous crossing the bar on a spring tide with a strong ebb running. He knew the dangers of the bar kicking up big seas with quicksand shifting under the surface. Even the old sailing ships fell foul of it. No-one could imagine that their father would have allowed it had he known, but he was away for the day. Owen must have persuaded Annie, their mother to let them out for a treat.We’ll never really know. Some misplaced sense of fun for the children? Or something more sinister, perhaps.”

“Sinister?” I asked, my story antennae on alert.

“When you’ve been a teacher, you see all kinds of rivalry in families” she said. "Blood isn't necessarily thicker than water, especially in a small community like this. John and Annie, his wife, were never the same after their children's deaths. John shut down even more than he was before."

I pondered this terrible event, rapidly becoming less keen to meet this man, to take on what dad had tried to do and failed.

"What about their mother?"

"Annie? She died of cancer about five years later. And a broken heart. Blamed herself, of course, for letting them go out to sea with their uncle. Owen still had his only son, your father who was younger than his cousins. You can see how it wouldn't be possible for them to work together after that."

I nodded. Totally impossible.

"So that's why he moved to London," she went on. "Took his family with him and worked as a tug-boat skipper on the Thames. And your father, of course, grew up and became a successful astronomer and quite famous wasn't he? I've got two of his books. Very readable for such a difficult subject. It was all in the papers when he was killed. A dreadful time you must have had."

I hadn't really thought about it, but dad couldn't have formed a career further from that of his father's if he'd tried. He simply turned his back on the family's maritime history and ventured into outer space instead.

I was grateful for her time and her empathic way of filling me in on details she must have found distressing, even after all this time, and the no-nonsense way in offering understanding of human nature and its vagaries, from head lice to family tragedy. Helen had the same streak as her Nain. She'd make a good doctor.

"So what should I do? Should I go and meet him?"

"I can't tell you that," she said, "but you'll know what's right when you get there. I would suggest you take a walk over the footpath, turn right at the bottom of the hill. You'll see the sign – 'The Boat Shed'. You can't miss it and it's not just a chandlery. He opened a small sandwich bar about five years ago at one end of the shed to tempt in the passing tourists. Angela runs it. She used to run the cafe down the road here, but that's another story. She makes an excellent prawn sandwich. Go and sit in the sun at one of the tables outside. It's all mixed in with old boats he's often working on or making a model. The tourists love it. Sit and decide whether you want to introduce yourself or just walk away. He won't know any different. You'll know what's right."

I was surprised.

"He's not always unsociable," she said. "Still has to run a business and make a living. And that's not easy. He's either intuitive or thick-skinned enough to know about the novelty of tradition in this glitzy world. Wears an old sailor's hat. Looks like Captain Birdseye."

I looked at her blankly. Captain Birdseye?

"Of course, you're too young to remember the advert for Birdseye fish fingers. Go. You can't miss him."

I wouldn't. I'd remember the white hair, bent back and the belligerent carriage of his head and the jutting chin with its frill of white beard. And that piercing gaze when I caught his eye.

"Have you told anyone about me?" I asked tentatively, including Helen in my query.

Helen shook her head.

"Not me" she said.

Her Nain shook her head. "No, I haven't either, as it happens. Haven't had time to spit with the guests in. Winter's for gossip round here. Why do you ask?"

I looked out towards the sea, the last of the ebb leaving a vast stretch of sandbanks as far as I could see over to the other side of the estuary.

"I don't know exactly," I said, "but would you mind if you didn't say anything to anyone local? I just have a feeling it would be better if no-one knew I was related. It's just a feeling. A bit lame, I know. If anyone asks, I'm a student journalist doing a travel feature for my course."

I felt better immediately. It was a half-truth if nothing else. I set off, feeling their eyes in my back as I climbed the steps leading out of the bay and over the other side towards the town.

CHAPTER 4

The footpath fell away steeply downhill, a tall conifer hedge shading it to one side. It opened out into a single track road leading towards the town of Porthmadog. To my right it ended in a dead-end leading to yard gates and the harbour wall.

I turned off the path, a sign in the trees on my right catching my eye, 'THE BOAT SHED – CHANDLERY and BOAT RESTORATION' painted onto a weathered board and hanging drunkenly where the fixing rope ends had slipped. Underneath it and attached by a piece of blue rope was another smaller notice, handwritten and simply saying 'ANGELA'S SNACK BAR'. I could have stopped then, walked into town, forgotten all about it, asked myself if I really wanted this; the potential for unpleasantness, rejection, opening a can of worms that might be best left.

My curiosity won. Besides, the old man wouldn't recognise me with my tatty shorn hair, a year older and in an unexpected place, camera slung over one shoulder and a notebook in my pocket. I began to feel like the journalist I wasn't, not yet at least, but I could always take a quick look and walk out again.

I walked past a long single-story building to my left and stood in the road in a parking space with the entrances for two boatyards either side of me. The gates faced each other, the one on my left wide open with heavy galvanised gates bolted firmly back, the ones on the right obviously belonging to my great-uncle, fabricated from flimsy wooden frames and filled in with chicken wire, one pushed back into brambles and the other open and sagging where it scraped on the gravel and patches of weeds. They couldn't have been more different.

I opted for the one on the left with the posh gates, stood in the opening then ventured into the yard, aware I was being nosy but really finding any excuse to avoid being in the other one and faced a sea of powerboats with gleaming fibreglass hulls, their bows lined up in ranks, sterns backing away from me onto the top of the harbour wall. Some were for sale, brand new and straight from the factory, some used, all with signs and breathtaking prices, some with outboard engines perched on the sterns advertising obscene fuel consumption. Jet-skis occupied an area near the main building, new ones swaddled like babies in layers of plastic, others for launch and ride, their owners storing them like horses in livery. Trailers filled in the gaps between a myriad of paint work in garish colours: purple and green, black and red, go-faster stripes and fancy writing.

At the far end of the yard, a modern slate building with floor to ceiling glass windows overlooked the yard. A triangular plaque was set on a post to the side of glass doors, big block letters in stainless-steel glinting in the sun – 'MADOC MARINE' it proclaimed, a flashy copy of the one outside Scotland Yard in London I'd walked past so many times. At least this one wasn't revolving.

I'd listened to Helen the day before describing the old wharf as it would have been in the eighteen hundreds. This would have been the old Cwmorthin and Meinofferen slate quays, a working harbour-side of trolleys and cranes, loading and unloading slates, dusty and dirty with a pervasive greyness and the clanging and banging of men at work. Now, a single blackbird sang from the cliff-face above, the gulls quiet for a change.

I fished into my back pocket and pulled out the guide book Helen's Nain had lent me, trying to imagine the stacks of slates brought down from the Ffestiniog quarries by train, over the cob and along the rail tracks to the wharf where I now stood. Schooners, sloops, brigs and barques would knock gently against the wall at high tide or with their keels wedged in the mud at low tide, a forest of spars and furled sails, their decks and holds empty in readiness for loading. I read on, lost in a world of wood and slate, surrounded by fibreglass and stainless-steel and engines the old sailing masters would never have dreamt of. The slate trade had opened Porthmadog to the world, the ships carrying slates from Ffestiniog to Hamburg, picking up new cargoes and sailing down to Africa and over the Atlantic, trading in salt, fish or grain from continent to continent and returning with phosphates from the Indies.

Even as I stood there, conjuring up visions and disappearing into a fantasy world of the past, I could feel prevarication nibbling away at my mission. I took some pictures, knowing I shouldn't without permission and hoping I hadn't been seen. I knew it was for my first term feature for uni to show the contrast between the old and the new but I was on private property after all. I could have taken them from the gate but didn't think it mattered that much.

I walked back out, suddenly aware of the CCTV that had undoubtedly followed me around the yard and turned to have one more look at the gleaming wealth of boats and the building at the far end. A figure appeared in the full length window above the reception and shop. Of course I'd been seen. A man, I could tell that at least, who would be naturally suspicious and dismissive of me at the same time. I hardly looked like a prospective customer in my grey combat trousers and striped top with Jesus sandals on bare feet. On the other hand, I could be part of a larger outfit and up to no good. I smiled to myself. Mine to know and his to wonder, I thought. I turned back and walked through the other set of gates to stand in my great-uncle's yard with my courage fading.

The yard ahead was littered with small dinghies, some upside down on trestles with their bottoms sanded and ready for varnish, others simply decaying with moss and plants growing out of split seams and rotting timbers. A few small sailing boats were propped up on balks of timber, the gravel under their keels speckled with abandoned paint pots and brushes stiff with faded colour in hopeful anticipation of a launch that might never come; not this year at least. There were timber wedges in untidy piles and rusted bolts mixed with crushed beer cans and polystyrene coffee cups around a rubbish bin, a gull squawking and pulling at tattered chip papers.

The intermittent buzz of a power-tool broke the silence. I peered over the harbour wall towards the piece of land now surrounded by water they called Ballast Island, the river deepening as the tide flooded silently in, inching its way up the wall below me and darkening the old wooden piles on the bank opposite. A line of small sailing boats sat quietly on their moorings in the channel.

Helen's Nain had filled me full of her childhood adventures, rowing across to the island in Swallows and Amazons style, to pick marsh samphire off the Traeth, catch flatties or dig for cockles in the sand, find blackberries in the mass of brambles and even sour apples from a stunted tree. Best of all she said, were the pebbles and stones surrounding the island, ballast dumped by the sailing ships when returning empty from their voyages. There were stones from all over the world: pieces of brick, coal, granite, lumps of volcanic rock, some with strange marks carved into them. She had a collection by her front door.

I wanted to be over there too, experiencing the solitude of being on a small piece of land surrounded by water at high tide, to sleep in the bushes in dad's old tent with the tide rushing past and not a person in sight. It was a far cry from London.

On the land side of the yard tucked in at the base of the cliff, there was a long single-story shed built completely from galvanised sheets, the roof once painted a deep red, now peeling to show the rusted steel underneath. There was an open door flanked by two small windows and a sign saying BOATSHED-CHANDLERY. At the gable end of the building nearest the gate, a mobile burger van was parked, a red and white striped awning shading the counter. White plastic picnic tables and chairs stood in a sheltered corner of the yard between it and a high stone wall, its chinks and crevasses bursting with pink and white flowers tangled up with ferns and brambles.

I walked over and stood in front of the counter. A woman in a green apron was polishing mugs with a checked tea towel. She turned, wearing a tired smile which didn't reach her eyes. Her hair was a nondescript brown, grey at the roots and tied back in pony tail.

"Yes, love?" she said, putting down the cloth.

"Cup of tea, please, and my friend says you make brilliant prawn sandwiches."

She opened a fridge at the back of the van.

"Can't be too careful in this heat," she said, putting a packet wrapped in cling film on the counter, the stainless-steel surface gleaming in the sun. I looked around at the van and the way it was organised. Too many kitchens during my holiday work and Milly's relentless cleaning in my childhood had bred an appreciation of people's standards. The sauce bottles were spotless. She placed my sandwich, two white china mugs and a matching pot on a tray.

"Brews better tea," she said as she caught my surprise. "Mind if I join you? It's quiet today. I'm Angela by the way."
She carried the tray to one of the tables, sat down and stretched her legs out, face to the sun and closed her eyes. She had an air of self-sufficiency that invited a relaxed silence. Blackbirds sang in the bushes above and the power-tool still buzzed in the distance. I opened my sandwich, a tiny slice of lemon and a sprig of parsley placed carefully across the top.

"This is truly, very, very good," I said, savouring the chunky filling and the sweet tang of the dressing. "Is this your own dressing?"
If I hadn't spent so much time with Milly and then all those holidays working in hotels and bistro kitchens, nibbling at leftovers and marvelling at the creations turned out by good chefs I wouldn't have known any different.
She tapped the side of her nose.

"Stays that way. No offence. My only claim to fame. I love cooking."
She swilled her tea slowly around in the mug.

"Never had a chance to do it properly, though. Too old now to be a chef and learn the clever stuff. Too many other things getting in the way."
I didn't ask. I didn't want my afternoon cluttered up with a confessional. I needed to be back on track.

"Can I take some notes about the yard. I'm doing an article for college on the history and change of use here since the slate trade. Do you mind?"

"No, why should I mind?"
I took another bite of the sandwich.

"Are these local prawns?"
She tossed her head back and laughed.

"Good God, no" she said. "There aren't any prawns in Cardigan Bay.

Might have been at one time, I suppose, but it's been fished out, scraped clean by the big boys in the trawlers from France and Spain."

I looked back at the menu at the back of the van chalked up on a black board in well-formed handwriting: prawn, lobster, smoked salmon, smoked trout, smoked mussels, dressed crab. She followed my gaze.

"The prawns are Best North Atlantic but it's the dressing that makes the sandwich special. Salmon comes from Scotland but the boss smokes it here along with local trout from the trout fishery down the road. The mussels are as near as damn it local, fresh from the Menai Strait. We used to be able to collect mussels from the harbour here but the licence died with the previous holder."

"What about the lobster and crab?"

"Definitely local. See the blue boat against the wall?"

The tide was well in now, the moored boats knocking gently against the slate blocks, the hulls poking above the edge of the harbour wall. She pointed to a working boat with a cabin and a large cockpit piled with lobster pots and a sign on the side saying 'ANNIE', hand-painted in uneven letters.

"That's the boss's boat, named after his wife. The lobsters and crabs come from Sarn Badrig. John's the only one to have a licence round here. Don't know how long it's going to last though. They're talking about changing the EU quotas."

I nodded, blessing Helen yet again for her history lesson about Sarn Badrig, the undersea causeway stretching eleven miles out into Tremadoc Bay, once an area of farm land and mythical villages. The causeway was built up into dykes and locks to protect the land from the sea.

"You know the legend of Sarn Badrig?" Angela asked.

I shook my head. "Only a bit about the geology."

According to the story, she told me, a man named Saethenin was responsible for maintaining the dykes. He always liked his drink but took to the bottle seriously one stormy night and in a drunken state neglected his duties in maintaining the dam. The sea rushed in and flooded the land, submerging the villages and drowning all their occupants. Only parts of the dyke were left.

"Could I go out there?" I asked, my list of places to explore growing by the moment, "and these quotas? Will they put him out of business?" She shrugged. "Maybe John would take you out. As for the lobster business, he's not bad at diversifying," she said, "Hence the snack-bar and me. The chandlery died a death when Doug Peterson took over the yard next door. He opened a new chandlery, called it 'The Yotshop' and started selling designer clothes as well as lifejackets and bits for boats with fancy packaging and astronomical prices. John should have made more of the traditional side, I thought then, but he's too old to get to grips with websites and advertising."

"I saw a tall guy in the window when I was leaving his yard. Is he the owner? Checking me out as a future customer probably." I wiggled my toes in the shabby sandals. "As if."

"If he finds you nosing around and you're not customer material, he can be a bit unpleasant. Thinks he's God's gift to women and customers and can be charm itself when he wants to sell something. I wouldn't want to cross him though. My partner works for him sometimes. Doesn't suffer fools gladly, that one. I'd steer clear of him if I were you, especially if you're just being nosy."

I couldn't see why. The gates had been open at both ends and despite my unlikely appearance, a stranger couldn't really tell who had money and who didn't.

"He's a strange one," she said, nodding towards the gate. "Took over that yard with money he'd made abroad, so they say. He tells people he used to be in the forces but he never quite says which one."

I raised a curious eyebrow.

"Anyway, he's been in negotiations with the Planning Department and Cadw for a new slipway off his yard, but been refused twice. He has to crane all his boats in and out over the wall. He'd like to get his hands on this yard with its slipway, I can tell you, but John would never sell. He says he'd die before he sold it to him, charm and all. He hates the man and his fancy boats and hates the jet-skis even more. All chrome and plastic in the yard, he says and not a decent plank of wood to be seen."

"Bit different to this place then?" I said, happy to listen to her gossip.

"Just a bit," she said looking around her at the scruffy yard. "But people want everything clean and easy these days, their shackles and cleats and bottle-screws off the shelf neatly sealed in plastic. They don't want to be poking around for boat bits in a grubby old shed smelling of smoke and fish. Except for a few," she added thoughtfully. "Funnily enough, some folk like to come and sit in the yard amongst all the grot and watch the boss caulking and sanding old boats. It's traditional, a bit of a lost art. They can sit here with their lattes and prawn sandwiches and imagine how the old quay would have been years ago."

It was hard to imagine.

"And then there's the models," she went on. "John's been making amazing models of the Porthmadog sailing ships for years. There's a locked room in the shed, sailing ships lined up against the walls on shelves, all made in detail. They must be worth a fortune. He doesn't allow many people to see them. I keep telling him they need to be somewhere secure but he won't listen. There are a few in the Maritime Museum in glass cases. Sometimes he sits outside in the sun and works on his latest project. It adds a bit more interest for customers. Traditional, you see. They like that. He's not daft."

I'd almost forgotten why I was here, great-uncle John opening up like a secret book. I scrunched up the cling film from the sandwich and finished my tea, the last dregs sticking in my throat. I must have looked uneasy. I coughed.

"You alright?"

I looked at my watch, needing a reason to leave and get on with the job. Or not. Helen's Nain said I'd know what was right. It just hadn't come to me yet.

"I'd really like to see the chandlery," I said, getting up, "perhaps a souvenir to take home. Something traditional. Also take some photographs of the yard. Is your boss around?"

"I expect so. He's always around," she said, picking up the mugs and putting them on the tray.

I thought hard and fast, the feeling about keeping my identity quiet returning with a vengeance.

"Your boss seems to run more of a traditional yard than the one next door. Do you think he would talk to me?"

"You can try but don't get too excited. He can be a bit abrupt at times."

"Not much to choose between either of them, then," I said, feeling even more disinclined to carry on.

She nodded. "Good luck," she called after me.

I followed the sound of the power-tool through the yard towards a slipway, the incoming tide now lapping at the top of the concrete ramp which fell away steeply into the water. Dinghies lay stacked in wooden racks leading back into the cliff face. The space in front was filled with an upturned boat on trestles and a man bending over the hull. The sleeves of his checked shirt were rolled back to reveal well-defined muscles with tattoos scrolled on tanned forearms and the backs of his hands. He wore a pair of paint-stained denim work trousers with baggy pockets and a hammer hanging from a strap on his hip, the generous waist band loosely held up with a pair of blue braces. As Helen's Nain had said, I'd recognise him from the peaked sailor's cap clamped on his head with white curls sprouting out over his ears. He was wielding an electric sander over the bottom of the boat, his back bent over his work. He didn't hear me coming, but I could hear my pulse pounding in my ears.

I stepped over a power cable, walked around to the opposite side of the boat and waited, almost faint with a sense of déjà vu, not mine but my dad standing there thirteen years ago. I stood still, watching while the sander buzzed and the gulls cried overhead. He looked up and stared at me, intense brown eyes under a bush of white eyebrows. He straightened up as much as his bent back would allow and switched off the sander, placing it on the upturned hull. Any words I had formed in my mind, any lies about student projects and travel features, souvenirs and the chandlery, any chance that he would not know me, dissipated like a breath of wind.

"You've cut your hair," he said.

Standing there like a silly schoolgirl, my mouth dry, I couldn't speak. He bent over stiffly, unplugged the sander, wound the cable up, ran his hand over the smooth surface of the boat, picked up the sander and gestured towards the chandlery. His voice was deep and gravelly.

"I usually have a mug of tea round about now," he said, showing no sign of surprise, as though he'd been expecting me. I opened my mouth to say something but he'd already turned to walk away. I followed.

He went on ahead, slightly stooped, walking with short steps and scuffling through the thick layer of wood shavings carpeting the gravel outside the door of the shed. He gestured to two ancient sitting-room chairs with plastic covers flanking a wooden cable-drum for a table, walked over to the snack-bar and back, lowering himself carefully onto a chair. I was still standing, frozen and tongue-tied. The lady from the snack-bar brought over two mugs of tea, raising her eyebrows as she approached.

We sat outside the open door. He took a packet of Golden Virginia from the back pocket of his dungarees and a packet of Rizlas from his shirt pocket. His forefinger was stained brown with nicotine. I lurched into an explanation, stammering and gabbling fast.

"I'm on holiday. I didn't think you'd recognise me. I've only a few days left. I'll come back tomorrow if you'd rather. I just wanted to meet you. I just wanted to meet you and tell you..."
I clammed up, the words sticking in my throat, unbidden tears threatening. It happened without warning, these moments of grief, the trigger not always clear, but this time the realisation that he was my only remaining link to my dad and my grandfather and that there were no other relatives left so closely connected. I didn't even include my mother.

He appeared not to notice my distress, teasing out tobacco strands from the packet, licking the edge of the paper and rolling a neat cigarette with thick fingers, the hands strong and brown with calloused palms. He spoke first, out of the blue, as though we'd been sitting talking for hours.

"It was a terrible thing, your father's murder. You must miss him a lot."
He was so direct, so matter-of-fact it gave me some space to collect myself. I thought about it, the security of a selective memory overriding the facts. Did I miss my dad? The child in me missed him, the memories of days when he was warm and close and spent time with me reading books or bird-watching or teaching me the stars. But when I grew older, his concern for me never seemed to stray beyond the immediate inquiries for my health and my school results before his attention wandered back to his research amongst the galaxies, his eyes glazing over under the monosyllabic information about my day to day teenage

life, if I talked at all. Had I pushed him away?

"Yes," I said. "Sort of."

He looked at me quizzically, took a drag from the roll-up and sat back comfortably in the old chair.

I talked for an hour, about myself and mother and dad and his work, the life we led in London with the big house and my relationship with Milly, the cooking and the dinners when he was home and entertaining his colleagues, how dad spent more and more time away and mother giving up her partnership in the successful interior decorating business she shared with Trish's mum. I didn't mention the depression and the drinking or the charming Uncle Frank. He nodded occasionally, rolled another cigarette. The tea cooled in the mugs and the sun slipped behind the cliffs.

Angela from the snack-bar walked over towards us. I didn't want her to know who I was.

"I'm just a tourist," I said to him quickly. "A student doing a project on the slate trade."

He took his cigarette out of his mouth and picked a piece of tobacco off his lip.

"I'm shutting up now, John. See you tomorrow. I need some smoked salmon for the weekend and Arnie Blackwell's coming for his lobster on Saturday."

He nodded. She was desperate to ask who I was, I could see, the curiosity deep in her tired eyes. She took a good, hard look at me then looked at him when he raised his head. He nodded towards me.

"This young lady's doing a travel feature for college, she tells me. She'll be back tomorrow, nosing around and taking pictures. She says she's interested in the history of the old sailing ships."

"Oh, right." She looked surprised. "Will you show her the models?"

"I might," he said.

"See you, tomorrow, then."

She walked to the gate and disappeared round the corner.

"Can I really come and see you again?"

He nodded. "You'll need some background for your work," he said. "Feature, is it?"

The bushy eyebrows rose in a white arc.

"That's right, if anyone asks," I said. "But I haven't told anyone I'm related to you except Helen and her Nain, Mrs Parry. They won't say anything. I asked them not to."

"Why?"

"For the same reason you didn't say anything to Angela from the snack-bar, I suppose," I said, feeling bold. "I just felt it was the best thing to do. I'm just a journalism student if anyone asks."

I couldn't explain why it seemed better to be anonymous. I needed to come back and spend more time with him before deciding whether I wanted to acknowledge it publicly or not. I hadn't asked him anything about himself. It didn't seem appropriate just then. Despite my natural penchant for asking questions, I'd retreated in the face of respect, for privacy, for good manners. I could hear Milly's words again.

"Learn when to keep your mouth shut, girl, and listen. You'll learn a whole lot more."

But I'd talked non-stop about myself and discovered nothing about the man I'd come to see. My mission had been transformed into a self-centred need that surprised me, the tentative exploration for a devoted, attentive, paternalistic figure, just like my dad had been, should have always been. I didn't know whether my uncle would fill that gap but I wouldn't find out if I didn't try. I didn't even know if I wanted it.

He picked up the packet of Golden Virginia and Rizlas from the table and put them back in his pocket, stood up for a moment, looking out to the harbour wall where the blue fishing boat rested against the slate slabs, its keel in the mud as the tide receded and the mooring ropes taut against the bollards.

"So can I come back and see you again, perhaps take some photographs?"

He nodded.

"I'll be here tomorrow afternoon," he said and disappeared through the open door.

CHAPTER 5

The snack-bar was shuttered for the night as I reached the gates, my head in a whirl hardly believing what had happened and I turned to see if he had come out again, to acknowledge the meeting if nothing else. But he'd gone, swallowed up in the dark recesses of the shabby shed, the door shut and the yard now silent. I'd hardly had time to process the self-congratulatory feeling of breaking the mould or conversely berating myself for the way I'd handled it, when a clatter behind me shook me back into reality.

I turned and faced a man closing the gates to the yard opposite. He had his back to me, pulling at the first gate, solid and heavy but swinging easily on oiled hinges. He bolted it into place and paused before starting to swing the other gate to. No rusty padlocks on this gate, I noticed, just a high security coded lock. He stopped, aware of my presence and turned to face me.

He was only just taller than me, slightly built but defined muscles filling out the shoulders of a blue short-sleeved shirt with 'Douglas Gill' embroidered on the pocket and soft canvas jeans with the bottoms tucked into suede boots. A silver Rolex flashed on his left wrist.

He straightened up and ran his hand over a dark no2 haircut as if checking, unnecessarily, it was tidy and fit to face the world. We stood facing each other in a moment of appraisal. I was uncomfortably conscious of his expensive designer clothes against my scruffy outfit of creased cargo pants and T-shirt faded from weeks on the road. If the gates to the two yards had been opposing pieces in a chess-set, then we were the players each waiting for the first move.

"Evening," he said, steel-blue eyes narrowed as he held my gaze, deep lines at the corners of his eyes more from analysis than smiling, I guessed. There was an intensity about him that discouraged chit-chat. I nodded.

"Hi," I said. It came out as a squeak.

"On holiday?" No Welsh accent here, just a hint of Scottish brogue. He pulled the heavy gate half-way, standing in the open space and turned to face me again. I just nodded, fiddling with the camera strap round my neck.

"I saw you chatting to Mr Jones. You must be interested in old boatyards. Unusual for a young lady."

He'd been the shadow I'd seen watching me from the office window following my every move while I'd wandered between his expensive powerboats, snapping away amongst the jet-skis and trailers. He'd seen me in his yard taking photos, taking pictures without his permission. He didn't mention it.

"You must have made a hit with the old man," he chatted on. "He doesn't have much time for people generally."

You can fish all you like, I thought, but you won't catch this one. I straightened my shoulders trying not to be intimidated. This was a different animal to the spotty sixth formers I'd had the occasional disappointing date with, leering Uncle Franks and pale-faced, pervy fertilizer salesmen of this world. This was solid maleness with piercing blue eyes, a deep voice that managed to incorporate interest and authority in an easy manner. It would be so easy to chat and simper, my feet rooted to the ground, fiddling with the camera strap. I stuck my hands firmly in my pockets.

"Actually, I'm doing a travel feature on the Welsh tourist industry," I said. "Mr Jones is an expert on the old sailing ships, I believe."

"For school, is it?"

That stung. I looked him straight in the eye.

"No, a magazine, actually," I lied. "I'll be coming back tomorrow to take some photos."

"Of course you will. See you around, then," and he flashed a brief smile.

I walked away, smarting at his patronising tone and easy familiarity. He'd known I was lying, my heart thudding against my ribs as I climbed the path. It felt like a physical intrusion, stirring something in me I couldn't or was unwilling to identify. His smile hadn't quite reached his eyes, the lines at the corners etched deeply in the weathered skin and the eyes searching and analytical.

He knew that I knew I'd been seen and caught on camera. I should have apologised for being in his yard for no good reason. I couldn't explain about the relationship with my uncle but I could have simply said I was interested in new boats and the change of use of the yards over the years. That would have been the grown-up thing to do but I blustered lamely and I was cross with myself for the pathetic schoolgirl subterfuge. I ran the rest of the path to try and shake off my embarrassment and down the steps to the bay, where Helen was waiting, sitting on the wall outside the house swinging her legs impatiently.

"Where on earth have you been? You've been gone ages. I'm dying to know how you got on. Nain says we can eat in the kitchen later after the guests. Come on."

She took my arm and frog-marched me over to a bench in the car park overlooking the beach. The tide was out, an expanse of damp sand stretching away from our feet to the cliff on the other side of the bay, the greyness speckled with reds and blues of small dinghies resting comfortably on their sides in the mud.

"Here," she said. "I thought you could do with this" and extricated half a bottle of Smirnoff and two plastic glasses from her jacket pocket.

"Tell all."

Ten minutes later I drew breath. "...and then," I hesitated, "on the way out from the yard I met this man."

She topped up the glasses. "What man?"

"The man from the other yard. God, he's a bit compelling, isn't he? I mean different. A bit gorgeous in a craggy sort of way. You know what I mean?" The look on her face said it all.

"Doug Peterson that'll be," she said, her mouth tightening in disapproval. "You know he's old enough to be your father? Keep away from him."

There was an uncomfortable silence.

"He only said good evening, Helen. What's the problem?"

"Sorry. Seriously though, he's not what he seems, even if you think he's gorgeous and... compelling, you said? Interesting description. Come on, I'm hungry."

We left the bench to the seagulls, walked over the road and round the back of the house to the back door, sat in the kitchen and ate left-over moussaka from the guests' dinner.

"Can't you stay on?" Helen asked. "I haven't got to be back in London until the end of next week. We could have a barbecue on the beach if the weather holds, and you did say you didn't want to go home until you had to."

"My train tickets are for Friday this week," I said. "I'll go and stay with friends in London."

"Change the tickets," she said simply.

My phone blipped a text message from my mother, enough to make me scrape my chair back suddenly and stand up.

"Excuse me a sec," I said and went outside to the front of the house, crossed the road and sat on the wall with my feet dangling over the edge above the beach. It was quiet, the endless procession of cars and people gone for the night, the fairy lights above the restaurant opposite framing the diners inside. I looked at the screen.

"Phone me urgently. Please."

We hadn't spoken to each other for six weeks. I swallowed, couldn't imagine what was so wrong that another text wouldn't do. There had seemed to be an unspoken understanding that talking was difficult. And something had to be wrong.

"Darling?" she said, breathless when I phoned. She never called me darling. Not for years, at least. Not since she gave up work and hit the bottle. A brittle, peremptory 'Cassie' was all I ever got.

"Darling, we need to talk. When are you coming home?"

I didn't answer.

"Cassie, he's gone," her words speeding across the ether so fast I could barely comprehend them. "I'm so, so sorry. Frank's gone, Cassie. He's not ever coming back here again. Cassie, are you there?"

"Yes," I whispered, the words sticking in my throat, questions crowding my brain and refusing to translate into sounds

"Felicity rang me, darling, and told me what he'd done. When Trish came back on her own from Abersoch on Sunday, she told her mum what you'd told her about Frank. She rang me. How could he do that after all those years? I threw him out, Cassie, there and then."

Her voice broke.

"Okay," I said slowly.

"And there's more. Felicity's asked me to go back into the

partnership. She's snowed under with work and she's doing the organisation for corporate events as well as the interior design commissions. Trish has taken over the floristry. I'm going back to work, Cass. I've put the house on the market..."

"Mum, stop. I can't take this all in. Back to London? We can't afford it."

"Yes, we can if I'm working. Felicity says we can rent the top flat in her place until the house sells."

"You? Working again?"

I choked the disbelief in my throat, couldn't help thinking about the bleary-eyed mornings, the afternoons spent sleeping and the evenings with slurred speech and the TV talking to itself. It hadn't always been like that but normality was so far way back in my early teens I could hardly remember it. I remembered when she'd backed out of the partnership with Trish's mum and I lost the close bond with Trish for a while. This was unreal, gloriously unreal.

"Back in business? With Felicity? The old business?"

"Yes, and I've stopped drinking. It shook me out of it, Cassie. I got some help," she said simply, "Grace and Favour Interior Design rides again and I can't wait. Come home soon. We've an awful lot to talk about. Please?"

"Next week," I said, " and that's brilliant news," trying to disguise the doubt in my voice.

"There's a package from the University for you. I opened it. It's a precourse assignment, a travel feature to be worked on in the first term. It says you're to collect notes and photos, and there's confirmation of your grant."

I laughed then, a laugh that came from my belly, unlocking the tightness I hadn't realised had built up over the weeks.

"I've already started on it," I said. "By the way, I've met great-uncle John."

It was her turn for silence this time. I wandered back over the road to the house with a sense of elation I'd almost forgotten I'd recognise again, my feet barely touching the tarmac. Thank God for Helen at the other end to share it with.

The following afternoon I changed my tickets at the train station, walked back down the lane to the boatyard, camera on my shoulder and notebook stuffed into my jeans pocket and turned into the gate heading for The Boat Shed. The yard was empty and the door was closed. There was no sign of my uncle. Had he changed his mind? Disappointment flattened the euphoria I'd felt since the last evening with the promise of a home to go back to and my mother working and normal again.

"Might be a good idea to hang on for a minute," Angela called from the snack-bar."He's got a visitor."

I waved my hand in acknowledgement and leaned against a rusting boat cradle perched on the edge of the harbour wall. The heat in the yard was almost oppressive, a hazy film of cloud sneaking in from the west and muting the sharp clarity of the colours in the estuary. The tide had turned, sliding slowly out towards the sea and creeping down the wood piles opposite on Ballast Island. I could make out the remains of the old crane driver's house and the decayed piles of the original wharf. I took a photograph, wondering if my rudimentary editing skills could superimpose the scene from two hundred years ago with ships tied up, a sea of masts and rigging and the crane unloading ballast to be dumped on the island.

Voices snapped me out of it, one voice stronger than the other rising through the galvanised roof on the shed. Silence returned, the shed door suddenly swung wide open forcing the door back on its hinges. The man I'd seen the evening before stood briefly in the opening then walked forward, slamming the door behind him. He marched through the wood shavings, kicking up dust, head down, past the tables and through the gates. He didn't see me. The door to the shed stayed shut. Curiosity and anxiety jostled for places as I stood there, unsure of what to do next. Angela gestured for me to come over. I raised my eyebrows as she sat down at a table putting two mugs of tea down.

"Is Mr Jones alright, do you think? That sounded like an argument." I looked towards the door of the shed which was firmly shut. There was no sign of life.

"He'll come out when he's calmed down. It's all about the planning permission for Doug's application for a new slipway on his land. Doug's been here for about three years and wants to expand the business. He's just had his appeal refused. This has been going on for a year now but this is the first time I've heard a row over it. It's just been letters up until now. John has been objecting to the application and Cadw and the council have refused because of the historical importance of the harbour. Doug's been blaming him for adding his own objections."

"What difference would it make to Mr Jones if there's another slipway?"

I couldn't see what all the fuss was about.

"John owns the only slipway this end of the harbour. It adds thousands to the value of the property. Doug's offered time and time again to buy this yard from him. Says it's too much for an old man and he ought to live out his days in comfort instead of worrying about running all this. No chance as I told you yesterday. John won't sell. Also..." She stopped mid-sentence. "I shouldn't be talking about all this to a budding journalist, should I?"

I shrugged, trying to look uninterested.

"I'm only a student," I said. "It's just coursework. I'm curious, that's all."

"John stays here most of the time. He's got a cottage in Borth-y-Gest but he only goes home to sleep occasionally, mostly in the winter. He bunks down on the chairs in the shed and cooks himself a meal on the old stove or eats food from the smoke-house or leftovers from the snack-bar at the end of the day. He's spent a lot of time this summer doing that. Likes to keep an eye on things, he says."

"What things?"

"Oh, comings and goings. You know."

Gossip's a wonderful thing. Listening was the next best thing, I reminded myself, sipping my tea.

"Really? But it's so quiet down here."

"Not always what it seems," she said and clammed up as a small boy about nine years of age appeared through the gates, head lowered and a fishing rod in one hand. He threw himself into the chair beside Angela, propping the rod against the table, his face pink and freckled below the crop of bright ginger hair.

"Mochyn," he spat out.

"Tomas, that's rude in front of visitors."

"Well, he is, that Doug. He never needed to tell me off again. I'm not stupid."

He scuffed his feet in the gravel under the table. Angela got up.

"I'll get you a drink while you look for your manners," she said turning apologetically to me. "This is my son Tomas. He knows about the fishing round here, at least in the harbour. He spends more time here than he does in school when he can get away with it. Trouble is..." she looked at him meaningfully, "it gets him into trouble sometimes, doesn't it love? He might be able to help you with your feature, though."

She fetched him a can of Coke, put it on the table and went back to serve a couple standing by the counter. I smiled politely. He ignored me, slurping his Coke and moving the can round in circles.

"Your mum's a good cook," I said, breaking the silence. "She makes brilliant prawn sandwiches but she says the prawns are brought in. She said there's not much fishing round here anymore. It's all shipped in from other places. She says the big trawlers from Spain and France used to come in the middle of the night and scrape the seabed with their nets and take everything, even all the young stock. The lady I'm staying with said you could sometimes hear the engines on a quiet night. Is that right, then?"

His head shot up and he wiped his mouth with the back of his hand.

"There's fish," he said, giving me a crafty look. "Different sorts of fish. You just have to know where to find them."

If I'd learned nothing else about extracting information from children in my time on the road, at least I'd picked up that a bit of casual indifference usually worked.

"Oh, right. It's just for a story for a magazine. I'm collecting photos and stuff, like pictures of the harbour and the boats. People like you seem to know what's really going on."

He drained the last of his Coke and bent over the can. He was still hunting for his manners, his face still cross.

"Oh, well," I said, getting up to go, "if you change your mind..."

He squirmed a bit in the chair.

"Show you the mullet if you want."

I could barely make out the words. He was desperate.

"When?" I looked at my watch. He sat up straight in the chair.

"Now, if you want. The tide's going out so we can get round from the slipway on the sand."

I took a picture of him, an air of self-importance in his face as he shouldered his fishing rod and led me from the table.

We skirted around the edge of the yard at the top of the wall and down the slipway onto a strip of drying sand and climbed onto the single pontoon which ran along the bottom of the wall. Boats were moored up against it with their keels touching the sandy bottom as the tide ebbed and we walked along the warm planks to a spot where one of the huge balks of timber had been bolted into the harbour wall.

"The old ships used to rest against these when the tide went out," he said.

A derelict rusting ladder next to it had snapped off half-way up to the top, bolts sheared off and the sharp ends festooned with tresses of seaweed. He carried on pointing and explaining like a well-informed tourist guide.

"Rain water runs off the yard down here. The rain pours off the cliffs at the back of the road and drains under the yard through the space where it's overgrown. Nobody bothers with it. It runs a bit wet all the time. The yard would flood if it wasn't there. JJ... that's what I call Mr Jones, says it's been there for over a hundred years. It's a dead good place for bouldering and the stones are tight so you can get a good grip. Some of them you get your hand in."

"But why would you want to climb up here? It's dangerous with all that weed and slime."

"It's cool for climbing but it ends just inside the fence to Doug's yard. It's a good short cut home if the tide comes in and I can't get back round the slipway. Sometimes I forget the time when I'm fishing," he said. "It's dead easy to climb up. I can sneak round the edge of his yard at the top and swing round the security fence and into JJ's yard and out through the gate."

He motioned me to sit down on the edge of the pontoon, the water a clear green below us. We sat in silence and watched the sleek mullet catching the sunlight as they wound in and out of each other like silver snakes.

"Buggers to catch," he said conversationally.

I raised my eyes at the language. It seemed such an adult comment. I chanced the question that had been chewing away at me.

"Is that why that man Doug was cross with you when you came into the yard because you'd been trespassing? You called him a pig in Welsh, didn't you?"

He turned and looked up the ladder to the top of the wall.

"Well, he is. A scary pig. Caught me in his yard a few weeks ago, didn't he? Got caught out by the tide and climbed up. I had to hang on just below the top of the wall 'cos he was standing on the edge talking on the phone and I couldn't go up and I couldn't go back down 'cos the tide had come in. I had to hang there and just wait 'till he'd finished talking. My fingers got cold stuck in the cracks. After he'd gone, I crept over the top and sneaked through the yard but he caught me on the CCTV. He said I'd scratched one of his boats with the rod. I never did. He told Gareth 'cos he works for him sometimes and I got belted. I was grounded for a week. That's why I'm mad. He warned me again, had a right go at me."

I sat and nodded. It sounded a bit of a harsh punishment. I waited.

"Me mam said it was wrong to eavesdrop on his phone call 'cos of what I'd told her I'd heard and that made it worse. She said I shouldn't listen to other people's conversations."

"Who's Gareth?

"Mam's partner. I don't like him. He drinks," he said shortly, "and other stuff."

He stood up suddenly as though uncomfortable with the memory. I stood up by his side and the mullet skittered away. He looked up at me, the freckles on his nose a warm brown against the pink skin. He stared out across to Ballast Island. I waited.

"I heard stuff when Doug was talking on the phone," he said simply. "I don't get it. If you overhear bad things even when you shouldn't be listening and then try and do something about it, it can't be wrong, can it?"

"I don't know," I said, having to think carefully. "It depends if it's going to hurt someone. Depends if the facts are accurate or it's just gossip. Depends if there's someone you trust who can do something about it," I said, knowing it was a complex set of issues he was struggling with and burning with curiosity to know exactly what he had heard.

"We have to go," he said. "JJ'll be looking for you. He lets me watch him work on his models sometimes. Gave me some smoked salmon once." He wrinkled his nose. "Didn't like it much."

"It's not to everybody's taste."

He scuffed his feet on the planks. Milly's words echoed in my ear. Shut up and listen, girl.

"That Doug said bad things about JJ on the phone. He shouldn't say bad things about him. I like JJ."

"What did he say?" I asked.

He put his head down and bit his lip.

"I heard him say he wanted him out of there, 'cos he was always around the yard, watching, never goes home," he said, so quietly I could hardly hear him. "Then he talked about Coke and money but I couldn't hear properly and my fingers hurt. My mum buys Coke in big boxes. She's got loads in the store room. What's Coke got to do with him?"

I shook my head.

"I don't know what you're talking about, Tomas. Just tell me what you heard."

"You won't tell me mam I've told you?"

"None of my business," I said. "If you've told your mam that should be enough. I'm sure she listened."

"She listened alright," he said. "She just got mad at me."

"Tell me," I said, frustrated now. "I like a good story, or is this just a wind-up? Or is it that you can't really remember? Or are you just making it up?"

He jumped at that. Got you, I thought. He screwed his face up, indignation flushing his skin.

"No, it's all true. I don't tell lies and I'm good at remembering. He was talking on the phone, like, and he said 'I don't care how much there is.' He said he'd sort it. Then he was quiet and I thought he'd gone away. Then he said, 'just make sure I get my money.' Then I heard his footsteps crunch in the gravel and I poked my head up and he'd gone. I couldn't hang on any more, anyway."

"What did your mam say when you told her?"

"She said I'd been watching too many films and it was a load of rubbish and what I thought I'd heard didn't mean anything."

He shook his head and looked up at the wall.

"I don't know what he was talking about. I just thought it sounded bad, like. But I really want to know. P'raps..."

"Sometimes you can get the wrong end of the stick when you hear just bits of a conversation," I said, trying to explain to a child the concept of Chinese whispers.

I filed it away, my head buzzing with questions I couldn't ask.

"We need to go," he said. "JJ'll be waiting for you."

I lifted my camera and took some shots of the wall and the ladder with its dripping weed, amused at being told my duty by a nine year old with a sense of responsibility. I thought back to Zoe and Dave's little girls at the festival and their independence, their way of taking all the angles into account.

"Is he a bad man, that Doug, do you think?" I ventured, as we padded back through the sand and up the slipway. "He seemed very nice when I met him yesterday."

"Ask me mam," he said abruptly, the sharing of confidences dissipating in the hot air and walked off.

"Thank you," I called after him, "for showing me the fish," but he'd gone.

I walked through the yard and stopped by the door to the shed. It was open now, the interior dark and quiet. I called out, feeling like an intruder, despite the fact that it was supposed to be a shop and open to customers. The smell of smoke from the open door at the back mingled with fish and tar, thinners and old rope, sunlight catching dust motes in the air. I headed for a door in the back wall and the sound of a shovel scraping the floor. He was bending over in a space outside between the two sheds, shovelling wood chippings into a smaller tin shed, the doors wide open, racks lined with fish against the back wall. He stopped and looked up.

"You've come back then," he said, tossing the shovel onto a pile of wood chippings. I turned to go back into the shed as he switched on a light, the fluorescent tubes running the length of the ceiling. The shed was crammed, jam-packed with stuff on shelves, ropes hanging from wall fitments, rusting Tilley lamps, fishing rods and old oars and an open glass case with lifejackets in packets covered in dust and shavings blown in through the door. I caught a movement out of the corner of my eye.

"Meet Neifion," he said, "Welsh for Neptune, the Roman god of the sea," pointing to a huge tank in a recess at the end of the shed, light casting a green glow on the bubbles from a filter. A lobster stirred at the bottom of the tank and waved antennae in greeting. "With a name like Cassiopeia, you'd know your Greeks and Romans, of course."

Of course. Obviously. I just nodded.

"Homarus gammarus, minus one front claw. I caught him and kept him. He's old and lame, just like me. Wouldn't have lasted much longer

on the reef."
He lifted the lid off the tank and tipped in some food.

"He won't live much longer. He's about forty years old now. Might as well see out his last years in luxury."

"Will you eat him?" I said, peering more closely through the glass as his one claw waved in the water, stirring the weed on small rocks placed carefully on a bed of sand.

"No. Couldn't eat anything that's got a name," he said.
I looked around, staggered by the amount of stock, the dust thick on every surface, clinging to the cracked window-panes festooned with spider-webs, understanding the enormity of organisation and maintenance in thc shed alone.

He coughed, a deep throaty smoker's cough, led me over to two old chairs either side of an old stove at the back of the counter used for customers. A till sat at one end. At the side of the stove a kettle stood on a dusty shelf next to a couple of blue and white striped mugs and some plates and pottery bowls. A cracked enamel sink with one cold tap was sunk into a work top beneath the window. He motioned to me to sit down in the chair opposite the window, filled the kettle from the tap and plugged it in. He sat down opposite me, leaned forward with his hands resting on his hips, elbows akimbo and stared intently into my eyes.

"What is it you want?" he asked directly.
I gathered my thoughts, determined not to repeat the garrulous outpourings of yesterday. The water fizzed in the kettle and a blue-bottle buzzed on the dirty window pane, its wings flailing in a spider's-web.

"I think I wanted to do what dad couldn't. You're my great-uncle, after all. It's not unnatural for me to want to get to know you. I didn't like my grandfather much and I know he was your brother. He was a very stern man. I'm sorry for what happened with your children but they do say that the sins of the fathers shouldn't be visited on the sons. I

thought I'd like to meet you. Family seems to be important suddenly."
I'd said too much. Too late now if I'd blown it, so while he was rolling a cigarette, I thought I'd ask about his visitor, my head buzzing with comments from Angela and Helen and then Tomas snubbing me and walking off.

"I'm sorry I was late. I heard the shouting from down in the yard. The guy from next door sounded pretty angry. I wasn't eavesdropping but you could hear it right down the yard. Angela said it would be best if I didn't disturb you."
I tried to put some apology into my voice but he seemed unconcerned.

"He wants my yard because of the slipway," he said, leaning back in the seat. "The council's refused planning permission for one on his own yard. They'll never let him demolish a chunk of harbour wall for his own slipway but he's not having this one. No-one is. It'll die with me and that's that. I don't like him and I don't like his dirty money. There's things about him I don't believe, all that stuff about the forces. He's a crook. He didn't get enough to buy that place from being in the forces or selling shackles in plastic bags."

"Is this yard worth a lot then?"
I looked around at the dilapidation and the dirt, the sagging timbers and tin roof and through the filthy window, the collection of rotting boats outside. He laughed until his eyes watered, coughing smoke from the cigarette, spluttering and clearing his throat, wiping his eyes with the back of his hand. He didn't answer.

"If you're still doing a story," he said, side-stepping the question and blowing his nose on an old rag, "you can come out to the reef tomorrow if you want. The pots need checking and the weather's on the change. Ten o'clock and bring a coat." He hadn't answered my question.

I stood outside, summarily dismissed and burning with questions. The air was stale in the yard, sandwiched between the cliff and the estuary, a breathless heat rising from the dirty gravel tainted with rotting garbage from the bins. Ferns and brambles hung limp and wilted from the cliff-face. Even the blackbirds and gulls were quiet. I had a sudden urge to get out of here, to be away from the old man with his rattling cough, run-down shed and graveyard of rotting boats. I remembered last evening's sense of elation after the phone call from my mother and the promise of the bustle of London, clubs and clothes and people like me getting on with their lives with optimism and purpose.

I reminded myself that's where I really belonged, not in this Godforsaken place chasing family history in a dirty yard with an expanse of soulless sand and a storm threatening. Just do it for the project for uni, takc photos and write a brilliant feature as my introduction to the term's work. That's what I came here to do, I told myself, and felt better for it.

CHAPTER 6

I was heading down the hall after breakfast the next morning, my camera and a light jacket tucked inside the rucksack. Helen's Nain came to the front door with me. She pointed to the barometer on the wall. It nearly filled the space with its long carved neck and brass fittings on the face. She tapped it but the hands didn't budge. I didn't ask why.

"Down ten millibars overnight," she said, opening the front door and scanning the sky. "You'll need a good coat out at sea. Here," and she handed me a heavy outdoor jacket. "John will take you out to the reef and back in again on the tide before the weather breaks so you'll be quite safe."

We stood side by side on the path. I felt uncomfortable addressing her suddenly.

"I keep calling you Helen's Nain," I said. "You've been very kind to me and I don't know what to call you. Mrs Parry seems too formal and Joan seems too... well too familiar. I'll always think of you as Helen's Nain."

She considered it for a moment.

"Helen's Nain would be fine," she said. "People have been called worse things, even if it is a bit of a mouthful. Go on now. Have a good

day. I hope you're not sick. The weather will hold, don't worry."
I glanced up at a hazy sky streaked with feathery wisps of white cloud and hoped she was right, my recent fascination with the legend of Sarn Badrig souring as I looked over the estuary towards Harlech Castle. The early tide was flooding into the estuary, a grey lumpy sea compared to the magical blue stillness of the last few days.

I'd googled the history of Sarn Badrig, the reef reaching out eleven miles into Tremadoc Bay from Mochras Point, a sandy headland between Shell Island and Barmouth and ending at the Causeway Buoy. It was out in the middle of a grey expanse of wet nothing, a focus for scientific research into the rare species of seaweeds clinging to the rock and stones under water, but on low water at spring tides it bristled above the sea in places like a partially submerged road. Bass and tope hunt in shoals and lobsters hide in weedy crevasses. People sometimes stand on the reef at low tide and take selfies, up to their ankles in the Irish Sea with captions like, 'Jesus, eat your heart out' and stick it on YouTube.

I quite fancied doing that but despite the geological interest, I preferred the myth of Saethenin and the terrible devastation his neglect caused when the sea rushed in through the hole in the dyke one stormy night and covered the land. I imagined the terror of the sleeping people and the farms and villages washed away. Helen used to crew in racing yachts out of Pwllheli when she was younger and said she'd been out to the end of the reef many times using the Causeway Buoy as a race marker. She told me it was the most melancholy sound she'd ever heard, the bell clanging mournfully as the waves pass beneath it, tolling the death of drowned sailors, she'd added fancifully. I laughed. Helen didn't do fanciful.

I arrived at the yard at ten o'clock, peered down over the harbour wall and saw my great-uncle already on the boat ready to cast off. I climbed the steel ladder down to the boat, the narrow side-deck rocking when I stood on it. The orders to sit in the corner of the cockpit were brusque.

"You've come, then," he said. "I thought the weather might have put you off."

I sat down obediently, tucked up against the cabin wall. He went below, flicked some switches and I watched as he lowered the engine into the sea. The Honda roared into life and water spurted out from underneath the engine casings. My hands gripped the seat but despite the slight resentment at his curt instructions, I told myself I better get used to it. Journalism was not for prima donnas with attitude, I'd been told at my university interview way back in June. It seemed a lifetime away.

"Well, push us off, then. That's a boat-hook," he called from the cabin, pointing to a large pole with a metal hook on the end. "Undo the mooring rope first and don't drop it. And bring that fender inboard, that white tyre hanging over the side."

I got it. I pulled the rope through that he'd looped around the ladder, pushing us away from the wall using the boat-hook as leverage and flipped the grubby fender over the side-deck into the cockpit. It seemed I'd done the right thing. He turned back to the wheel without a word.

I sat down again as he steered the boat out into the current, the bows turning towards the sea. I looked back as we passed a green conical buoy at the entrance to the harbour. The man I now knew as Doug Peterson was watching us, silhouetted against the backdrop of his yard with its gleaming white powerboats lined up like soldiers. I started to compile all the information about him I'd heard, from Tomas's eavesdropping to Helen's brief description of why she would never crew for him again. Once was enough with him, she'd said, despite crewing for different skippers who needed a competent pair of hands in her teenage racing days.

"Why?" I'd asked, thinking of her description of the sleek racing boats she'd grown up with and the excitement and social whirl she'd described in the racing weekends.

"Wandering hands," she'd said briefly, "and the arrogant assumption I wouldn't mind. He thought I'd be just another one of his quick screws to be flattered by the attention. It was the first time I'd crewed for him in a race although I'd been crewing for my dad and others all my teenage years. I'd been warned.

'It was rough that day but it was a capable boat, a Sigma 38 and an important race, blowing about a 5 and the seas were as choppy as you'd want for a race. We were off the Tudwal Islands just past the Bell Rock and on a windward leg out to the Causeway Buoy. He'd asked me if I'd like to take the wheel, knew I was experienced and probably thought he'd flatter me with the chance to helm his bloody boat. No problem, I said.

'I was concentrating hard to keep her on the wind and he was sitting on the cockpit seat behind me. The guys were busy with the winches. He got up suddenly and stood behind me, pressing his belly hard into my back and put his hands over mine on the wheel. I couldn't say anything and I couldn't take my hands off the wheel. Well, it was his boat and the wind was howling. I was stuck for a minute. Then I got angry because he was overriding my helming more than anything else."

"So what did you do?" I asked, scarcely able to imagine it.

"I slipped my right hand out from under his, took it off the wheel for a second and jabbed my elbow straight back into his ribs. It took him by surprise. I never offered to crew for him again and he never asked me. He got the message."

"You don't much like him, then, do you?"

"Can't stand him," she'd said. "Smug bastard." End of conversation. We motored out past Borth-y-Gest and Danger Rock and picked up speed after the eight knot limit, the wake a creaming white curve behind the boat and the outline of Cnicht and the Moelwyns now hazy in the distance. The Ffestiniog train chugged over the cob with a comfortable head of steam, its passengers enjoying the security and comfort of a land-based journey, a bleak contrast to the vastness of open water in front of us. The channel buoys disappeared one by one as we passed them, a line of greens and reds bobbing like coloured marbles against the grey water and then finally a red and white buoy larger than the rest. Uncle John came out of the cabin and the boat sped on out to sea all by itself.

"Autopilot," he said, clocking my worried face. "That was the Fairway Buoy we just passed. We'll go right out to the Causeway Buoy so you can take pictures. We're in clear water now for half an hour or so. Feeling alright? Pannad?"

He seemed a different man out here, more relaxed, the gruff voice and abrupt clipped phrases softened to a normal politeness. I nodded, flipping my hood up against the cold. He turned back into the cabin and I stood up and held onto a solid wooden handle by the cabin door and watched him. He'd put a kettle onto a gas ring and it was already spitting steam. He took two mugs from a cupboard, wiped them out with a grubby tea towel, threw in tea-bags and filled them with the water.

"Milk?"

I nodded again.

"Mind your head," he said, gesturing me to stand back. He put a spoon in the mugs, fished out the tea-bags and bending the teaspoon back, flipped them expertly through the open door and over the side into the sea.

"Never fails."

I laughed, sat down and he brought out the tea and a rusty tin. More surprises, as he revealed double chocolate-chip cookies. I sipped the tea and nibbled on a biscuit, despite the nagging nausea that had crept up as the wave formation seemed to change, the waves shorter and steeper, bouncing my gut around from one side to the other. We sat in the cockpit in silence.

"Is it hard, coming out here?" I asked, thinking of his drowned children. It seemed okay to talk about it out here, less intrusive, ironically.

"It was a long time ago," he said, rolling a cigarette in the shelter of the cabin, leaning back against the bulwark.

"Why didn't you turn me away, like you did to dad?"

He drew on his cigarette, the tip glowing in the wind.

"I remembered you at the funeral in that big hat and long plait over your shoulder. You were curious about me then, weren't you, even with all that sadness? I could see your face and the angle of your jaw. I wondered if my daughter or my granddaughter would have looked like you."

He stared back towards the Fairway Buoy, the long stretch of Black Rock Sands away to the right and Harlech beach away to the left, two golden arms fringing the bay and the reef in front out to sea. His sudden intimacy silenced me.

"I'm an old man," he said without self pity. "There's not a lot of time left to spend it on hate. A young face in an old man's life is a good thing."

He picked up the cups and the biscuit tin.

"Journalism, you said? Plenty of good stories out there to write about."

Was this a thawing, an emotional tag to tether me for his own needs, someone to assuage his loneliness? The strength of yesterday's feeling flooded back. I didn't want this.

A bell clanged in the distance.

"That's the Causeway Buoy," he said and went down below.

We motored round the end of the causeway although there were no rocks to be seen and the dangers that lurked beneath the surface were well hidden by the surge of water against the north facing side, steeper than the other as it fell away to the south. Helen was right about the buoy clanging its eerie warning to shipping to stay clear. I took some pictures, thinking of the sailing masters I'd read about who had made mistakes in their navigation into Porthmadog and headed straight for the reef instead of rounding it safely in deep water. In their desperate last bid to avoid it, some had tacked away to the west only to be wrecked at Hell's Mouth. Out here in a rising wind on a lee shore, with fog or driving rain, I could only imagine the horrors.

"Look for black flags," I heard him call above the thrum of the engine.

I looked ahead as we motored down the other side of the reef. The boat rocked gently in the swell as he cut the engine to idling speed, came out and picked up the boat-hook, leaning over the side to a black flag floating flat in the water. He went back in the cabin and motored forward repeating the process a few times. He hadn't said a word, heading towards the land and down the south side of the reef to a navigable channel now fully covered by the tide. I knew something was wrong. He gunned the engine and headed back towards the Fairway Buoy, re-engaged the autopilot and came out into the cockpit staring back towards the reef.

"What's happened?" I dared to ask.

"Some bastard's had my pots."

He sat down heavily on the seat, flexing his fingers where they'd stiffened on the wheel. I waited.

"Do you know who it is?"

He shook his head.

"Would they have had lobsters in them as well? Your lobsters? Would they sell them? Where would they go to with all those pots? Wouldn't someone notice?"

He shrugged.

"Good questions. They'd have been unloaded in the dark, put on a truck somewhere and the lobsters sold to a dealer. I'm the only one with a permit round here. It'd suit someone to put me off, take over the licence."

He was quiet for a minute.

"Mind you," he said, relaxing a little. "Times are changing. There's new legislation on the way for shellfish quotas. Stocks are down and there's no money in it any more. The pots might have been empty. Just keeps a few of my customers happy."

"Would whoever it was have come from Porthmadog?"

"Unlikely. Everyone knows everyone else's business in Port. It's too busy in the summer and too difficult to unload on the quiet without someone noticing. More likely a boat out of Barmouth or Pwllheli. Someone who's already got pots. A few more on the back of a boat wouldn't raise any eyebrows. If it's about the pots at all," he said, almost to himself.

"What about the man Angela said is coming for his lobster tomorrow? What will you do?"

"You do ask a lot of questions," he said, irritation creeping into his voice. "I'll give him some smoked salmon instead."

"Will he mind?" I said.

I couldn't believe this was just all about lobsters. Someone didn't want him out there, buzzing around in his boat picking up pots and aware of anything unusual going on. My brain was knocking off facts like a row of dominoes; Tomas's eavesdropping on the phone call about stuff he didn't like but wouldn't tell me, his mother's reluctance to listen and the punishment he'd received from her partner Gareth for trespassing in the yard. Was I jumping to conclusions, trying to create a bigger story out of hot air rather than just a tourist feature? Had the slate trade evolved into something more sinister? Could I, should I, investigate?

"Don't you let it bother you," he said, taking my silence for distress.

"Oh it won't," I said. London and a new life loomed on the horizon. A feature might emerge from all this, a topical issue on fishing stocks or smuggling, even better. I filed the potential away for future reference. Property wars and arguments between two men, neither of whom I liked very much interested me as much as a cold haddock. Lobsters interested me even less. I looked longingly ahead for the Fairway Buoy, the sea empty except for a fast boat in the distance heading in the direction of Pwllheli.

"Wonder who that was," he said. "He doesn't want to be out here for much longer. Wind's picking up," he said, ignoring my discomfort and obvious nausea. We passed the Fairway Buoy and crossed the bar in short steep seas, the bows throwing up spray and soaking my face and hair. It was calmer in the estuary and we nosed into the wall and tied up.

I couldn't wait to get off, picked up the rucksack, thanked him for the trip and with indecent haste leaped off the boat and climbed the ladder up to the yard. I waved to Angela as she was winding in the awning at the front of the snack-bar, the scalloped edges fluttering red and white against the grey background and headed back to Borth-y-Gest. The wind snatched at my hair as I negotiated the steps down to the bay, still feeling unbalanced from the boat's motion. I headed for the warm comfort of the kitchen where Helen's Nain was measuring out flour for brownies.

"Enjoy your trip?" she asked, preoccupied with her baking and not waiting for an answer. "You're to sleep in the house tonight." It was not a request. "There's a storm on the way. I've made up a bed in the sitting room. The guests don't use it at night." She pointed through to the

barometer in the hall. "Dropping like a stone."
She spooned the cake mixture into tins on the table. I didn't argue. I'd had enough of the great outdoors. I'd already decided I was not cut out to be a mariner and preferred my feet on dry land, preferably in a warm dry kitchen with brownies baking in the oven. You could stuff the sea and its crabby sailors.

"So how did you get on?"

"Okay," I said. I didn't really want to talk about it. I hadn't yet had enough time to assimilate the mixture of brusqueness and familiarity and his tentative attempts at friendliness. "Someone stole his pots, though." I wandered down the garden, picked up my clothes from the tent, trod the tent-pegs hard into the ground and closed up the flaps. Beyond the end of the garden, tired leaves rustled in the oak wood as the wind blew in fitful gusts. I was glad to go inside.

We were sitting cross-legged on Helen's bed later, backs against the wall and snuggled into cushions facing the TV in the bay window and waiting for 'Casualty' to start. It had been my turn to supply the vodka. I basked in an alcoholic glow of well-being, of being warm and full of chicken casserole and cake, of leaving the day behind me with its mixed emotions and grey wildness and relishing the blanket of land-based security. The wind rattled the sash window and spattered the beginnings of rain against the glass. Between the gusts and even over the muted sound of the TV we could hear the insistent roar of the waves breaking on the bar.

I'd been out there, seen it for myself in its benign state on the way out to the reef and the difference on our way back in with a gale on the way. An ugly swell had been gathering at the Fairway Buoy, the waves marching in towards the No.4 where the sand bar crossed the entrance to the estuary. I imagined it at its worse with shallow water threatening to ground the boat and slew it sideways at the mercy of a breaking sea, the shifting quick-sands below the keel churned up and holding it fast. I shivered at the thought. I'd told Helen about the missing lobster pots but kept my ideas to myself. She would laugh and berate me for ridiculous notions and tell me to get real, not to get involved and to enjoy the rest of the holiday. I told myself not to stick my nose into something unpleasant, something deeper and guaranteed to spoil my fun. I was still on holiday. The vodka took over and I concentrated on the screen as the signature tune of 'Casualty' blared out the first two unmistakeable notes just as blue flashing lights bounced through the window and reflected onto the wall behind us. Helen shot off the bed and peered through the window.

"Coastguard... and a police car... and the Harbour Master. Something's going on."

Tomas Jenkins, the Tomas I'd spent the afternoon with only the day before, nine years old and wearing a red sweatshirt, blue shorts and carrying a fishing rod, was missing. He had been due home at five o'clock for his tea. It was now eight o'clock. 'Casualty' played out its dramas to empty front rooms as the whole village seemed to mobilise, gathering for news and instructions in the car-park, swelled by diners from the restaurant as they hurriedly finished their meals and joined the press of people now heading for the pillbox and the beaches beyond. The tide had turned, the strong southerly kicking up white horses across the estuary. We'd grabbed coats and joined the mass of people in the car-park, the coastguard and police directing operations and Doug Peterson wearing a bright yellow sailing jacket leading a group up the footpath to the cliff-top.

"Well, he would, wouldn't he? He's ex military, so he says," Helen said, her mouth pursed in dislike.

I heard Angela's voice carried on the wind before I saw her. She stood, a lone figure on top of the pillbox on the headland, a short green coat over her gingham overall, her hands cupped to her mouth, swaying precariously in the updraft from the rocks below. When I reached her, the wind and tears had streaked her face, her eyes hunting wildly from left to right, searching the rocks below the cliff where the incoming tide ran strongly below us, desperation in her voice as she shouted for Tomas.

We could see the group of people led by Doug Peterson: some walking along the path, calling, peering into bushes covering the cliff-face, some running down the steps into the sandy bays, ignoring the cold and wet, scrambling up Danger Rock and up over the cliff towards Samson's Bay. Angela teetered on the edge of the cliff.

I grabbed her by the arm, fearing for her safety in the gusts of wind, Helen on her other side and shouted in her ear to step back from the edge of the cliff, her voice muffled by sobs, her legs buckling as we walked her up the slope and sat her down on the bench below the church. Her voice came in choked sobs, trying to explain.

"We've been searching for hours, Gareth and Doug and me. He's never this late. He always comes home when the weather's bad. He never answered his phone. Gareth said he was probably up to no good, messing around in Doug's yard again. But he wasn't there. Doug checked in all the boats and Gareth looked in the harbour. He wasn't there either."

Anger crept into her voice.

"He's not supposed to come fishing here.We only allow him in the harbour, except he's been talking about the bass off Danger Rock. Gareth told him he'd be in trouble if we found out he'd gone there on his own."

Someone brought a coat and put it over her knees.

"Come back to Nain's," Helen said. "Leave it to the others. They've called out the lifeboat and the helicopter. You can't do any more here except get hypothermia."

"Did you check on the pontoons?" I asked, the picture in my head of the sun-baked planks of the pontoon and the silver mullet only the day before and Tomas's fascination with his 'bouldering' wall. And the beating he'd had from Gareth for trespassing.

She turned on me, a scathing look that would have sunk a ship.

"Of course we checked. Gareth went down and walked all along the pontoons and in the boats tied up. He called and called. I could hear him. I checked John's yard. He goes to Morfa Nefyn visiting friends on Fridays so I was on my own in the yard. Tomas never misses his tea on Fridays. Ever. We always have fish and chips from Allports. Then I rang the police."

Well, he wouldn't answer, I thought, if he'd been up to no good and was hiding, would he? I caught Helen's eye.

We told the coastguard where Angela would be and took her back to the house protesting only feebly. She'd been running up and down for three hours, sick with anxiety and exhaustion. Helen whispered a few words into her Nain's ear, picked up the big torch on the dresser and we left the house by the back door.

"What are you thinking?" Helen said, as we ran up the steps from the bay.

I shook my head, my breath coming too fast to talk. The gates to both yards were closed and locked.

"There's a hole in the fence," I said. "Tomas told me it was his escape route."

We squeezed through, brambles scratching our arms and stood on the harbour wall in Doug Peterson's yard at the top of a ladder.

"You must be bloody joking," Helen said. "Look."

The pontoon at the bottom of the ladder rose and fell with the waves on the incoming tide, banging against the metal steps and creaking against its moorings to the steel pile attached to the wall. The boat I'd been out on strained at its moorings against the wall as the waves rolled in beneath the hull.

"I'm going down," I said. "You can stay here if you want. Give me the torch."

I tucked it into my coat and zipped it up to the neck, the rubber cold against my skin and felt my way down the rungs, placing each foot carefully and relying on my hands like I'd never relied on them before. There's nothing like fear to give you strength, I thought wryly. I reached the bottom, the pontoon bucking and kicking under my feet like a mad horse and the spray breaking against the sides soaking my trainers. I held onto the ladder and looked up. She was right behind me.

"Thought I'd see if you got there alive first," she joked, hanging onto the ladder. "God this is awful."

The pontoon lurched like a demented animal as a wave passed underneath us. I felt my way along the pontoon to the balk of timber and the slab of harbour wall Tomas had proudly shown me with its huge slate blocks and nooks and crannies where the mortar had pitted and worn away. Tomas said he liked to use it for climbing up into Doug's yard. The rusting remnants of the old ladder to the right gripped the wall with sharp bolts and skeins of seaweed.

"Cass, wait," Helen called, "I can't see you."

This was Tomas's secret place, his climbing wall to the short cut through the yard he'd boasted about, the wall slimy and dripping with water. Pieces of rotten planking, a polystyrene cup and a plastic beer bottle had washed into the gap between the wall, the pontoon rising and sinking with the swell. I clung on to the bottom rung of the ladder with my right hand and pulled the torch out of my coat, shone it onto the surface of the water rising and falling beneath the rubbish.

I swallowed, not wanting to acknowledge the glimmer of red shirt under the planks, the flash of white skin and copper hair beneath the black weed as it lifted in the swell.

Helen made the call.

CHAPTER 7

There is something profoundly and quietly shocking in the proximity of a life ended, a bizarre feeling that something ought to be done when there is nothing that can be done. This was my first time at the scene of a death. There would be more to come with my chosen career, I knew, with traffic accidents and house fires and all the horror stories covered in the daily round of newsworthy tragedies. But I'd known this child, if only briefly, alive and vibrant with a sharp tongue, quick wits and a love of fishing, putting his trust in a total stranger and desperate to share secrets no one else would listen to. I battled distress with disbelief as I looked down at the still body. But I hadn't forgotten what he'd told me; every word.

When dad had been killed, my only glimpse of him in death had been in the funeral parlour, the neat, tidy body lying sedately in the coffin while the central heating hummed in the background and a vase of sickly sweet lilies permeated the room. Here, I was buffeted by the wind and rain, lurching to keep my balance on the pontoon as the rolling swell of grey waves marched down the harbour. This was death in the raw.

We pulled him out onto the wet planks. I stood looking down at his feet in its cheap trainers and striped socks, his body lying like a bundle of rags, the eyes wide and staring and glazed over, the freckles on his face now blended in with the white skin. Helen had checked methodically for vital signs. There were no histrionics, no frantic attempts at resuscitation. It was too late. I took my coat off and laid it over his legs, an automatic response that earned me a critical glance from Helen, her expression acknowledging the futility of my actions but understanding the gesture. We kneeled down by his side, holding onto the cleats on the pontoon for safety as the tide gathered pace and the wind increased. It howled in the shrouds of the yachts moored out in the river. We had to shout at each other to be heard.

"What on earth was he doing here in this weather?"

"He might have been climbing the wall to get out, caught out by the tide. He's done it before, he told me. It leads into Doug's yard. He must have lost his grip on the wet stone and fallen from the top."

She looked up at the wall and down to the gap at the bottom where the water surged between the bottom of the wall and the pontoon.

"He would have been trapped in that narrow space."

"Do you think he drowned because he couldn't get out?"

What was left of the words catching in my throat at the awfulness of it was snatched away by the wind, a vision of the child scrabbling at the pontoon to extricate himself from the narrow space as the waves broke over his head and the debris battered him under the surface.

Helen shuffled backwards on her knees as the motion of the waves beneath the pontoon increased. I stood by his feet, keeping my balance with one hand on the harbour wall, my brain on overload, fact and emotion racing through my mind and scrambled together like the mess of flotsam and jetsam heaving below at the base of the wall. Even then, with the tragedy unfolded in front of me, I could hear Tomas's words, the words he'd thought he'd heard Doug speak on the phone and the confusing effort to make sense of what he didn't understand but knew intrinsically that it was wrong. He had shared his thoughts with me as an adult who should know what to do, what action to take for the best, concern for an old man he liked.

But I had kept them to myself, taking my own advice in relation to the passing on of gossip, of unclear meanings and the damage caused in the wrong hands. I added it all up. My conscience pricked at me and questioned my part in his death because I hadn't shared his worries with someone: the pressure on great-uncle John to sell the yard, the row I'd overheard in the shed between him and Doug Peterson, Helen's open dislike of the arrogant man with his wandering hands and snippets of information from Angela. It all piled up in my mind. I knew that any interference from me, any divulging of information, could make life unpleasant for my great-uncle and I would be far away, back to London and carrying on with my studies leaving a mess behind me. But deep down I just hadn't wanted to know. It was not my fight, any more than lobsters or fishing rights, veganism or New Age life on the road. I had my own life to lead. I also knew I would have to face my conscience. But not now.

Sirens wailed above us and the first figures peered down from the top of the ladder. The bright orange of the Criccieth lifeboat emerged out of the fading light at the same time, lurched into the pontoon on the swell and tied up by the side of us. We were moved to one side by the crew, the rain was heavy now, my hair plastered to my face and my jeans soaked. Police and paramedics climbed down the ladder, and Helen responded to all their questions clearly and competently. Tomas was surrounded by bent figures as they strapped him to a stretcher lowered down the ladder. I stood shivering, isolated in my misery, my coat lying on the planks where they'd removed it from his legs. They slid the stretcher carefully into the boat and motored to the bottom of the slipway and the waiting ambulance. We were told to go back to the yard and wait in the shed.

I heard Angela's screams as I reached the top of the ladder, the yard alive with uniforms and cars, the flashing blue lights eerie in the grey light. She ran towards the slipway, teeth bared like a wild animal. They lifted the stretcher from the boat onto a trolley as the ambulance backed up to the top of the slip. A man I assumed was Gareth followed behind her, a short man with a stooped posture. He was wearing a donkey jacket and boots, a black baseball cap pulled down over his forehead. He kept looking uncertainly to the left and right like an actor in a stage-set, unsure of his cues. We were ushered through the open door of the shed as the stretcher was loaded into the back of the ambulance, Angela held back by the Harbour Master, his shoulders wide and protective as he tried to restrain her. I didn't want to look.

It was dark in the Boat Shed. Helen found a light switch and a fluorescent tube over the counter flickered into life. There was still no sign of my uncle. My legs started to shake and Helen pushed me round the back of the counter into one of the old chairs I'd sat in two days before, the cold and the shock hitting me. I started to shake, nausea rising in my throat, my teeth chattering uncontrollably. Helen picked up an old rug from the back of the opposite chair, threw it over my knees, lifted the kettle from the shelf and filled it from the cold tap. It was as though she'd been here before. She found the mugs and took milk from the mini fridge under the counter and sat down in the chair opposite, the silence shattered by the rain clattering on the tin roof.

The door opened, the shadow of my uncle filling the space, his look directed at Helen busy with the kettle and mugs. Even in my state of shock, I thought irrelevantly of the easy familiarity between these practical people, the polite rituals of greeting seemingly unnecessary but of course he'd know who Helen was. He was at school with her grandmother. He nodded to her briefly, leaned on the counter and looked down at me shivering in his chair.

"They've told you," Helen said.

He brushed his hand over his face, pale beneath the tan and shuffled around the counter shaking his head. He opened the door to the wood stove, threw in a firelighter and dry sticks and lit them, then reached under the counter and pulled out a bottle of Grouse. Helen poured hot water onto tea-bags as he fetched a wooden stool and sat between us, his back to the counter, the light dim and the sticks crackling in the stove, the heat already thawing my numb fingers. Nobody spoke, our individual thoughts separate yet blended; the terrible grief of the mother, the relationship with the man she'd sent to look for him, the way forward for her with a lifelong sentence of bereavement. It didn't merit words.We sat in silence, sipping the hot tea and whisky.

"The snack-bar," my uncle said, out of the blue, more to himself than us. "There's food ready for the weekend. Angie'll not be coming in. There's fish ready in the smoke-house waiting to be packaged. Maybe I should just close it down. The food will have to be binned. I can't see what to do."

It was a statement not a question. I remembered after dad died, how the practicalities of life carried on; dishes to be washed and folk to feed as though nothing had happened, the need to keep busy paramount.

I snapped out of my shocked torpor, the problem he'd voiced thrown into the air like a lifeline. It was too early to give in to shock and grief. I remembered all that from dad's sudden death. It would happen when it was ready and usually without warning. It still did. I thought about the next few days and how people cope in the aftermath of a tragedy. Statements had to be given the following day, they said, and I had to decide how much to tell the police. They'd offered us support but we'd said no. We had Nain and each other's company. I needed to be busy.

"I'll do it," I said, blurting it out without even thinking. "I've done it before in cafes. I don't know Angela well but she takes pride in that little place. I know how she does it. I'll run it for you for a few days so the food isn't wasted."

"I'll help," said Helen. "They won't let us go anyway until all the statements are completed. We'll be better if we're busy. But will you cope, Mr Jones? Will you be alright on your own?"

Helen looked at him directly. He acknowledged her concern with a nod of his head, her unspoken allusion to the death of his own children.

"It was a long time ago. But thank you for asking. I've work to do. I'll stay here the night. You two go now. Your Nain will wonder where you are."

He scraped the stool back, threw some logs on the fire, turned his back on us and disappeared through the door to the smoke-house. I'd stopped shivering and the whisky soothed the misery for a brief moment. We informed the police we would be available there in the morning for statements.

"Will Angela have someone to look after her?" I asked as we left the yard. "I know she's got a partner but Tomas said..." I couldn't go on.

"What? That Gareth? Waste of space he is. Nain's told me all about him. Fingers in the till when Angela ran the shop and Post Office. That's where the money went, people say, when they closed her down but she didn't tell the police what she suspected. Too scared of him. They've got a tiny cottage in the village now. Gareth works for Doug Peterson sometimes. Why she stays with him God only knows. Police liaison would be with her, anyway."

The gates to Doug Peterson's yard were wide open. Two police cars were parked in front of the showroom and the lights were on in the upstairs office.

"Wonder if they're thanking him for doing a brilliant job coordinating the search?" the sarcasm in her voice unmistakable.

"Or if they're asking him why he and Gareth didn't find Tomas when they were searching the harbour. They can't have looked that hard. We found him. It wasn't rocket science, was it?"

"He's such a smooth-talking bastard," she said. "I bet they'll believe anything. Come on."

We headed up the footpath and down the steps to the village, guilt and fear catching my throat. I needed to talk. A strong south-westerly had whipped up the waves in the bay, the water already slapping against the slate wall with the approaching high tide. It was nine o'clock and nearly dark. I stopped by the gate and grabbed Helen's arm.

"I need to talk to you," I said.

She caught the urgency in my voice and steered me over the road to the bus-shelter out of the wind. I told her everything that Tomas had told me, what he'd overheard and his curiosity to know what Doug had meant by the words in the phone call.

"Tomas said his mum hated Doug. Perhaps he meant for protecting Gareth? I don't know. He couldn't understand why she was angry with him for telling her about bad things he might be doing now even if he didn't understand the words. Then Gareth punished him for being in the yard but that didn't put him off.

'I got the feeling he might have gone back to the yard to see if he could listen in on any more conversations. I tried to tell him that eavesdropping sometimes got people into trouble because they didn't always know or understand the whole story, but it's difficult explaining that to a nosy child. He just walked off. He was such a bright, confident little boy. Is it my fault he's dead?"

I choked up. Helen put her arm round my shoulder.

"I knew that if I told someone Tomas would get into real trouble and I couldn't say anything to Angela. She already knew and warned him off. She's his mother after all. I'd have been intruding and making a worse muddle. I was just hoping he'd made it all up."

"Shit," she said quietly.

"What do I do now? I can't live with this," I said.

She was quiet for a moment.

"Suppose he was right, suppose we both suspect Doug Peterson is involved in some sort of shady dealings; drugs, people, I don't know. Why wouldn't I be surprised? All that money for a new yacht and a flash car, that pressure on your uncle to sell his business to get him out of there. That land and the slipway must be worth over a million. He'd have to have the money from somewhere and it wouldn't be from flogging the occasional Skidoo."

"That's a serious accusation," I said.

"Yeah, but I bet you thought it too. And didn't you tell me your uncle sleeps in the shed a lot to keep an eye on things? Bet he suspects something."

"And that makes him vulnerable as well, doesn't it?"

"Yes, it does but he'll know that."

The wind rattled the bus-shelter roof and an empty drinks can rolled down the car-park tapping against the line of boulders on the grass verge and out into the water. The tide crept higher up the wall.

"But if there was something seriously criminal going on, the police would already be investigating it," I said.

"They're not going to share it with the general public, are they? Don't be naive, Cassie. You've got to tell them everything in case it's information that might help. Drug stuff goes on round this coast all the time, it's just we never get to hear about it unless it's a biggie that's been planned and then resolved. You know the damage caused by drugs on the street. Didn't you say your father was killed by a crack addict?"

Helen's bluntness brought the bigger picture into focus. Even in the aftermath of the tragedy of a drowned child fencing my brain in, I started to think. Helen echoed my thoughts.

"There's Angela who wouldn't and didn't want to listen to Tomas because she was scared, Gareth because he's up to no good and works for Doug and poor Tomas who was just a nosy child in the wrong place at the wrong time and overheard stuff he shouldn't. I could understand why someone would want to stop the gossip at source."

"What do you mean?" I said, a sick feeling in my stomach.

"Did Tomas just fall, I wonder?" she said, "or did something frighten him so much he had to let go? Then he might have hit his head on one of those bolts on that ladder or something. He'd have been unconscious when he hit the water and been submerged under all that debris. That's why he couldn't scramble out."

"But why would anyone be on the edge of the wall unless they were moving trailers?" I said. "Unless possibly making phone calls away from the office, like the story he told me when he was eavesdropping. He got into trouble for that. It's still unthinkable that anyone would do something like that deliberately, like frighten him as he put his head up above the wall to climb over into the yard and knowing he'd fall."

"Ain't it just?" she said. "Maybe it was just a simple thing that went wrong with no malice intended. We've no proof it was anything else."

"What do I do, Helen? I can't keep this all to myself, can I?"

"No," she said. "Not anymore. Talk to the police when you give your statement tomorrow but stick to the facts. You can't go round accusing people of causing the death of a child, Cass."

"But what about Tomas's story and what he heard about my uncle and the threat to the yard? I'll be going go back to London as an interfering fly-by-night and leave him on his own with the whole episode tainted with suspicion and accusation. I can't believe there wouldn't be some sort of revenge if the police start asking questions. He's an old man, even if I don't like him very much."

We stood up. She looked me straight in the eye.

"Your decision," she said.

"Yeah, right, as if I don't know. And don't call me fucking naive, either," suddenly cross with myself for not grasping all the facts as quickly as Helen. "I just think differently to you."

We crossed the road heading for the sanctuary of Helen's Nain's kitchen, my sharp retort earning a swift look of appraisal. She squeezed my arm. No hard feelings.

The wail of sirens and blue lights flashing across the bay stopped us in our tracks.

"God, what now?"

A police car and an ambulance swung round the corner past the bus shelter and turned sharply up the steep hill leading to the primary school.

"Angela lives up there," Helen said." That's where she rents the cottage. Come on."

We ran up the hill. The close bordered by terraced cottages was blocked off by a police car. From the cottage in the middle of the terrace we could hear Angela's voice even from where we stood, the words overriding the conciliatory voices of the police, the medics ushering a man into the back of the ambulance. He was holding his arm encased in a white dressing with a dark stain showing up in the dim light.

"Oh my God, that's Gareth," said Helen, catching her breath. "That's his van parked outside."

A white Transit with the back doors open was surrounded by piles of clothes, bags and bedding. Angela stood in the doorway of the small cottage, throwing objects down the path. A boot hit the side of the van and bounced off onto the gravel. Neighbours watched from the other side. Nobody moved.

Angela's voice echoed round the village, every word clear, a torrent of verbal abuse, screamed at the top of her voice, the anger and despair cracking her words apart, having to listen seeming like an intrusion into the worst, personal and private grief imaginable. I cringed, physically and emotionally at the passion.

"He'd have come home for his tea if you hadn't said you'd beat the living shit out of him. I'll fucking kill you if I ever see you again," were her last words screamed before the police woman turned her around and bundled her through the door, a kitchen knife held firmly in her spare hand.

The medics shut the doors to the ambulance and drove off.

We stood in stunned silence. Helen put a foot forward.

"Leave it," I said to Helen, holding her arm. "She's got people there. They'll deal with it."

"She stabbed him, didn't she? I saw a knife in the policewoman's hand. What'll happen to her? Will they arrest her?"

I felt a subtle change in our relationship, my new, practical medical student friend sure of herself when it came to bodies but not so easy with the consequences of such profound and disturbing emotion. Even with my schoolgirl experience toward the daily stuff of tragedies for newspaper fodder, I knew that the police would have to work with a difficult set of circumstances of grief-fuelled assault. She needed professional, personal care now, before the media descended. There would be no peace for a while. We crept down the hill, my phone already ringing, my mother concerned after the national news had picked up the story of the missing child and now the breaking news of his death. It hadn't taken long to hit the media.

The comfort of food and warmth dispelled only a small fragment of the day. I thought of Angela and her impossible grief, her trust in a man she now accused of the loss of her son. The story of Angela's misfortunes unfolded as Helen's Nain sat with us at the table.

"She couldn't make ends meet," said Helen's Nain. "Tesco had just opened, The Post Office was closing branches everywhere anyway and... she told me once in confidence, she couldn't balance the books at the end of each day, no matter how careful she was. Every one suspected Gareth of having his fingers in the till but you couldn't tell her. He bought a van and had a new fishing kayak but he never seemed to work much. She was very defensive. Frightened, I thought, of the consequences of confronting him."

"So what happened?" I asked.

"The shop closed and she moved up the road to the cottage she's in now. She had no money until John took her on to run the snack-bar. Gareth's been working for Doug Peterson on and off."

"Pity she didn't cut his throat never mind his arm," said Helen, loading the dishwasher.

I slept hardly at all that night on the sofa in the front room, the gale howling through the village and rain slamming at the big bay window leaving a misty, washed-out Saturday morning. My rash promise to run the snack-bar mingled with trepidation about giving a statement to the police and how much to explain what I'd heard from Tomas. I also didn't know how I'd feel going back to the yard with the stark cameo of the ambulance and Tomas's body being loaded into the ambulance imprinted on my mind and Angela's screams still ringing in my ears. But I'd said I would.

A deep silence had settled over the bay, an absence of the usual early morning footsteps and dogs barking, of children's voices over buckets and spades and footballs on the sand below the sea wall. We walked in silence. Even the sea was quiet. The gate to the yard was already open when we rounded the corner, my uncle's Toyota still parked by the door from the night before. Smoke curled lazily from the chimney-pot on the smoke-house at the back of the shed. I glanced down through the open gates to the yard next door, already busy with boat owners waiting to have their boats craned in and jet-ski owners hitching up the trailers to take to the beach. I'd expected a subdued silence, I suppose, then realised that none of these folk were part of the previous day's tragedy; many would not have heard the news and would go about their weekend pleasures anyway. Holidays are precious and what could they do?

The shed door was open. I negotiated boxes stacked to one side and ropes coiled on the floor and found my uncle shovelling wood chippings for smoking the last batch of fish in the smoke-house. It was as though nothing had happened.

"You've come then," he said by way of greeting, showed me through to the tiny kitchen adjoining the snack-bar where Angela vacuum-packed the fish and prepared the sandwiches. It was spotless.

"I'll deal with the fish for packing later," he said. "You'll find plenty in the fridge for sandwiches."

"Did you get some sleep?" thinking he might be too upset to talk, imagining the uncomfortable old chairs by the fire. He didn't reply, just handed me the keys to the snack-bar.

"When Arnie Blackwell comes for his lobster, tell him to come and find me," was all he said, "and you and the Parry girl can use the shed for your statements when the police arrive. I've lit the stove against the damp."

He turned his back abruptly and disappeared through the back door to the smoke-house, the shovel scraping the concrete under the wood shavings as he stoked the fire and checked the fish already hanging on the hooks.

Helen had unlatched and pulled out the awning and set out the plastic tables and chairs, wiping the rain off. I investigated the small kitchen and checked the fridges and hot plates. I thought I could manage if I did a lot of apologising for delays. I had a feeling that customers would be few and far between, the yard tainted with the death of a child. Would I buy a prawn sandwich here so close to the event? Probably not, but I was glad to be busy, knowing full well that shock would rear its head eventually. I kept reminding myself this was a process I needed to get used to, to assimilate the disasters that befall people and carry out the task in hand.

"It goes on, doesn't it?"

Helen's voice broke the silence as I straightened up from the counter, her arm gesturing around the yard.

"What does?"

"Life," she said, "it just goes on."

Not for Angela I thought, as I wiped down her shining stainless-steel counter. How does anyone go on after the death of a child? Or a father, come to that. But here we were, my uncle, Helen and me, the holiday makers next door, making lives, getting on with stuff. I chewed it over as I wiped and tidied, wishing the police would arrive so I could give my statement and unload the information that had festered in my head all night.

The blue and yellow paintwork of the police car flashed through the gate at last and I was summoned to the shed. I felt better after they'd dismissed me, the police woman was kind and sympathetic but her colleague listened intently when I told them of Tomas's story of the phone conversation. Be careful, Helen had reminded me, just stick to the facts. Forget suspicions and suppositions. It's not your job. Eyebrows were raised when I mentioned 'coke'. Make of it what you will, I decided.

I took over the snack-bar from Helen, already on her way to the shed to give her statement. Wheels crunched on the gravel as a white Range Rover nosed its way through the gate and pulled up in the yard. The windows were down and a baby's cry pierced the silence. I stood behind the counter remembering my uncle's instructions for the man called Arnie Blackwell and his order for the regular holiday lobster. A man emerged from the driver's seat, opened the rear door and bent over for a few minutes. He stood up, turned around and faced me.

He was built like a wrestler, about six foot two of solid muscle encased in black jeans and a close–fitting T-shirt that defined his muscles. Long black hair slicked back from a broad forehead was tied in a pony tail and a gold hoop glinted in one ear. His fore arms were tattooed down to the wrists, the left arm across his chest cradling a baby wearing a blue sunbonnet, his brown legs kicking happily, wide awake and smiling up at the man's face, a black Zapata moustache framing his mouth and a baby's dummy gripped firmly between his teeth. He pulled it out with his right hand, sucked it and placed it in the baby's mouth.

"I told you not to do that, Arnie," a sharp voice called through the window. "It's dirty."

"Nothing wrong with my mouth, darlin'," he said, turning towards the car. I could hear every word. "You don't seem to mind it."

He turned back towards me with a grin on his face and winked. I think I blushed.

He walked over towards me and stood in front of the counter, the baby gazing up at him with big eyes.

"Angela around?"

I put the cloth down and told him quietly about Tomas, the baby wiggling brown toes in the air.

"Hell," he said, turning and calling to the woman following behind him. "Shelly, you hear that?"

A woman picked her way carefully over the gravel, white high-heel sandals and long, tanned legs disappearing into the hem of a short denim skirt.

"What? The ginger-haired kid? The one with the fishing rod?"

"You do mean Angela's boy?" he said, as if he hadn't heard first time.

The woman touched Arnie's arm, leant into him, her head only just reaching his shoulder, staring at me.

"Mr Jones says could you go and find him. He'll explain about the lobster. I'm afraid he hasn't got any today. Somebody stole his pots," I said.

"Hell," he said again. "And Angela's boy's dead? Here, Shelley, take the kid, will you?"

He strode off down the yard to the shed. She took the baby back to the car and strapped him into the seat, leaving the door open and tottered back to the counter.

"Give us a skinny latte, love."

I turned around to prepare it, could hear her nails tapping on the counter.

"How did he die then? Up to no good, was he?" she said, her conversational tone shocking me.

"Why do you say that?" I asked, barely able to conceal my dislike.

"He was always snooping around the yard next door, used to drive Doug mad. Our boys keep their jet-skis there. They don't miss much. So how did he die then? Can't imagine him being careless. Can't believe he drowned. He was pretty clued up, you know?"

I knew.

She took her coffee, hands all red nails and gold bangles.

"Arnie'll settle up," she said. "Shame about the lobster. Got any smoked salmon?"

I was speechless.

Unfeeling bitch, I thought and handed her the coffee. She sat down at one of the tables. It promised to be another hot day despite the storm that had battered the coast in the night. I looked over to the Range Rover and the baby strapped into the car seat.

"Will the baby be alright in there? You can bring him over in the shade if you like."

"Arnie will carry him," she said. "He's heavy."

I looked over. The baby was kicking its legs happily against the car seat. She got up suddenly, scraping the chair legs in the gravel.

"Keep an eye on him, will you? Won't be a sec. Just going to get the boys."

She disappeared through the gates and into the yard opposite out of sight but not out of earshot.

"Jem! Zac!" her shrill voice echoing around the cliffs behind me and came back with two young men in tow, her walk brisk and determined despite the short skirt, and directed them to the table. Boys pretending to be men more like, with slim, toned bodies clad in designer shorts and cutaway T-shirts like their father. That's where the similarity ended. They had tanned smooth faces and blond hair, as alike as two peas in a pod. Their faces would have been attractive if not for their sulky expressions. They threw themselves ungraciously into the plastic chairs, rocking dangerously on the back legs.

"Don't do that," the woman snapped, catching my eye and glaring at them. They fidgeted and whispered between themselves as they looked over towards me behind the counter, "you'll break the chairs... and where's your brother gone?"

One of them pointed towards the gate. A younger boy appeared from behind the gatepost. He scuffed over the gravel in old Nike trainers, creased shorts covering his knees and a baggy shirt hanging off his thin shoulders

"For God's sake, Jason, where have you been?"

He shrugged and stood in front of her, picking his nails.

"I'm ordering food for us. Go and see if the girl's got anything you can eat. Got any veggie burgers?" she called.

The boy sidled up to the counter, lifted his head and stared at the chalked-up menu. He was about fifteen, I guessed and a sorry specimen of a teenager. Poor lad, I thought having a mother with the maternal instincts of a house-brick. I knew about that, feeling a lurch of compassion for his thin frame and spotty face.

"No meat, then?" I asked.

He shrugged. "Can't stand crappy meat and not knowing where it's from, like. Minced up shit you don't know what's in it, yeah?"

"Yeah, right. Veggie or vegan?"

"Just veggie, but no dairy." He bent his head and mumbled into his T-shirt.

"An' I hate veggie burgers."

I could see the raw patches of eczema on his elbows and a rash of acne on his chin, a startling contrast to his tanned, well-groomed older brothers. They were still twitching their feet and kicking the gravel around, making loud comments and sniggering, irritating their mother whose face had tightened into a frown. I looked at the boy called Jason with his high forehead and sharp cheekbones and acne and well remembered the agonies of my early teens. I gave him my full attention and thought hard about the contents of Angela's small but well-stocked kitchen and Milly's comfort cooking from my childhood days.

"Eggs?"

He nodded.

"Special breakfast for you, then. Bet you're hungry."

He flashed a look of gratitude and walked over to a table on his own.

It felt surreal, flipping over onions and burgers, slicing buns and peeling cheese slices out of their cellophane envelopes, such mundane tasks only the day after finding Tomas, the pale dead face swimming obstinately into my vision in the seconds when I wasn't occupied. I shook myself, knowing my buried emotions would emerge eventually. I would deal with them then.

For now, my feelings extended in sympathy to the kid sitting on his own, immersed in his phone. In the freezer, I found bananas used for smoothies and the sliced white bread Angela kept for prawn sandwiches and on a shelf, a shaker of cinnamon for topping cappuccinos. I beat up two eggs and soaked triangles of bread, sliced two bananas into lengths, brushed them with olive oil and coated them with sugar and cinnamon. I fried them on the griddle away from the burgers, the eggy bread puffing up golden and the bananas crisp and brown.

I plated it up carefully and called him over.

"Water?"

He nodded and took the plate and the bottle of chilled Volvic I'd taken from the fridge.

"Wow," he said. "Cheers," his eyes brightening and went back to sit at the table on his own.

"That was nicely done," Helen's voice from behind startled me. "Bit sad, isn't he?"

Arnie arrived, the baby now extricated from the car seat cradled in his huge arm, the older boys noticeably quieter as he talked to them, gesturing towards Doug's yard.

"Pleasant family," Helen said as they were filling their faces."Do you think they feed burgers to the baby?"

"He's lovely. A happy baby," I said. "Seems to have bypassed the genetic makeup of the others. Let's hope their dad pays the bill."

"Funny combination," Helen said thoughtfully leaning on the counter. "Those twins are blue-eyed blonds like their mother but the baby and spotty kid are brown-eyed like their dad."

"Do you fancy them, then? The older ones, I mean?"

"You're joking. Those arrogant bad-mouthed little shits? Think they're God's gift to women. They haven't stopped looking at you. And twitchy? They can't keep still for a minute. Have you noticed?"

"Probably excited about getting the jet-skis out onto the water."

"Yeah," she said gazing thoughtfully out to the yard. "More like tanked up on something."

I left her to clear up after they'd gone and went to find my uncle. He was standing by a rowing skiff, running a cloth over the hull, the varnish so bright I could see my reflection. Two long oars rested on the seats. He looked strained and tired and barely acknowledged my presence. I could hear him wheezing when he straightened up.

"Is this your own boat, as well as the big one we went out on?"

He nodded, swiping the rag along the deck and over the brass fitting on the bow.

"I've sold that man Arnie some smoked salmon instead of the lobster. That's what his wife wanted. Is that okay? Was he alright about the lobster? I told him the pots had been stolen. Was he annoyed?"

He turned his head towards me, leaning with one hand on the hull.

"Don't you ever stop asking questions?"

"Not very often," I said, "which is why I get to know lots so I can learn how to write stories and fill them full of juicy titbits for the not so discerning public to read."

I don't think he knew whether I was being facetious or not and grunted in response. He pulled up a round of timber and sat down, cleared his throat and fished in his pockets for his tobacco. It was late in the afternoon, the day redeeming itself once again in hot sunshine. He motioned towards another log of wood for me to sit down.

I felt flat and exhausted, only vaguely listening to him telling me the background of Arnie Blackwell and Sons, Scrap Dealers from Dudley and his ill-mannered twins who were constantly in trouble with the Harbour Authority over excessive speed on the jet-skis. They buzzed yachtsmen in the narrow channel risking their boats going aground and blared out loud music at barbecues on the beach. It seemed they were within an inch of being banned from the water altogether if their father didn't keep a tight grip on their behaviour.

Then there was Jason, the middle child, about fifteen he said, with the acne and long, sensitive fingers and bitten nails which I'd noticed when he took his plate from me. Not scrap-dealing material, my uncle said, but doesn't stand much of a chance to do anything else in his life with that lot dominating him.

"Wouldn't be surprised if he runs away when he's older," he said. "Likes to talk about the old ships and the way people lived round here in the slate days. He comes over here to escape from his brothers when they're messing with their jet-skis. They bully him and make fun of him. He just mooches around on his own. He used to talk to Tomas a lot. He's welcome any day."

"He'll be upset, then," I said, "but he didn't say anything when I served him. His mother's a cold fish. No use him looking to her for a bit of comfort and understanding."

I remembered Helen's Nain telling me about my great-uncle John as a child and how he was bullied by his brother, my grandfather. He must have remembered and was happy to give Jason the space to be on his own. I looked at him with different eyes; briefly.

We sat in silence again, it suddenly occurring to me that we were having a conversation. Sort of.

"That baby's an after-thought, then," I said, musing on Shelley's obvious reluctance to handle the baby, "and that boy Jason's vegetarian as well," I added inconsequentially. "Skinny kid and lovely hands but nails bitten to the quick. He's miserable. Shame."

I stood up quickly, a wave of unwanted compassion threatening to engulf me, the tragedy flooding into my head like a spring tide. Not now, I promised myself, not here.

"I'll close up," I said. "I've emptied the fridge.Will you keep the shop open in case Angela comes back?"

He shook his head.

"She won't be back. Would you?"

I looked around the yard, imagining the child with the bright shock of ginger hair and the fishing rod. How could she come back with the ghost of her child flitting between the upturned boats and sitting like Banquo's ghost in an empty plastic chair waiting for his mother to bring him a can of Coke? I couldn't imagine it.

"I have to go back home on Monday," I said. "My course starts in a few weeks. I have to do some work to get ready for the start of term."

"There'll be Tomas's funeral," he said, an unspoken question in his voice as I turned to go. I wasn't promising anything. I couldn't even think about it.

"Yes, I know. I'll call and say goodbye tomorrow. If that's okay?"

CHAPTER 8

I slept in the tent that night, the mozzies kept at bay by a light breeze. There was a chill in the air that heralded the beginning of autumn and I tucked my nose well down into the sleeping bag. In the morning, I slid around and lay on my stomach with my head by the open tent flap and my nose in the wet grass shimmering with spider-webs, planning my last day saying goodbye to my great-uncle with whom on reflection, I felt no connection with whatsoever despite the shared awfulness of Tomas's death.

They say tragedy brings people together but there was too much distance and too little shared history for our relationship to be meaningful. Even his attempts at friendliness on the boat when we were motoring out to the reef had felt uncomfortably forced. I was glad I'd made the effort to meet him, desperately sad about the little boy I'd met briefly and gutted for his mother but wanted no part of my life cluttered with this shabby boatyard and failing business and the shed crammed to the rafters with dusty relics for obsolete sailing boats. I hated the peeling paint and leaky tin roof and the pervasive smell of fish from the smokehouse. I didn't much like him either.

I missed my writing and chatting to like-minded people, sitting at my computer and downloading photographs, planning and designing layouts for stories and features. I knew that even when I finished my degree and then worked for a newspaper with more exams to take, it would be a good few years, if ever, that I would have the opportunity to write features. Dream on, I thought. I had a long way to go and couldn't wait to get started. Helen's voice shook me out of my reverie.

"Breakfast's ready. And news," she shouted down the garden. "You have to come and see this."

Helen's Nain placed bacon and eggs in front of us and turned up the sound on the portable TV tucked in between plates and dishes on the dresser.

"Told you there was stuff going on," said Helen, her mouth full of buttered toast.

"A powerboat in Pwllheli Marina has been seized by officers from the National Crimes Agency on suspicion of connection to a major drugs haul linked to the interception of a yacht yesterday off the southwest coast of Ireland," the TV blared.

'The 28 foot powerboat, 'Fast Lady' had been escorted back to Pwllheli from Rosslare after a call to the RNLI Officers from the Border Patrol searched the boat before releasing it for its journey back to North Wales. Indications are that the powerboat was intending to rendezvous with the 40 foot yacht 'Andromeda' on route from the West Indies to North Wales with a cargo of cocaine destined to be unloaded for the UK Market.

'The 3,000 mile journey for the 'Andromeda' ended 200 miles off the coast of Ireland when military personnel from an Irish naval frigate boarded the yacht and escorted it to Cork harbour where a large amount of cocaine was impounded. A combined task force had been tracking the yacht across the Atlantic before its entry into Irish territorial waters."

"I know that Pwllheli boat," said Helen. "One of these Launch and

Ride deals people use if they're only here occasionally. Don't know who it belongs to now, though. How did they think they were going to offload that amount of drugs onto the shore without anyone noticing? Kilo bags on the back of jet-skis?"

We stared at each other. I mused over the news item as we cleared the dishes, remembering that Helen had said she'd crewed on boats out of the marina since she was a teenager and knew most of the boats and the people who owned them.

"Tomas said..." I started.

Helen flashed me a warning look across the table and slammed the dishwasher shut.

"I'll miss you two," said Helen's Nain, bustling around unimpressed by the news. "The guests will disappear for the winter and Helen won't be back until goodness-knows when and I still haven't quite got used to being on my own. Will you come back for a visit, do you think?"

"I don't know," I said. "I only came to try and make a connection with my uncle. He doesn't like me much and I seem to have brought nothing but trouble. I don't really belong here, do I? You've been so good to me and I shan't forget it but I think I belong in the busy world out there."

"But your roots are here, you know; your grandfather and his father. You can't ignore it. Maybe in time you'll think differently."

I bent down and gave her a kiss on the cheek, which surprised myself as well as her.

I left the house and made my way through the bay, late summer tourists already filling the car-parks and cafes, up the steps and down the other side under the trees to the corner of the boatyard where the sign still hung at an angle on the fence. My brain chewed over the story of the cocaine haul, the potential connections and food for a story. It would make a brilliant feature, following the lines of communication and the sheer audacity of the guys who'd set it up. Helen had said they must have been nuts to leave the Caribbean in the hurricane season so they were either clever risk-takers, desperate and greedy or just plain stupid. I didn't know much about hurricanes and couldn't imagine a month at sea cooped up with bales of cocaine and a couple of other guys in potentially lethal weather. But what did I know?

I followed my feet up the steps and down the path on the other side in a story-board day-dream not watching where I was going until I looked up at the entrance to the Boat Shed gate. Doug Peterson stood in the gateway, legs apart and arms folded across his chest, his dark hair slicked back from his forehead and pale blue eyes staring straight at me. I nodded briefly and made to walk around him.

"Come back for your photographs, then?" he said, and looked meaningfully at the little Sony slung over my shoulder.

I wanted to push past him, the man who'd been sent to hunt for Tomas. I'd found it hard to believe he'd looked thoroughly, remembering Angela's screams when they brought Tomas out of the lifeboat and placed him on the stretcher, the torrent of abuse she'd hurled at her partner Gareth as he climbed into the ambulance clutching a bloodstained arm while she threw clothes and shoes at him before the police took charge. If he'd looked properly in the first place, would Tomas be alive now? I tried desperately to keep my emotions under control, suspecting he could read the accusation on my face.

"What's your problem? You think we didn't look properly for the kid, is that it?"

"I found him easily enough," I retorted. "Perhaps I looked a bit more carefully than you did."

I swallowed, scared and knowing I'd overstepped the mark.

"Well let me tell you this, missy," he said, his head jutted towards me and the muscles stood out on the powerful neck. His tone was sharp, the words enunciated slowly.

"I knew perfectly well he'd be frightened to come out if he'd been hiding in the yard in the first place, climbing over the wall when he'd been told not to. He knew that but he still kept doing it, sneaking around and listening to people's conversations, always flitting around under my boats."

"But he was only a child..."

He cut me off.

"I checked every single boat in the yard in case he was hiding: every cabin, every trailer and every tarpaulin. He wasn't there, not anywhere. Gareth checked all the boats on the pontoon and there was no sign of him then. If he fell off the wall he must have been hiding somewhere else and fallen after we left to look for him on the cliff top."

"I didn't think..." I began.

"That's your problem, isn't it? You don't think. Snooping around with your immature inflated sense of your own importance just because you've got a camera slung over your shoulder. This is private property and you're on my land with your dangerous, snap-happy accusations and taking photographs without permission. Reporter on a newspaper, eh? Doing a feature? Interested in the history of the place? I don't think so." He poked the air in front of me and jabbed his finger in my face. I stepped back. My foot caught the tow-bar of a trailer and I stumbled, twisting and catching myself on the metal. My camera strap slipped off my shoulder and the camera fell between me and the hard metal edge. I heard the crack as my foot landed on it. I bent down and picked it up. The lens was shattered.

"I can't believe you just did that."

I stared at him holding the camera out towards him.

"You've wrecked my camera," I said, my face burning.

"And you're trespassing on my land." He stared me down. "And you've

taken pictures in my yard without my permission."
He'd seen me snapping away blithely, caught on camera, even the last defiant act as I walked through his gates a few days before. I should have known better.

"I don't know what you're doing here but I suggest you go back to where you came from and take that friend of yours with you."
The colour rose in his face and suffused the tan into a deep red. He was angry and I was too scared to confront him about the camera. I'd been in the wrong and knew it.

He walked away and I choked back tears in a mixture of fear and humiliation. My face burned as much as his, not so much with the intimidation as my own ineptitude at handling both the encounters I'd had with him. My suspicions had been based on facts and opinions as flimsy as the cobwebs I'd buried my face in that morning in the garden, dreaming of big stories and journalistic fame. Helen had said I was naive and I'd snapped at her. Naive? Of course I was fucking naive, making assumptions and jumping to conclusions and listening to the chatter of a child, like building a house on sand. Not only that, I squirmed with the memory of the knee-trembling attraction I'd felt the first time I'd met this man. Even so, as I swallowed back tears, a part of me wondered whether his anger was disproportionate to the presence of a mere schoolgirl taking pics in his yard for a project. There were only boats there after all.

I stood by the harbour wall and collected myself, watching the tide slide out sluggishly and unwelcoming without the sun to pick out the greens and blues and flashes of silver on the skins of the grey mullet that I would never have known about, save for the observations of one small boy. The world felt grey, ironed out, the end of the season reflecting my mood. It was time to end it, time to go home. I went in search of my uncle who was deep in conversation with a man, the state of his paint-stained work clothes and the mouldy small yacht they were standing beside just another sad case of over-enthusiastic lovers of old boats who'd got nothing better to do. I waited until he turned and saw me.

"I've come to say goodbye."

He nodded.

"I'm leaving tomorrow."

"So you said."

"Well, goodbye then," I said. I offered him my hand. I didn't know what else to do.

"It's terrible, what's happened, with Tomas and the snack-bar and everything," I stumbled on. "I hope it'll be alright, without Angela and all that."

He coughed, a deep hacking cough that took his breath away and touched my hand briefly.

"Good luck with your course."

He turned abruptly and walked away. It was like a slap in the face, but what did I expect? He'd be devastated over the death of the child, I knew, but would never show it. We'd nothing in common after all, only a few tenuous blood ties and some ghosts laid to rest. He'd acknowledged me, seemed he hadn't much liked what he'd seen and would be glad when my train chugged over the cob on Monday back to my real life away from here.

I took one last look at the boatyard, the tired vegetation drooping from the cliffs behind and the fading pink flowers and gossamer seed - heads of the willow herb poking out from the wall by Angela's snack-bar. I could hardly believe that just a few days ago I'd sat under the bright awning and drunk tea, eaten her special sandwiches and soaked up the sun, the copper-headed child with his bright eyes supping Coke and scuffing his heels in the gravel. I stared at the Boat Shed with its peeling paint and a seagull perched on the chimney poking out from the smoke-house, the bent gates and the lop-sided wooden sign. I left the yard, avoided looking down between the sea of boats towards Doug Peterson's glass and stainless steel signs and the CCTV cameras and the office window from where I knew he'd be watching.

Would I return, Helen's Nain had asked? No way. I'd got no intention of coming back.

I caught the train on Monday morning and arrived at Paddington in the rush hour. My mother met me, stopping stock-still on the platform. She looked brilliant, bright-eyed and impeccably groomed in a cream linen suit. Her hands flew to her mouth in disbelief.

"You've cut your hair off."

Where had I heard that before? The picture of the boatyard swam in front of me with my great-uncle's first words as he stared at me only a week ago.

She whisked me off to Felicity and Trish and dinner in their grand dining-room to celebrate the new business arrangement. The upstairs apartment of their house was to be our new home. There was a large box on the table in front of my place setting, wrapped in gold paper and a gauzy gold ribbon.

"A present for your course," she said. "Open it."

Presents? From my mother? With clear eyes and a bounce in her voice? The camera sat in my hand, a selection of lenses unwrapped on the white tablecloth, a shoulder strap with 'Canon' embroidered in large letters.

I cried a bit. She couldn't have known about the little Sony, smashed beyond repair. We talked and drank champagne and discussed the latest fashions for flowers and decor for weddings. It was a world apart and I put aside the tragedy and the disasters of other people's lives. Just for tonight, I basked in the sheer opulence of it all, cosseted in safety with a future ahead of me.

It would be three years before Wales and the town of Porthmadog entered my life again.

It was entirely unexpected and certainly not welcome.

PART TWO

JANUARY 2018

CHAPTER 9

I was bored. It took me a while to discern the mixed bag of feelings creeping up on me that Monday morning briefing in the Editor's office when I'd been allocated my work load for the week. Okay, so I was a junior on the staff and expected to jump through hoops until I earned the privilege of covering bigger, juicier stories, but I swore if I had to attend any more court sessions hanging around outside the magistrates' court on cold pavements with the culprits and victims, I'd get a job in Debenhams.

But court was where I was going to be tomorrow, amongst the fat bellies and fag ends, the grubby pushchairs and wailing kids, wondering whatever happened to the dreams of feature writing and my name in by lines on a major newspaper. I needed to move on and up, look for a different job as soon as I'd finished my next round of exams and head back to the city instead of reporting this provincial Northampton shit. I felt better already at the thought.

A letter arrived on my desk at lunch time.

"Is that a letter, a real letter?"

I shared a desk with Tim, my junior colleague, now peering over my shoulder at the rare occurrence of paper communication.

“Mind your own business,” I said, as curious as he was at the classy white paper and posh but indistinct franking at the top.

“Looks official.”

“Piss off, Tim.”

“You in trouble then? A summons, it looks like.”

He pushed his glasses on top of his head, turning him into a goggle-eyed space creature and leaned further over. I shoved the envelope under a pile of papers, rooted in my bag and handed him a ten pound note.

“Go buy some decent coffee. I’ll treat you.”

“Only if you promise to tell.”

“I might. Now fuck off and make yourself useful.”

I opened the envelope and read the letter, pushing back my chair and made my way through the office with indecent haste. The brass plaque with Edward Martin, Editor, fondly known as ‘Ed,’ engraved on it had been newly polished that morning. I knocked briefly on the door, fell through it in my rush and stood like a fool on the grey carpet, letter in hand. He swivelled round in his chair.

“Ed, I need a favour.”

He stared at me, pale grey eyes fixed on my face.

“Knocking would be good. Waiting would be even better.”

“Sorry,” I said, trying to sound convincing.

He was a big man, body gone to seed with too much sitting. The skin on his neck hung in folds over his collar with the top button undone. His tie was loosened at the neck, the yellow and black zig-zags a testament to his total lack of taste and little care about his clothes in general. It didn’t matter: his mind was sharp as a razor, his wit acerbic and his reputation for not suffering fools gladly was known far and wide on the press circuit. I took a deep breath. He sighed and ran his hand over the remaining strands of grey hair on his otherwise bald head.

“What do you want, Cassie? I’m busy. Reading your work on the old colliery site as it happens. You do know we don't do features on this paper. This was supposed to be a story with word limits."

"I know, but it seemed too good to cut and I need to practise. I've done the short piece as well. You'll find it at the end. Ed, I need a favour."

"Favour? You've only just started here. Favours have to be earned."

I thrust the letter at him. He read it through, glancing at the letter head.

"Gerald Hughes and Partners, Solicitors."

He'd punched it in to the keyboard as quick as a flash.

"Well, you'll have to go, won't you? You never know, you might have been left some money. Was he a close relative, this great-uncle of yours?"

"Hardly," I said. "I didn't even know he'd died. I only met him a couple of times three years ago."

I remembered so clearly the way he'd dismissed me as I left the yard to go home after those few awful days. Even with my new-found experience on my degree course with its challenging work placements and a lot of growing up, I still felt uncomfortable at the memory; it still felt like a slap in the face.

"I spent a few days trying to get to know him before I went to uni. He was rude and grumpy. He didn't like me much. Some horrible things happened while I was there. A child died...and other stuff. I've had no contact with him at all."

He was quiet for a minute.

"Interesting that you're a beneficiary if, as you say, he didn't like you."

"He's probably left me his pet lobster," I said, "just because he knew I thought it was revolting. Old, ugly thing kept in a tank. It only had one claw."

"Ah, well," he said. "We all get old and ugly eventually."

He cleared his throat, linked his fingers and propped his jowls up on them. Nobody interrupted Ed when he was thinking. But I chanced it.

"I was thinking of doing some research while I was there," I said, hoping he might let me have a working break. "You know, the County Lines thing and drugs trafficking by sea? It goes on, I know it does and there might be a local connection from here."

"No. Take a week out of your holiday allowance," he said, turning back to the screen. "Unless you want to do it as a practice feature, of course, as you're so keen on making your way up the ladder. I'll read it, that's all. In your own time, Cassie, not mine. Right? And good luck with your inheritance."

I shut the door quietly.

The coffee was cold by the time I came back from Ed's office. Tim was waiting impatiently.

"You've gone a bit pale, Cass. What's the letter say, then?"

I swivelled my chair round.

"Looks like I'm away for a few days. Up to North Wales, as it happens. Guess who'll have to do the court reports next week?

"I don't mind. So who's the mystery letter from, then?"

I sighed. It was no good keeping anything from Tim. He'd make a really good journalist when he grew up and packed in the silly jokes. He never stopped asking questions – just wore you down until you gave in. One of these days he'd pick on the wrong person with a short fuse and end up with a bloody nose.

"Solicitors," I said. "Looks like I'm a beneficiary of a will."

"Cool. Does that mean money?"

"More like a one-clawed pet lobster owned by my great-uncle."

It was dark when I parked the car that night and depressing to go back to the one-roomed apartment I lived in during the week but I'd had to start somewhere and Northampton was as good as any place. London and its highlights were a weekend treat when I wasn't on duty for the paper.

The room was small and claustrophobic, the urban greyness outside lit up by the street lights and neon signs from the takeaways. I'd picked up a Waitrose lasagne and a bottle of Pinot Noir to help drown the memories of my short stay in Porthmadog, the hostility of the man Doug Peterson and my great-uncle's abrupt manner interspersed with overtures of friendliness flashing through my mind. I tried to lose myself in rubbish television while I ate, then rang my mother and told her about the letter. Once over the surprise, she agreed with me about the possibility of inheriting the lobster or being left something revoltingly equivalent out of sheer spite.

"It would be just like him," she said. "He wasn't a nice man. I know you tried your best, but leopards and spots and all that. You won't have to arrange the funeral, surely?"

"I've no idea," I said, "and I don't know anything about funerals. Why would I have to bury him? I hardly knew him."

I drowned my disquiet in the last of the wine. I needed to stay somewhere in Porthmadog and thought briefly about Helen. We'd lost touch when she qualified and disappeared off to Africa to do voluntary work with some disgusting diseases but I knew the name of Helen's Nain's guest house in Borth-y-Gest. I rang.

"You can have Helen's old room," she said, her pleasure bubbling down the phone. "I'm closed for the winter so there'll be no guests here. I had no idea how to get in touch with you when they found John and it was the solicitor's job anyway. So sad. I can't wait to see you."

Tomas crept into my dreams that night, his pale face washed by the waves and the shirt a red stain beneath the water. I couldn't shake off the feeling there was a secret he'd shared with me, the feeling that this was unfinished business I was about to be thrust back into. I woke in a cold sweat as a lobster claw waved in front of my face and dragged me down to a dark hole in the reef I'd seen from my uncle's boat.

Prophetic? Rubbish. I rationalised it out over a cup of tea in the morning and read up on the recent upsurge of cocaine trafficking in North Wales. For the first time in months I was buzzing with enthusiasm for a change and a good excuse to hone my journalistic skills, one-clawed lobster notwithstanding. I could always eat it.

On Sunday, I drove to Wales, a mixture of nostalgia and selective memories taking me on the route I'd hitched before, the warmth and comfort of my newly acquired Corsa a far cry from the hitch-hiking trip with aching feet, wet clothes and the narrow escape with the pervy salesman. I could laugh at it now after three years of growing up. I turned off down the road into Borth-y-Gest and parked outside the guest house where Helen's Nain greeted me with a mixture of delight and intense scrutiny, turning me round on the pavement.

"You look so different. A proper bob this time," she said, running her hand over my hair. "I like the way it follows your jaw line and curves up at the back. It's lovely."

"Bit better than hacking it off with a pair of nail scissors," I said, uncomfortable with the appraisal, tucking one side behind my ear, conscious of her eyes on the diamond nose-stud my mother had given me as a graduation present. She was still gushing over my hair.

"Like velvet curtains. It frames your face beautifully. And the colour...it's very purple."

"Damson, actually. And it's only streaks. I decided there wasn't enough colour in the world this winter."

"Well it's certainly different. I'm not sure what our Mr Gerald Hughes will think. He's very conventional, even for a solicitor," she said, standing back and scrutinising my face. "All grown-up now. Bit pale, though. Three years at university. It's gone so quickly and now you're a proper journalist. Your eyes look as though they could take on the world. But you've still got a face like a pixie."

"Pixie? I thought they were mischievous, with pointed noses."

"Elvin, then. Delicate, I'd say. Not exactly the face of a hard-bitten journalist, thank God. I bet it fools the clients. Come in, cariad, out of the cold. You're food for an old woman's eyes."

I wasn't used to pertinent comments about my face, embarrassed at the close attention.

The kitchen was wonderfully fragrant with the aroma of dinner in the oven and a batch of her brownies cooling on the table on a wire rack.We settled in to gossip and news of the people I'd known so briefly and under such tragic circumstances, not to mention the details of my great-uncle's death.

"The postman found him. The door hadn't been opened that morning and his truck was still in the yard. He must have died in his chair. He hardly ever came home to the house up the road, you know, even over Christmas. It hasn't been lived in for months. He must have just found it easier in his shed. The regular boat owners using the yard kept an eye on him. He seemed to be alright, they said, just protecting his property. He always had food in and kept the stove going."

"What was he protecting?"

"His model ships, I suppose. They must be valuable. He worried about them being stolen. He used to say the only people who'd appreciate his life's work would be something like a maritime heritage trust. I can't imagine there's anything else of value in that old place. It looks more like a scrap-yard now, lots of people coming and going and dumping stuff."

"What sort of stuff?"

"Just rubbish. He was not quite himself for a while, you know. People took advantage of him and left things in the yard. There's even an old caravan."

The feeling I didn't want to go anywhere near it was almost one of pure revulsion. The strength of it unsettled me. Whatever he'd left me, claws or no claws, someone else would have to deal with it.

I changed the subject.

"And Angela?" I asked.

"Working in Tesco. She went away for a while and came back only last year. Tomas would have been nearly a teenager now. How she copes, I don't know. She has a dead look about her, like a walking ghost."

"And Gareth? She threw him out, didn't she?"

"He's still around. Does a bit of yard work for Doug and sits in the pub most of the time, so I'm told. Not a nice man. Always trying to pretend he's better off than he is."

Cocky little shit, I thought, remembering him strutting through the yard at Angela's heels as she screamed at the stretcher and the men in uniforms carrying her son's lifeless body. I tucked into Helen's bed that night with the sash window open a crack. I wanted to hear the roar of the sea on the bar and drifted off to sleep with my unwelcome recurring dream of lobsters and waving claws and dark caves far under the reef.

My appointment with Gerald Hughes and Partners on Tuesday left me free on Monday to start my research. I needed all the experience I could get if I ever wanted to work in London and the Northampton newspaper seemed to churn out the same grind day after day, road traffic accidents notwithstanding. I made some phone calls, drove to Pwllheli, the coastal town halfway down the Lleyn Peninsula and found the local youth leader sipping coffee in the office of a dilapidated building in the back streets.

"Cocaine, you want to know about? Crack? All over the place. How it gets here is anybody's guess," he said. "The police haven't enough resources to check every lead. It's well organised. Even the phone links between dealers are so cleverly concealed the leads are usually cold by the time any one responds."

"Sounds like an impossible job," I said, jotting down notes. "What can you do to help?"

"Our biggest success is education of the young people who come to the centre so at least they can make informed choices. We listen, watch and pick up info on the main distribution centres; the new dealers have to operate from somewhere. And kids like to chatter. The dealers pick on regular users in their squats or flats or whatever, bribe them with a couple of freebies, take over the flat and target the streets from there. The tenants are too stoned out of their heads to do anything about it and if they weren't serious addicts, they soon are."

"But it's only a small town," I said. "The police must know where everyone lives, surely? It's not exactly like the middle of Birmingham or London."

"Yeah well, the numbers of coppers on the ground are disproportionate to the size of the area. Not many to cover a big stretch like the Lleyn coastline. Do you know it?"

No, I thought, but it was time I did if I was going to write convincingly about it.

"Anything can come in by sea and get dropped off in secluded bays and inlets and not be noticed unless there's a lead."

"Have you got any leads at the moment?"

"Possibly, but I'm not going to share them with you, am I now? Press nosing around'll only shift it somewhere else.Who are you working for, anyway?"

"Part of my training." He'd seen my press card. He wasn't to know it was only an exercise, was he?

"I'm interested in how drugs get onto the land from the sea. I saw a poster in Criccieth asking people to report suspicious movements on beaches with dinghies and jet-skis. Does more come in by sea than by road? What about small shipments?"

"Well," he said, getting up from the chair, "if you want to spy on the bays and beaches for trafficking in the middle of a January night, you're welcome. Just remember it's not all pink and fluffy. Dealers don't take kindly to nosy young journalists after a big story. We're talking millions of pounds in street value. It puts our kids at risk too. Our job is to help them resist it. Now, if you don't mind..."

Thanks a bunch mate, I thought, getting into my car, banging on the heater and the wipers full pelt. I took a turn back to the centre and drove down to the marina, my next port of call.

It was a desolate scene, grey, wet and windswept. A sea of masts tossed from side to side like pendulums as the boats surged against the pontoons in the gusts. I licked the salt from my lips as I made my way along the front of the marina office, the air full of drizzle blown in from the sea. The guy in the marina office shrugged when I asked about commercial fishing boats.

"There's a few fishing boats for the bass and the lobster and Gwilym Thomas runs fishing charters locally in the bay and well out into the Irish Sea during the summer. Big red boat. You can't miss it. It's hauled out for the winter. You'll be lucky to catch him in the yard, though, this time of year. Try the shed."

I found him in a huge boat shed, warming his hands near an industrial heater blowing hot air futilely into the vast space of galvanised walls and roof. He wore an old blue duffle coat buttoned up to the neck and a canvas hat with fake fur ear-flaps. I asked him if he ever saw any unusual activity out on his fishing trips. It was a naive question but I was cold and he wasn't friendly. He picked his own soapbox.

"Are you asking me about the fishing stocks? Brexit legislation stuff? Giving us back our waters? Too late for that. French have taken all

the bloody fish and what rights we had those bastards down south sold them to the Spanish. Is that what you're asking?"
He was angry before I even started. I let him talk for twenty minutes and took notes until he ran out of steam.

"Have you ever been warned off being in any particular areas?"

"What, because of the fishing? No, too small for the big boats to bother with the likes of me out there. Bit different close in, mind. I used to have my own pots for lobsters. They got nicked last year. I bought new ones and they got nicked as well. I thought I knew every bloody boat round here and their owners but I couldn't pin it down. Police don't want to know."

"What about the NCA and the Coastguard?"
He just laughed. "You're joking. These are lobster pots, not drugs hauls. Not even worth telling them. Not that there's any coastguard bases left round here. All comes from Holyhead now and that's a fat lot of good sixty miles away. There's only the mobile units for emergencies."

"I'd heard there was somebody in Porthmadog who had his pots stolen off Sarn Badrig. It was three years ago, though. He thought someone was trying to warn him off just being out there. He couldn't find out who it was, either."
He raised his eyebrows. "Yeah well, there's things go on. No good bitching about it all the time."

"Isn't that called complacency?"
I knew as soon as I opened my mouth it was a mistake. His face shut down like a blind on a window.

"You go back to your English newspaper, young lady, and write a story about sandy beaches and suntans. You don't want to be poking your nose in where it don't belong, right? You'll bite off more than you can chew. Got it?"
He turned on his heel and walked out of sight to the other end of the

shed, disappearing behind a wall of outboard engines stacked up for winter maintenance. I didn't blame him. I deserved that.

Next stop I'd go to the horse's mouth. I parked in the centre of town and systematically quartered the main street and all the streets leading of it. It was term-time and kids under sixteen were dutifully in school. What I needed was the welcome sight of a homeless individual in a doorway. I gave up and headed for Costa Coffee, warming my toes and thinking about the charity shops on the High Street and negotiated a couple of alleyways I'd spotted before the drizzle turned to cold rain. The heap of rags tucked into a recess in the wall could have been mistaken for rubbish if it hadn't been for a pair of boots sticking out onto the cracked concrete.

"Alright, mate?" I said, standing well back. The heap moved and a head encased in a hoody poked out.

"Whadda you want?"

"Bloody cold out here," I said, rubbing my hands together. "Haven't they got anywhere in this God-forsaken place you can stay? Where I come from at least they've got shelters when it's cold like this."
I squatted down and waited.

"Stayed at a mate's house last night. What's it to you?"

"I was wondering if I can buy you a coffee and a bite to eat. I'm doing a story for the paper on the increase in homeless young people in North Wales. Interested?"
He didn't ask which paper and I wasn't going to mention drugs. He said his name was Pete. I didn't tell him mine and he didn't ask.

He led me to a cafe and ordered a full breakfast, his thin hands and dirty finger nails handling the menu over and over, adding toast and an Eccles cake and two coffees. The cuffs of his jacket rode up over thin wrists, bruised with old and new needle marks. I heard Ed's voice in my head about getting old and ugly like the lobster and the youth leader's words about vulnerability. I lurched a bit, tendrils of sympathy threatening to ruin my plan. Then I reminded myself why I was here and who he was and why I needed to tighten my grip on my shoulder bag. A fix at any price would include not being nice towards other people's purses.

We sat at a table by the cafe window, the glass misting up with steam from damp customers, figures flitting by on the pavement outside bundled up in coats and woolly hats, frozen fingers clasped around handles of carrier bags, heads down against the drizzle. Only one walked past bareheaded, shoulders stooped and the top half of his body leaning forward as though braving a full gale, his head turning from left to right scanning the pavement. I caught a glimpse of dark hair and a moustache, a swarthy figure in a green, old-fashioned army Parka. I'd seen that strange gait before but couldn't place it. He turned into the road, hesitated, then crossed, weaving across in between cars to the other side and stood for a minute or two by the lamp-post opposite. I watched absently for a moment then turned my attention back to Pete.

He slurped coffee as we waited for the meal, the liquid spilling a little over onto the table when he picked up the full mug, happy to talk at first, his eyes constantly shifting to the window. I tried not to stare. He cut the food up when it arrived, shovelled it into his mouth as fast as he could chew, crammed the Eccles cake in and washed it down with gulps of coffee. I could feel the vibrations from his foot tapping on the floor. I wondered how long since the last fix of whatever he was on and how long to the next one and how long I was going to keep him in his seat before he shot off like a jack-rabbit.

He gave me the life story, a sad past about being thrown out of the house at sixteen, living in squats and dabbling in drugs. Bit more than dabbling, I thought. He couldn't keep still. He was beaten up on the streets of Liverpool, he said, and moved into Wales where he had a mate and thought life would be kinder. More like he'd just followed the traffic of whatever he was hooked on and thought it'd be cheaper, or easier. He was twenty-one: gaunt, dirty, jittery and wrecked.

I put my journalist's hat firmly on my head and listened as he spluttered in between the mouthfuls of pastry. Milly's voice floated over the aroma of my cappuccino. Listen and wait, girl. I waited.

"And before you ask," he said, catching my eye on his thin wrists, "I've been straight for two months. Looking for a job now. Going to work hard and get qualifications and start a business. Don't take stuff no more."

Liar.

"Good for you," I said. "I bet it's tough going, trying to get clean."

"Too bloody right," he said. "I'm getting some help now, though. Tell you what, if the kids round here knew just how tough it was to go clean, they'd think twice about touching any of it."

Gotcha. He'd mentioned the drugs, not me. I reckon he'd tried to give up and failed and was back on something with a vengeance. But he wasn't going to tell me.

"Must be expensive," I said, looking out at the wet streets deserted in the rain, imagining him begging for cash in the summer, being moved on from shop to shop, corner to corner. "Not much passing custom for coins in the winter, I don't suppose, when the tourists have gone home."

He shrugged.

"You can get a wrap for peanuts round here. There's loads coming in from the cities. Local guys don't like it, but hey, you've gotta buy from whoever, yeah?"

I nodded.

"I thought that's why you said you'd come here – to try and get away from it. Start a new life," I said.

"Reckon it's followed me round. There's a lot goes on round here.

You'd never believe."

He was enjoying this now, almost forgot I was doing a story. He knew stuff I didn't. He leaned over the table conspiratorially, the crumbs from the Eccles cake clinging to the stubble on his chin.

"Yeah," he said. "You'd never believe."

"Really?" I said, all wide-eyed and innocent.

He turned to look out of the window, clammed up, scraped his chair back and wiped his mouth on his sleeve.

"Gotta go. Ta for the meal."

He'd gone before I'd put my cup down, banged the cafe door and ploughed across the street with his head down and hoody up. A figure emerged from behind a lamp-post and they walked off together. Why did I get the feeling I wasn't welcome round here? I shrugged it off. It wasn't the reason I was up here in the first place. On the other hand, it was a start. It was all good practice. I decided to review my interviewing techniques when I got back to work. I closed my note book and shoved it into my bag, wondering how the rest of his day would pan out.

I clattered down the stairs for breakfast the following morning, my appointment with the solicitor at ten o'clock.

"You can't go looking like that, Cassie," Helen's Nain said, eyeing me up critically before I sat down.

"He's very formal, you know, is Mr Hughes, Senior. Very traditional."

"I can't see what difference my clothes make," I said, on the defensive before I knew it, looking down at my best jeans and sweatshirt, the leather jacket draped over the back of the chair, my boots laced comfortably.

She sighed.

"You young people don't seem to see the need for making the right impression. He might be more useful to you than you think."

"How?"

"I don't know. Just a feeling. I think it would be a good thing if you looked a little more...conventional."

She left the table and pottered upstairs, returning with a smart black and white checked jacket, black trousers and a white blouse.

"These are Helen's. She kept clothes here for formal dinners and meetings at the sailing club. You're the same size. She wouldn't mind. There's a pretty scarf to tuck into the neck."

She studied my face.

"Oh and the nose-stud. And the rings. Best out, don't you think?"

I glared at her but she held her ground.

She meant it. I decided not to argue. I didn't know everything, after all and dress codes were not my forte.

"I just think that he would be a good person to have on your side. You're very English despite your Welsh background and whether you like it or not, this is a very traditional Welsh community. Play the game, cariad. It's only for an hour."

I drove into town, bumped the Corsa over the cobbles by the harbour and parked outside the Pen Cei, the cafe bar in the square. It was early in the day and too early in the year for tourists, the road to the solicitor's office empty and the park deserted. A lone swing creaked in the blustery wind and dead leaves rustled and blew in fitful circles round the waste bins. I was ridiculously nervous. Interviewing members of the public for stories was one thing with the protection of the paper to go back to and the justification for being in awkward situations but facing a stern solicitor on personal, formal business was freaking me out.

I reached the building, a forbidding edifice in grey slate with a brass plaque on the wall, straightened my jacket and tucked the scarf back into my neck where the wind had whipped it sideways, took a deep breath and pushed open the door to a dark reception area and a blast of warm air. A bespectacled little woman rose and came round from behind an old-fashioned desk. The smile was reserved.

"He'll only be a minute," she said, gesturing to a hard-backed chair against the wall. She sat down again, her fingers racing along the keyboard on the desk. She looked up.

"We were sorry to hear about Mr Jones. We didn't know he had relatives."

I nodded.

A door opened in the panelled wall to my right and a tall man filled the space. He was dressed in a charcoal-grey suit with a faint stripe which accentuated his height, an immaculate white shirt with the starched cuffs at his wrists displaying gold cuff-links with a monogram. He wore a grey tie, a small pin with a gold head carefully inserted half way up. His neck seemed to grow out of the collar, long and thin and wrinkled like an ancient tortoise, his face almost gaunt and the eyes hidden behind thick-framed glasses.

I stood up. He bent his head briefly and held out his hand.

"Miss Jones? Please come through."

The room was panelled in dark wood and dominated by a huge desk with a traditional green reading light. There was nothing else on the polished surface except a note pad and two gold pens side by side. He gestured to a comfortable leather chair and sat behind his desk. I sat down, my knees together and my feet flat on the carpet like a naughty schoolgirl in the head's office.

He started off with the preliminaries. I was scarcely listening to the details of names, addresses, the formal language and then I heard the word ' lobster.' I knew it. I was right all along.

"...and to care for the unfortunate creature in a befitting manner until its natural demise..."

I must have snorted. He lowered his glasses onto his nose, peered at me over the top and cleared his throat.

"...and in order to ensure that there are means to ensure its well-being, I therefore bequeath the whole of my estate to my great-niece, Cassiopeia Meyers-Jones."

I'd misheard.

"Sorry?"

"This will include the premises known as The Boat Shed, all its contents and the freehold land on which it stands."

Someone poured ice through my veins. I froze on the chair.

"Also included in the estate, the cottage in Borth-y-Gest known as No. 4, Tai Pilots, the fishing vessel 'Annie,' and all other vessels or part thererof currently on the land unless otherwise owned by private owners."

I couldn't speak. It was too much for mere words. I could feel the silence.

He coughed. "A considerable inheritance, Miss Jones."

A gust of wind sneaked through the old windows and fluttered the blinds. I found my voice.

"No. You can't be serious."

He sat with his fingers laced.

"He can't... he didn't even like me. I don't know anything about boats and yards. I haven't any money to look after it. And I've got a job and a career and exams to take. I'd have to sell it. I don't want it." Shock gave way to blustering panic, my voice cracking in protest

"Ah, yes," he said, clearly uncomfortable. "I haven't quite finished. There is a matter of money. Your great-uncle was very clear about that. There is a sum of fifty thousand pounds which can be made available to you."

"Wow," I said, wishing I hadn't. It sounded infantile.

"Indeed."

There was a long pause.

"I think we'll have some coffee," he said, speaking quietly into an intercom, "before we continue. I'll give you a few minutes to digest it so far."

So far?

He spoke into the intercom. The secretary opened the door and placed a tray on the coffee table in front of the desk, poured coffee and handed me a delicate bone china cup and saucer.

"There are some conditions attached to the inheritance."

I put down my coffee cup, clattering it on the saucer.

"There has always been a covenant on the yard itself and the buildings. It is to be used for maritime purpose only, part of the industrial heritage of the slate industry. The caveat inserted by your great-uncle states that the money available to you can only be released on the condition that it is used to restore the yard and the business to its former, traditional use."

You old bugger, I thought.

"Which means," he said, looking up, "the re-development of a traditional boatyard and the retail of materials suitable for wooden sailing craft. I believe your great-uncle collected and sold materials to classic boat owners from all over the world. It's a specialist field, you understand, in the restoration of wooden boats."

"You're joking."

"I never joke, Miss Jones," he said.

CHAPTER 10

I drove back to Borth-y-Gest, the sea and the bay and the houses blurring into a hazy grey mist, speechless with the enormity of it all. I couldn't even begin to work through the ramifications of the legacy, the effect on my career, who to go to for sensible help, what to do next.

"Duw Mawr," was all Helen's Nain said in disbelief as the kettle over-flowed under the running tap.

"I'm meeting with one of the partners this afternoon to show me round. He's been responsible for overseeing the yard. I can't think what to do first. There's still a load of paper work to be done and I have to come back for more appointments in the next few weeks to finalise it all. Help."

She turned off the tap and put the kettle on the hob.

"We'll have a pannad," she said, her voice quavering slightly. "Then we'll make a list," her voice firmer now, as she gathered mugs, warmed the pot and reached for the biscuit tin, the kettle gathering steam and whistling quietly to itself.

"List?"

"Yes. It helps clarify things. Write everything down that comes into

your head, including how you feel about it."
She placed a mug of steaming tea in front of me.

"So how do you feel? Right now?"
I shook my head. I didn't know how I felt. It wasn't real and I didn't think she'd appreciate the expletives that came to mind. She certainly wouldn't know about the overriding fear of meeting my new neighbour, the man in the yard next door, the one who smashed my precious Sony and made me feel like a two-year old and wanted to buy my great-uncle out for the sake of a slipway. I hadn't forgotten. It almost wiped out the news of the inheritance.

I walked to the yard in the early afternoon, still in my tidy clothes but with a long black wool coat lent by Helen's Nain. I protested.

"You're always lending me coats."

"My husband bought this for me just before he died. I've never worn it. It's expensive and classy and you're meeting another partner from the firm. Remember what I said about appearances. Make an impression. Trust me. You're a woman of property now. Look the part."

"Okay," I said, "thank you, but the stud goes back in."
The grey skies were already darkening in the late afternoon. Every step of the path was familiar even though I'd only been there before for such a short time, every step imbued with mixed feelings of sadness as I reflected on the death of the small boy, the hurtful rejection from my uncle and the intimidation from the man in the boatyard. I prayed he wasn't around.

But that was three years ago, I told myself. But now? Not such easy prey any more. Three years at uni and all those holiday jobs in between terms had taught me a lot. I'd worked and lived on farms fruit picking and mending holes in the not so salubrious accommodation of old caravans allotted to students, fended off groups of drunken fun-lovers at bars and clubs, waited on in hotels till my feet were sore and cleaned house for a university professor with a fussy wife. I wasn't wet behind the ears any more. I even coped with chipped nails when I had to and learned to wear gloves. I squared my shoulders and turned the corner at the bottom of the path.

The Boat Shed gate was open a fraction, just as sad and flimsy as it had been three years ago and now sagging on its hinges. A black Audi was parked outside. A man unfolded himself from the driver's seat and stepped out. He was tall and slim, wore casual trousers, blue shirt, a snazzy tie and a brown leather jacket, unlike the suited patriarch of Gerald Hughes and Partners I'd spent the morning with. There was mud on his shoes, slate-grey splashes from the puddle he was standing in. He didn't seem to mind and looked ruefully down at his feet. He smiled, an open smile in an open face, green eyes, dark eyebrows and a mop of unruly black curls.

"David Hughes," he said, holding out his hand. "Miss Jones, I presume?"

I shook his hand which was warm and firm.

"Cassie," I said.

"I've been looking after Mr Jones' affairs since he passed away."

"Does that include feeding the one-clawed Archie?" I said, liking him already.

"Naturally. All in a day's work for a junior partner. We specialise in injury claims. I'll take the car through into the yard, if you don't mind."

I laughed for the first time that day, pushing both gates open and fixing them with the hooks attached to posts in the gravel. He drove through and parked outside the shed. I stood in the open gateway, staring at my inheritance. It was worse than I could possibly have imagined.

Apart from one sailing boat in a state of obvious restoration with some scaffold planks and a ladder propped against the stern, the whole area resembled a scrap-yard: old dinghies piled up in a corner, planks and pieces of paint-spattered timber, paint pots, a rusting boat trailer, even an old caravan and a battered Ford Fiesta tucked in under the cliff. There were steel girders piled up against the wall of the Boat Shed, one sheet of its galvanised roof lifting in the breeze where the fixings had torn away.

He parked the Audi outside the Boat Shed and stood like a sentry by the battered door waiting for my inspection. I stopped by the snack-bar, now closed up with rusty streaks oozing from the bolts for the shutters and tried to imagine Angela in her overall behind the immaculate stainless-steel counter, the beautifully written blackboard menu and the bottles of ketchup and mustard and vinegar. I blinked back the image of the ginger-haired boy with his angry face sitting at the table cradling his fishing rod, lost for a moment in a world apart.

"Can I help you?"

The deep voice with the Scottish burr I'd remembered cut through the memories.

"It's alright, Doug, she's with me," said David.

Sandwiched between David and the man I'd dreaded meeting, I turned to face him. He stared at me quizzically, head on one side, the sheepskin collar of his jacket turned up against the wind, studying my face as David left his post and splashed through the puddles towards us.

"Friend of yours, David?" the man said, his eyes running over the expensive coat and the diamond stud in my nose. The thick wool collar reached halfway up the back of my head and I'd tucked my hair behind it, sleek and glossy and not a hair out of place. Apart from the parting straight down the middle of my head, my hair bore no resemblance to the ragged bob I'd hacked three years ago.

He didn't recognise me.

"Doug, this is Cassie Jones. Miss Jones, Doug Peterson. He owns the yard next door. He's been good enough to keep an eye on things since

Mr Jones passed away. Let's go inside, for God's sake," said David, hugging his chest. "It's freezing out here."

An electric fire had been plugged in by the old chairs. Someone had thrown old clean curtains over the seats but the plaid rug was still there. The shed was as filthy as I'd remembered and I was glad the light was so dim I couldn't see the full extent of the junk I knew filled the room. A faint light glowed from the lobster's tank in a corner and the florescent tube flickered overhead.

David warmed his hands.

"Not general knowledge yet, Doug, but Miss Jones has inherited the property from her great-uncle. She was only made aware of the situation this morning."

A stunned silence cut through the creaks and clatter of the tin panels overhead. David chattered away, leaving out the details of the conditions attached. It was nobody's business except mine, after all.

"So there it is," said David cheerfully into the dusty silence.

"Neighbours, I think? You're the first to know, Doug, and of course there is still a lot of admin to complete, but Miss Jones should be able to take possession in early March. Of course, you have a great deal to think about, Cassie. It's a massive commitment. I'm sure Doug here will be very helpful if you need him."

He got up.

"I'll just feed Neifion while I'm here and leave you two to get to know each other." He disappeared into the dimness of the shed.

I waited, sensing the change in the air.

"So," he said, leaning back in the chair. "John Jones's great-niece, eh? Not just a schoolgirl pretending to be a rookie journalist."

"You owe me a camera," I said, looking him straight in the eye.

"You were the one who stood on it. And you were trespassing," he fired back.

"You should have found Tomas easily. I did. It wasn't rocket science."

"And you shouldn't have been nosing around my yard blabbing unfounded suspicions to the police," he said, his eyes narrowing.

This was like a game of tennis. I sat back and folded my arms. "Being nosy is a pre-requisite for being a journalist," I said.

"But you weren't a journalist."

"No," I said, enjoying the banter, "but I am now. Fully-fledged and paid up."

That shut him up. David emerged out of the gloom.

"Getting to know each other?"

I carried on, fired up now, ignoring his presence.

"I was only standing in the yard taking photos for a project. You were a bit over-reactive, don't you think?"

"You were snooping around," he said his finger pointing at me.

"Was there something worth snooping for?" I asked.

His face hardened. That's enough I thought. I'd overstepped the mark. We stared at each other, the memories of a child's death and unspoken dislike between us. I waited.

"My yard was, and is, none of your business," he said.

There was no answer to that. The silence was painful.

"I didn't realise you knew each other," David said, bemused, looking from one face to the other.

Nobody enlightened him.

"I thought John had left this place to some Maritime Heritage Trust," Doug said, addressing David, "he always said he would. He wouldn't sell it to me, you know. It's no use pretending I didn't try."

He turned to me, hostility veiled in politeness.

"So what will you do with it, Miss Jones? Would you consider re-opening the idea of a sale at some time? You'll surely not want to take over this place. It's gone to rack and ruin the last few years. You've got a career in journalism ahead, I imagine."

Whoa, this was too fast. The rescue came even faster.

"I think Cassie needs some time to herself, Doug. There's a funeral to arrange first and a lot to take in. I'm sure you'll meet again soon when everything's finalised. I'll lock up, shall I?"

I knew I liked him. Doug Peterson nodded a brief goodbye and headed for the door ahead of us, his shoulders filling the frame and blocking out the light.

"You owe me an apology as well as a camera," I wanted to call after him as he negotiated the potholes in the yard but decided that it would sound childish and petulant. He rounded the gate-posts and disappeared from view. David turned to me waiting in the doorway, his face thoughtful.

"Of course, there's still the house in Borth-y-Gest to look at. I've got the key. Would you like to see it now? And we need to have a talk, I think."

He started the engine and turned round fast in the yard, splashing grey mud from the puddles. I followed the car and closed the flimsy gates behind him, looking back at the bleak yard through the chicken wire nailed between the wooden frames.

"We'll have a coffee first," he said, sensing my perplexity as I got into the passenger seat. "I'll explain why I rushed that a bit and you need to explain what all that conversation with Doug was about. It sounded rather acrimonious to me. We can't work together if I don't know half of it, can we? Then we'll go back to the yard and look at the Boat Shed properly after we look at the house in Borth-y-Gest."

Relishing the warmth of the coffee shop in the High Street and spooning the cappuccino foam absently into my mouth with the spoon, I told him the story. He stirred his coffee and dunked a biscuit.

"I know Doug pretty well. We sail together," he said, "at least not exactly together. We race against each other in the summer. He took over the yard here in Port a few years ago and joined the sailing club in Pwllheli. He owns a Sigma 38. He's very competitive, takes part in all the big races over to Ireland and some bigger national events like the ISORA. He races to win and doesn't balk at a few dirty tricks."

He grinned. "Loads of fun, racing, if you've got the bottle. Do you sail, Cassie? Ever raced?"

I shook my head, remembering Helen and her tale of the wandering hands whilst helming his boat and her intense dislike of the man.

"Helen crewed for him once she told me. Only once though. She wouldn't go again."

"He's an arrogant bastard," said David but there was no rancour in his voice. "He's also a charmer and a womaniser with a reputation for getting exactly what he wants, by fair means or foul sometimes. And who he wants," he added. "You'll certainly have your work cut out fending him off. He wants that yard of yours badly – make no mistake. He's got big ideas for development in the harbour and a slipway is one of them."

"So where would he get the money from if I decided to sell it? It's only a boat business he's running."

He shrugged.

"Forces pay off? An inheritance? I've no idea. It's a bit of a mystery locally. Just be aware, that's all. There'll be pressure from him. Of course, he doesn't know the conditions of the will. It's none of his business and there's plenty for you to think about without any added complications."

He leant back in his seat and looked at me critically, narrowing his eyes and studying my face with his head on one side. Helen's Nain had done that. For the second time I was beginning to think there was something wrong with me. His gaze flickered to my hands clasped round the mug with my proudly manicured nails and black polish I'd indulged myself in when I started working and earning proper money.

"Although," he said, "I have a feeling you're a bit of a wolf in sheep's clothing. You can't be a journalist and a shrinking violet, can you, if you'll excuse the metaphors?"

I got up.

"Too right," I said. "Can we see the house now?

We drove past Helen's Nain's house in Borth-y-Gest to a line of terraced cottages overlooking the bay. I was lost for words as David put the key in the lock at No.4, Tai Pilots and put his weight against the door to open it. A wave of damp, rot and mildew flooded out. Peeling wallpaper hung in strips from the walls in the tiny hall and net curtains at the windows in the front room were frayed and grey with dust and cobwebs. There was a kitchen of sorts at the back and two bedrooms down a flight of stairs. Light bulbs hung from bare wires. It was too dark to see any potential in it, any way of living in it, any way of selling it.What could I say?

"Oh...My...God." It seemed appropriate.

"Quite," he said.

We drove back to the Boat Shed in silence. He glanced down the yard opposite.

"Doug's car's gone," he said. "Good. I'll park here. I could tell you were desperate to see the place properly and I didn't want him nosing in just now."

I remembered where the light was in the shed and flicked the switch, finding more switches that lit up the dark recesses. The lobster waved its claw as I walked around the main counter and down the centre of the shed.

"You'll have to go, revolting creature," I said in passing, mindful of the clause in the will and wondering if natural death from old age would affect the inheritance.

Shelves on both sides of the centre corridor were stacked with chandlery, some in tattered cellophane packets, nuts and bolts in boxes and unravelled ropes with ends escaping down the walls like investigating snakes. There were labels peeling away from pieces of wood crafted into strange shapes and metal pulleys the use of which I couldn't possibly imagine.

The shelves ended, merging into planks and balks of timber stacked from floor to ceiling stood up end upon end with thin strips of timber allowing gaps in between. A beam of torchlight lit up the top plank as David appeared from nowhere.

"Do you know what that is?"

"Wood?" I said, trying to keep the sarcasm out of my voice. I looked again at the reddish-brown plank.

"That's mahogany," he said, whistling through his teeth, pulling the planks away from each other, "and here's some teak and this looks like iroko. He certainly knew what he was doing, your great-uncle John. This lot is worth a fortune. These are all protected hard woods now."

The planks covered the whole side of the shed to the far recesses where it was pitch dark apart from a glimmer of a dirty white painted door. He pushed it open.

A small room had been lined with shelves like an old-fashioned pantry. Each shelf held a model ship, some tiny, some at least three feet long, with rigging and sails, even miniatures of sailors working on the deck. He shone the torch close into the models, his voice breathless, a little awed as he lit up the shelves.

"This is his collection. I haven't looked properly in here before. These are the models of some old Porthmadog sailing ships. Look at the detail. He's even made anchors and windlasses. This is something else,

Cassie. This is a treasure trove. Have you any idea...?"

I hadn't. Not a clue. He shook his head and closed the door carefully.

"Does that explain why he wouldn't leave the place?" I said. "I can see there's a lot of work and skill but are they valuable?"

"We can find out," he said. "I think we need to discuss security before anything."

"What about the funeral?" I said suddenly overwhelmed. "It's bothering me. I haven't a clue what to do. In fact, I don't know what the fuck to do about anything."

I didn't mean to, but I slid down the planks and sat on the filthy floor and cried. He handed me a handkerchief, seemingly unperturbed. Gates, locks, CCTV, funeral dates...there wasn't any time left to do any more research for myself. Any enthusiasm I'd had for investigating cocaine, heroin, migrants and trafficking generally, leached away over the next few days. I was more concerned with the ball and chain of my inheritance hanging round my neck and the visits to the solicitor to finalise details.

I walked to the office on Wednesday morning and returned the washed handkerchief David had mopped me up with.

"I didn't think people carried old-fashioned hankies any more. Beats a soggy Kleenex," I said managing an apologetic smile.

"Habit picked up from my father," he said. "He carries one folded in his top pocket with just a corner showing, a new one every day washed and ironed. Drives my mother mad."

"I don't fall apart very often," I said. "It's just that organising the funeral and sorting out the security measures for the yard are out of my league. I don't know where to start."

"It's all taken care of," he said. "Mr Jones left instructions and funds with us and the funeral director a long time ago. All you need to do is attend, perhaps afterwards an open invitation at a local pub? People will want to meet you, you know."

Oh God, I thought, wrapping myself around a bottle of wine that night in the sanctuary of Helen's bedroom. I needed to phone my mother again, having lied that the first meeting on Tuesday was delayed. I couldn't face telling her the whole news; even more, I couldn't face her response. I could almost hear the shrieks down the phone before I'd picked it up. I had just said I had to look after the lobster. Truth by omission. It was all I could face that first day.

A draught of cold air sneaked through the sash windows and stirred the curtains. A gale was forecast, Helen's Nain said at supper. I thought of great-uncle John's boat left out for the rest of the winter with its expensive engine exposed to the weather, moored up and leaning against the harbour wall at the mercy of wind and wave. I thought of his Toyota, a hefty pickup simply covered with an old tarpaulin and tucked under the cliff near the snack-bar, batteries flat and engine at risk from freezing. Did I care? The realisation that they were now mine suddenly hit me. I needed to do something. But not now.

I poured another glass of wine and phoned my mother.

CHAPTER 11

I put off visiting her until the Friday. I drove straight to London and planned to stay just the one night. I psyched myself up to answer the barrage of questions from my mother as well as Trish and Felicity and escaped on the Saturday morning back to my flat with its grey urbanity and the roar of the motorway. Helen's Nain's list was in my head as well as my back pocket. I was running out of paper. I was on overload with emotions and couldn't pin down how I felt, my usual ebullience for a challenge fading with the reality. Journalism or the Boat Shed? I didn't see how I could do both.

I waited for briefing to finish on the Monday morning, my tasks for the week to include court reports and a weekend duty covering the local sport. There's nothing as miserable as reporting on a local football match on a Saturday afternoon in freezing fog when you hate the game anyway and are expected to deliver action-packed photos as well as the copy.

I sat at my desk waiting for a clear space outside Ed's office, my mind wandering to the alternative. Unasked for plans sneaked into my muddled head when I wasn't watching: clear the yard, clean the shed, learn new stuff and then there was that appalling cottage with its glorious view overlooking the bay compared to my dismal flat. How far would fifty thousand pounds go as well as giving me a meagre salary? Now I had to make a decision and tell Ed the news. Avoiding Tim and his inevitable questions, I headed straight for Ed's office. I knocked on the door. This time I waited.

"Inherited a lobster, then?" he said, waving me to a chair. "Done some research? Bet you went to Pwllheli. Did you meet Gwilym Thomas, then? Runs the fishing charter."

"You mean the fisherman with the manners of a pit bull? You know him?"

"Known him for years. He's not known for his pleasantries, is Gwilym, but he runs a good business. He takes me on fishing trips in the summer."

" I didn't even know you knew the area. You never said."

"Ah well, if I'd given you all the leads you wouldn't have had to work so hard, would you? It's all good practice and it'll go down on your CV, don't forget. Did your uncle leave you the lobster, by the way?"

I stood up and handed him my letter of resignation. Then I sat down while he read it. I'd never seen Ed lost for words.

"Good God. That's some inheritance," he said finally. "Congratulations."

He rubbed his hand over his face and sat back in the chair.

"Bloody hell," he added unnecessarily. "What will you do?"

"I can't do two jobs," I said. "I've thought about it. I don't want to give up my career as a journalist but I can't see any way out. It's a challenge, if nothing else. There's a shabby cottage as well and a fishing boat and a Toyota pickup and clients using the yard all the time. Oh, and a snack-bar. I've worked out I can pay myself a living wage for a couple of years and get it into some sort of shape."

"Do you know anything about classic boats, Cassie?"

"Course not. Can't be rocket science, though."

"Learning your fids from your baggy wrinkles, eh?"

I hadn't got a clue what he was talking about.

"I can learn," I said with a confidence I didn't feel. "What I don't know I'll find out. I can't bear not knowing things."

"I'd noticed. Do your feature anyway if you can though. And stow it away. It might come in useful if things don't work out and you still need a CV."

I crept out of the office to face Tim, two coffees in hand, barring the way to my desk.

"Got to be important," he said, glancing through the glass to Ed's office. "I can see his face from here."

The coffee grew cold as I told him.

A text from David arrived next morning. Funeral arrangements were in place for the following Friday at the tiny church, Eglwys S. Mihangel, built on the lane up above Black Rock Sands, the crags of Moel-y-Gest to the north and the estuary to the east and south. He'd organised a wake at The Sportsman Hotel in Porthmadog. 'Not to worry, all is settled including invitations. Wear black.'

No problem. Nearly all my clothes were black anyhow. My mind-set was similar at the thought of meeting people I didn't know and their inevitable opinions.

I worked all that week and into the next, ploughing through a list of charity fundraising events, a centenary birthday in an old people's home and complaints from residents near a primary school on the speed-bump restrictions. I covered a story of a farmer who starved his dogs and horses and threatened the RSPCA officers with a shotgun. It rained every day and it was cold and I dropped my phone in the liquid shit that passed as a farmyard. By Wednesday, I was almost looking forward to the funeral.

"It'll be cold up there at the church. You can use my coat again," said Helen's Nain on the phone when I begged a bed for the weekend.

"Oh, by the way, one of the boat owners from the yard was looking for you. He came to the house, sent by Doug Peterson, he said, who seems to know everybody else's business and whereabouts. Something to do with a caravan? I took his number."

The funeral came and went; a short, solemn service in Welsh attended by a small group of solemn men, my solicitor amongst them. He took me by the arm after the burial and showed me the tiny grave of Uncle John's children, a slate gravestone at the head with two doves carved above the inscription.

"That's so sad. They didn't need to die," I said. "Why did my grandfather take such a risk?"

He shrugged. "You'd have to ask those who knew him best."

"But he was my grandfather. He was so stern and strict I can't imagine him taking risks."

We moved on. The children's mother, my great-aunt Annie, rested in the next plot. And then Tomas. A simple headstone with a fish carved into the slate. That was enough. I turned my head away quickly so he wouldn't notice. I blamed my tears on the wind and swallowed hard. I looked up towards the crags of Moel-y-Gest where black crows wheeled in the breeze and listened to the wind soughing in the huge pine tree next to the church, then turned to watch the surf breaking white on the bar to the south.

Helen's Nain had said my roots were here. There was a community here, a sense of belonging. I felt it suddenly, comfortingly, as keenly as the wind around my legs, more than I ever felt standing at my dad's grave in the impersonal London cemetery, the simple casket lined up with row upon row of strangers in death and probably as well in life.

"A good place to rest," Gerald Hughes said, steering me towards the car. "He'll be at peace here amongst friends and family. He wasn't a happy man for many years, you know."

David appeared at the hotel for the wake and hosted the introductions. I shook hands with local business men, a bank manager, an accountant and the Harbour Master, a burly man in a navy jumper. Apart from the waitresses, I was the lone female. They were all tall men, their heads inclined towards each other as they grouped in deep conversation. Occasionally one would remember my presence and leave the group to cross the room where I stood with David.

"What are you thinking?" he said, in between visits.

"They look like corvidae," I said.

He stared at me.

"Know your birds, do you?"

"Dad was a keen bird-watcher when he wasn't watching stars. He dragged me along with him until I rebelled. These guys just remind me of old crows."

"And powerful ones at that," he said. "Don't underestimate them and don't let it faze you."

I knew I liked him just as much as when I first met him, easy-going and comfortable.

I didn't speak Welsh but the guests inquired politely as to my intentions for the yard. I felt like a diminutive blackbird in a closed clique dismissive of me to the point of rudeness. I didn't know whether it was my nationality or my gender. I didn't much care. I was glad I'd left my nose-stud in.

"You'll be looking for a yard manager, I expect?" was the general inquiry. "You'll be looking for someone who knows about boats."

I made vague comments. I was more interested in Will Roberts, the Harbour Master David introduced me to. I didn't waste any time.

"I'm worried about my uncle's fishing boat," I said to Will Roberts. "I can see it's been okay so far this winter but I was looking at the long-range forecast. They're predicting gale force winds from the east. That means it's going to bash straight onto the wall where the boat's tied up. It could smash itself to bits or even do some damage in the harbour if it broke loose. And there are spring tides next week. I wondered if you can help me move it. I'll pay."

I was gratified to see his jaw dropping. I carried on chatting boaty stuff as though I'd been doing this all my life, throwing in what terminology I'd learned from the Internet as naturally as I could.

"It's got a Honda 90, petrol engine I know, but I don't know whether the main batteries will be too flat to start it. I bought a charger with me and a long extension cable to hook up but it might take overnight. I know what to do to connect it all up."

He raised his eyebrows, saucer in one hand and coffee cup half way to his mouth.

"The thing is, Mr Roberts, I have to go back to work on Monday. High tide's at fourteen hundred tomorrow. Could you or one of your staff help me move it where there's some shelter further into the harbour? If you've got a space, that is? I just need to get used to it with someone beside me. I haven't been at the wheel before."

"I do know the boat, young lady."

He was a bit frosty, I thought, but I didn't care as long as he did what I asked. Besides, it was his job, after all.

"I don't usually work on Saturdays," he said.

"Oh," I said, "what a shame. We journalists rarely get Saturdays off. The best disasters often happen at weekends. Always makes a good front page story ready for Monday's paper. Not to worry. Let's hope the weather holds, then."

"Journalist, you say?"

It seemed to work.

"Two o'clock then?" he said and turned away, already on the phone. I kept the smile off my face.

Then it was all over. I thanked people graciously for attending, the response from them one of solemn politeness tinged with vague curiosity. But mostly disinterest. Too young, wrong sex, city girl...and English. I could feel the disapproval and almost interpret the conversations. I didn't need to be Welsh speaking.

I headed for the yard, shucked off Helen's Nain's expensive wool coat and grabbed an old jacket from the boot of the car. This time I'd come prepared. I picked up the engine key from the shed, climbed down the ladder and opened the cabin door to the boat. It stank of damp and diesel, the tin mugs still on the shelf and the biscuit tin thick with rust. It had been three years after all. I had a feeling the boat hadn't been used at sea for a while.

I turned the engine key, watching the lights on the console flicker unexpectedly then glow bright and stay on. I made sure the button on the throttle was in neutral, found the control to lower the engine and turned the key all the way. It coughed reluctantly into life. I checked the cooling water siphoning out of the engine casings, remembering my first and only experience of this, or any other boat, come to that. God bless Google. I let it run for thirty minutes. The charger stayed in the boot.

Helen's Nain was waiting for me as the light faded. She made tea and was unusually quiet.

"Are you alright?" I asked, as she stirred the tea slowly in the pot and put the lid back on.
She brought it to the table, sat heavily down in the chair and sighed, asked me about the funeral.

"I'm sorry I didn't go, in a way," she said, "but I'd had nothing to do with him for many years and it's only a year since my Gethin passed and so many more of our age as well. I couldn't face another funeral at the moment.

'We were the same age, your great-uncle John and I. Just focuses your mind for the moment when one's peers pass on. I'm sure the funeral went well, though. Quiet, I expect. It would have been what he wanted. It's a good place to rest."

"Plenty of old crows to see him off," I said, the image of the gathering of suits at the funeral fresh in my mind. "I don't think they liked me much, though. I've got an awful lot to prove, haven't I?"
She nodded. She knew exactly what I meant.

"I've been thinking," she said, brightening up, "about what you call me. Do you think you could bring yourself to call me Joan, now, being as you're all grown-up and a property owner as well? I don't feel like a Nain when you're around; more of a partner in crime, actually. Not real crime, of course, just a figure of speech. But I do think there are things I'd be able to help you with if you're going to build up this business. What do you think, Cassie?"

"Okay," I said, rolling it round in my head. I wasn't sure. "Joan. What sort of help?"

"Not climbing up and down ladders, cariad, that's for sure, but I'm pretty good with the Internet. There'll be a lot of things you'll need to find out about classic boat bits, for example, and cataloguing the stock you've got. I've got time before the season starts. I'm not ready to join your great-uncle John under the ground just yet."
The tears welled in my eyes.

"Thank you," I said, "and you're not going anywhere. That's just brilliant."
I sniffed and blew my nose. She pretended not to see.

I went to the yard late Saturday morning. There was no sign of Doug Peterson. The lights were off in the office and the gates were shut.

I was so relieved he wasn't there that I just stood with my eyes shut for a minute, the tension draining away. Nobody had ever exerted such an unpleasant influence over me before and I wanted to make my own mistakes without his critical eye. His CCTV watching my every move was bad enough. I was trying to decide what to do next about moving the boat, what to check, how to handle the ropes so I didn't look stupid when the Harbour Master and his mate turned up. A high-pitched voice out of nowhere cut across my thoughts.

"Excuse me. I was looking for Mr. Jones."

I turned round. A slight man in a green anorak straight out of the sixties faced me, pale with a faded tan and a black Beanie perched on his head. He had green corduroy trousers tucked into ankle socks above muddy walking boots. He looked about fifty but his face was unlined, pleasant enough and bland as though life hadn't touched him much. He blinked a lot behind rimless glasses, his eyes pale blue and staring intently at me. I knew him.

"We've met before," I said, wishing I hadn't. How ridiculous was this for coincidences, the nerd on the railway track three years ago boring me with the tourist spiel and inviting me to visit the engine shed. I searched around for a name. Did he remember me, though? He did, his eyes widening in surprise.

"You're the lady with the long plait. Unusual these days.We met on the Cob, goodness me, all those years ago, too." He smiled and cocked his head on one side. "What a coincidence. I was looking for Mr. Jones, though, the owner. Is he around?"

I explained.Whatever colour he had in his face drained away in the cold air.

"I'm so sorry to hear that. I haven't been here for a while. He was well enough when I saw him last."

He looked around the yard, his gaze settling on a green tarpaulin.

"I've been coming here for a good few years now, renovating an old boat and working on the railway in my spare time."

He pointed to the tarpaulin spread over the deck of a small wooden yacht chocked up on balks of timber nailed together. He coughed and shuffled his feet in the gravel.

"So you're the new owner? I have business I needed to attend to with Mr Jones. Do I deal with yourself now? I'm Hugh Phillips, by the way."

I remembered his name then, calling out as I backed off down the track, the creepy little man I'd created a story around and made fun of, laughing with Trish and Simon over my first pint of lager at Spooners. It seemed rude now. I'd moved on.

He held out a gloved hand, green knitted gloves with holes in the fingers. I took it briefly. He looked cold and perturbed. I remembered my manners, ushered him into the shed and switched on the heater by the two chairs.

"Now," I said. "How can I help you?"

He took his gloves off and stuffed them in his pockets and then his Beanie, to reveal a high forehead and a bald head, holding the hat in his hands and turning it round and round.

"I owe Mr Jones some money, you see, and there's the matter of the old caravan. I only intended to leave it here for a few months and pay some rent, but time's slipped by..."

I nodded. "Did you stay in it?"

"Only for one season while I was working on the boat. Then my work sent me up to Scotland. I've only just returned. It's a bit of a wreck now, I can see. I feel really bad about this, Miss...?"

"Cassie. Cassie Jones."

"I need to move it out of here, Miss Jones. Scrap it, I think and pay you whatever I owe for the rent."

My brain clicked into gear.

"How long will it take you to finish your boat?"

"Finish it?"

He laughed and shook his head.

"Never, probably. It's a restoration labour of love, really. I have a passion for classic yachts, you see, and steam trains, of course. This is the nearest I'll ever get to affording one. It's more about the journey, the restoration, you see. I'm not really interested in going to sea in it, just returning the boat to its former glory."

"You know a bit about classic boats then? And all the bits that go with it?"

My brain clicked into overload.

His face lit up. He gazed around the shed, as much as he could in the gloom.

"Oh my word, yes," he said, a faraway look in his eyes. "Blocks and tackles and..."

"...fids and baggy wrinkles?" I asked, showing off and remembering Ed's knowledge and how I'd Googled the strange words; a fid was a tool for opening up ropes for splicing and baggywrinkles were soft coverings sometimes made out of frayed rope to stop sails chafing against hard rigging. I'd remembered it word for word.

"Indeed," he said, looking at me seriously. "Everything has a purpose on a sailing ship. Everything is meaningful."

"Do you work with boats, then?" I said.

"Goodness me, no. I'm a wind turbine engineer. I'm working out of Holyhead in Anglesey for the next year or so, maintaining the wind farms out at sea."

He sat very still and upright in the old chair, his knees together and the Beanie still in his hands.

"So will you be carrying on with the work on your boat here?"

"If I may. When the spring comes and the weather warms up. I'll pay my way, of course."

"I wondered if you'd be interested in a deal," I said, my thoughts racing.

He cocked his head on one side like a sparrow, the shiny pate catching the light, listening intently.

"If I scrap any money owing on the caravan and cover the cost of having it removed, would you care to consider helping to catalogue all the stock in here? I haven't a clue. Nothing is labelled, everything's piled up on the shelves. Maybe at weekends until you can work on your boat again? I want to have a website built as soon as possible but I need to know what stock is here."

"A website?"

"Yes. I want to recreate the Boat Shed, bring it into the twenty first century. There's a market out there, even for fids and baggy wrinkles."

"Oh my word," he said, running his hand over his face, "Oh my word."

He was very old-fashioned, I thought. He must have special skills to survive in the world of alpha-male wind turbine engineers. A true nerd, but I quite liked him.

"Think about it," I said. "I'll be here tomorrow morning before heading off back to work. I have to finish working my notice and then I'll be back living here for the foreseeable future. I'd really like to see the place up and running before the end of the summer."

I couldn't believe I was saying all this. I turned the heater off and shook his hand again, hearing the engine of the Harbour Master's launch over the stillness in the harbour. It was two o'clock.

"You'll have to excuse me," I said. "I've got a boat to move."

It sounded grand and confident. I was about as confident as a jellyfish but I reminded myself that when you tell people something enough times it often become more real. Then you feel duty bound to do it. I shut the door and crossed the yard to the ladder.

CHAPTER 12

I said a quiet prayer and the engine roared into life first time as the harbour launch moored up alongside. Will Roberts, short, thickset and every inch the Harbour Master in working clothes was clad in a heavy-duty navy jacket and woollen hat. He clambered into the cockpit leaving a young man at the helm of the launch. I hoped he was in a more amenable mood than the previous day at the funeral. He wasn't.

"Ready?" he said, by way of a greeting, his voice deep and his face unsmiling. "Life-jacket on correctly?"

I nodded. I wasn't going to make that mistake. He glanced cursorily at the buckles I'd fastened and was glad I'd put it on before he saw my clumsy efforts.

I'd looped a rope around the ladder to hold the boat in to the wall as I'd remembered Uncle John doing and left the boat-hook ready on the seat in the cockpit.

"You know where the throttle is, I presume."

I'd assumed he would take the wheel, despite my blasé attitude at the funeral.

"But I thought..."

He gestured towards the cabin door.

Now was not the time for argument. I'd felt the same way when I went out with my great-uncle three years since; instinct said to do as I was told. I didn't like it much but I wanted the job done. Niceties could wait.

"That way," he said, his voice as brusque as the day before, pointing out to sea. "If you're going to drive this thing you might as well practice first before you pile into something and damage my harbour. Head out down the estuary slowly. Red buoys to starboard and green to port on the way out. Reverse buoys coming back in. All the way to the No 4, if you please and circle each buoy close in without hitting it."

I'd only ever driven a Corsa. I pushed the throttle forward and turned the boat into the channel, cursed inwardly for a whole hour as I did as I was asked and congratulated myself as we glided back through the harbour, past the boatyard towards the bridge. Not a word was spoken.

Will Roberts' assistant, Mark, had moored the harbour launch at the end of the pontoon and was waiting to take the ropes. I put the throttle in neutral as instructed and nosed into the pontoon. The boat bumped into the edge, but only gently, and lay alongside while he secured the lines to the cleats. Will Roberts threw one hefty leg over the side-deck and stood on the pontoon. He turned briefly to me as I ducked out of the cabin door into the cockpit, the engine left idling comfortably.

"It'll be safe enough here for tonight," he said. "I'll find somewhere more permanent tomorrow. Mark will see you tied up and secure. Not bad, Miss Jones. Better when you've learned your port from your starboard."

He walked off without looking back.

Mark stood on the pontoon grinning, fresh-faced and confident.

"Missed a couple of buoys, did you? Went the wrong way round them, yeah? No matter. There's plenty of water out there at high tide to let you make a few mistakes. He wouldn't have let you go aground."

I stared after the burly figure now at the far end of the pontoon as he disappeared through the security gate and up the ramp to the car-park outside the yacht club. I looked at my watch and the grey sky and the gathering gloom and thought of all the work I had to do. I blew my nose which dripped in the cold and despaired at my chipped nail polish and the oily black marks on my coat sleeve. I was cold and cross.

"Alright for some," I said. "Not surprised he doesn't like working Saturdays. He's just in time for the rest of the match on the telly and a few beers with his feet up."

I was smarting from his criticism and surly manner and almost glad I'd spoiled his Saturday afternoon. I thought I'd done brilliantly out there and missing a few buoys didn't seem that important. Mark was squatting on the wet planks by the side of the boat checking the ropes. He looked up at me.

"Not likely he'll be putting his feet up," he said. "He'll be going home to change a bed, check a drip and make sure his wife's as comfortable as possible. I know. I've been in the house since they sent her home. It's like a miniature hospital ward."

I hoped I'd misheard him. He stood up, his face serious.

"His wife's in the terminal stages of cancer. He's looking after her at home with the help of carers and nurses. It's difficult at weekends to get extra care in at short notice. That's why he rushed off. A neighbour's with her for the afternoon. She can't be left alone."

He took a quick look at my face. I felt the colour burn in my cheeks despite the cold.

"You weren't to know," but he couldn't keep the reproach out of his voice.

I wanted to run after him but he'd gone. I was mortified. Another lesson to be learned, Milly would have said. Things are not always what they seem. Be careful with your assumptions. I knew what it meant working for the paper and delving into the tragedies of other people's lives. After all, a journalist's job was to ask questions to get to the truth, we were told, and nothing should surprise you. Take the notes, write them up and move on to the next story. Nothing personal.

But this was different. I was beginning to understand that my life up here and success or failure depended on relationships. Every minute something new reared its head. I needed to tread more carefully. And keep my mouth shut. Had I learned nothing at uni? I stood in the cockpit in a fog of shame and embarrassment, creating apologies in my head and desperately glad I hadn't said anything to the burly man with a sick wife about his leisure time at weekends. It would have been unforgiveable.

"Fancy a drink tonight, then?"

Mark was standing waiting for me, a grubby peaked cap clamped down on his head, hands on slim hips and broad shoulders straining against the donkey jacket. I'd thought he was just a teenager standing at the helm in the launch but now I looked twice. Why not? Tomorrow could wait. Maybe I could wash away the sour taste of guilt and dull my embarrassment.

"One thing," he said, as we turned to leave the boat. "I nearly forgot. Those mooring ropes must have rubbed against the harbour wall, with them not being checked for a few weeks after Mr Jones passed, like. They're nearly worn through. You'll need to replace them. Must have been a sharp bit of wall to do that. Clean cut right through, nearly. Funny that. It's only been a few weeks. We've had no wind to speak of. I've pulled them through to sound rope for now so the frayed ends won't matter."

He was thoughtful for a minute then ushered me along the pontoon out of the marina, the security door closing with a quiet click behind us.

"See you at eight, then," he said as we parted company. "The 'Ship' is just along there. There'll be a crowd of us and some music, probably.

Will you come?"

"You'll be talking in Welsh, though, won't you? I can't speak Welsh. Not yet anyway. Will they want me there? Didn't you lot try to burn out the English once?"

He laughed. "It's not the seventies anymore. That's bad history, that burning holiday homes stuff. We're all bilingual anyway. We won't shut you out. Besides, you're Welsh, aren't you, with your great-uncle being Mr Jones? Welsh as they come, you are, deep down. You'll be alright."

I went that evening with misgivings but desperately needing to feel young and reckless and forget about the day's events and my new-found responsibilities. I drank too much, predictably, propping up the bar after a few pints of the local brew and God knows how many vodkas, listening to the music from the group in the corner and singing along to 'Galway Girl' and 'Fishermen's Blues'.

Instead of the indifference I'd expected from the group Mark introduced me to, I seemed to be a novelty. 'Girl turned boatyard owner' sort of novelty. I answered some questions but I wasn't that drunk to have forgotten the afternoon and my promise to be more circumspect in my chatter and to take more care with my assumptions.

Mark soon forgot about me as Saturday night gathered pace, lapsed into pure Welsh with his mates and knocked a pint over one of the girls. They drew together in a group and I retreated to a corner of the bar on my own in a warm, alcoholic glow of independence, my new and unusual status boosted by the interest. I felt safe and secure in the crowded pub just listening to the music. I wasn't one of the crowd and never would be, but I didn't mind. They'd been pleasant enough. Even the walk back along the dark path to Borth-y-Gest passing other late drinkers worried me not one jot. In London I would never have contemplated it.

It was three in the morning when the hammering on the front door woke me. Blue lights flashed outside the bedroom window, a familiar portent of disaster, my heart thudding and bile rising in my throat remembering the blue lights of the police and coastguard in the boatyard when they lifted Tomas's little body into the ambulance.

I stumbled out of the bedroom. Joan was already at the front door as I reached the top of the stairs.

"There's been a fire," I heard a man say. I'd already bundled back into the room and threw clothes on. Somehow I was not surprised. They drove me to the yard in the fire-service car, the single fire-engine parked outside the gate which had been forced open, uniformed guys now reeling in the main hoses and walking in and out of the yard carrying shovels. They'd taken a while to find me, apologised for the gate and the mess.

"It's the old smoke-house," the fire officer said. "The piles of wood chippings in the bunker round the back were on fire. It's too early to tell if it was deliberate. We got here just before it broke through into the chandlery. It's mostly smoke damage."

"How did you find me?" I said, checking the front door to the shed.

"Late night drinkers you were in the pub with saw the smoke, phoned us and the police. You were lucky it hadn't spread. They seemed to know where you were staying. There's no sign of a break-in. Bit of a mystery, this."

I had to remember that everyone seemed to know everything in this small town, including where I was staying.

"We were sorry to hear about Mr Jones. We used to buy our Christmas smoked salmon from him." He chatted away as though nothing much had happened.

"How could oak chippings catch fire in February outside in the cold?" I asked. "The smoke-house hasn't been used for ages."

He shrugged.

"The police will look into it. There's nobody around now anyway."
It was four o'clock in the morning and my head was thumping with the beginnings of a hangover. The strangely frayed mooring ropes and now a fire in the yard so close to the shed took on a significance that made me uneasy. My warm glow was beginning to fade. I needed a pannad and a good stiff talking-to: my propensity for over-indulgence in stories was threatening to compete sensibly with hard facts.

"It's all out now and damped down," he said. "There's a lot of water in the shed, I'm afraid. Going to start up the business, are you? And the snack-bar again? My wife'll like that."
They packed up and drove off, leaving me alone in the dark yard, the air thick with the stink of smouldering wet wood. I checked the front door was locked and pulled the broken gate together as best I could.

Joan was waiting up for me, pannad at the ready. My mere presence was beginning to affect other people; I felt guilty about dragging the Harbour Master away from his dying wife, guilty about keeping Joan from her bed and suddenly guilty about the bloody lobster I hadn't given a thought to. At least David was feeding it but that couldn't go on forever. I explained to her how I felt, the confusion over the enthusiasm and support from some I'd met standing alongside a deep unease about my welcome here. I hadn't ever forgotten the row I'd overheard between Doug Peterson and my uncle over the planning permission, the pressure to sell the yard and his offer to me. But Doug Peterson was away for a month, I'd been told by Mark.

"He goes every year to the West Indies for a holiday before the summer season starts over here. His secretary Denise keeps the business ticking over but he won't be around for a few weeks yet."
Thank God for that, I thought. Perhaps things will be different when I move in.

"Go to bed," Joan said. "It'll unravel itself."

Sleep evaded me. I lay in Helen's bed as the dawn rose over the estuary. A cold draught sneaked its way through the sash window and did nothing to dispel the headache. My tongue felt like sandpaper. The sky was grey when I pulled the curtains back and white horses were whipped up out in the estuary by the easterly wind then broke against the sea-wall protecting the promenade. This must be the beginning of the cold spell they'd forecast. I had to go back to work today, fire or no fire, gales or no gales, suddenly remembering the strange little man with the caravan who said he would give me his decision about the caravan and the stock that morning. I brightened at the plan I'd hatched and shared with no-one.

I'd mulled over the most important things to deal with: the lobster with his one claw had to go somewhere else to be looked after, the Toyota needed attention, the boat, which at least I'd now moved to a place of safety couldn't stay there forever and there was the smoke-house and the mess to clear up after the fire. Overriding it all was the nagging feeling that I wasn't wanted here and the list of jobs to be done had all seemed an impossible task in the early hours before dawn. Then I pulled myself together. I had a plan.

It was still early when I left the breakfast warmth of Joan's kitchen.

"Take milk," she said. "Just in case you have visitors."

A Sunday morning winter silence followed me back to the yard. Not even the blackbirds greeted me as I pushed open the gate. It sagged even further on its hinges and the wooden plank along the bottom edge caught on the gravel but I was grateful to the fire crew for their work in the middle of the night and the damage to the gate was a small price to pay. I looked over to Doug Peterson's heavy-duty galvanised gates with the security code and the solid fences protecting his yard.

"That's what I want," I said aloud to a passing gull.

Then I looked around at the yard full of junk and derelict boats, the peeling paint on the shed door and the black mess that had seeped from the smoke-house where the fire crew had poured water onto the chippings. I wished, just for a second, that the whole place had burned to the ground.

"Good morning."

He'd crept up on me, Hugh Phillips with the Beanie firmly planted on his head, on a bicycle this time. He sat astride the saddle with his feet barely touching the ground and his trousers tucked into his socks.

"Did something happen?"

He followed me to the shed and propped the bike against the wall.

"I cycled from the Bed and Breakfast," he said. "It keeps me fit."

I wasn't interested in his fitness and had almost forgotten the suggestions I'd made the day before to this perfect stranger who could have been a serial killer for all I knew. Then I remembered his caravan. I pushed the door to the shed open, switched on the electric fire, and filled the kettle.

"Tea?"

He stood behind the counter with his hat in his hand, turning it round and round just like the day before. You're just nervous, I thought. Wonder what you've decided?

"I'd like to take up your offer," he said. "But what happened here?"

The smell of smoke permeated the whole shed. I explained. He was very quiet. In fact, he was so quiet I felt I could be quiet as well. We sat on the grubby chairs in silence while the kettle boiled and switched itself off leaving only the faint hum from the pump in the lobster tank.

A noise broke the silence. A noise, not of timbers settling or beams creaking, more of a rustling noise from the darkness at the bottom of the shed where the model room hid its secrets. Hugh Phillips started in his seat.

"What was that? You said there was no sign of a break in."
I shook my head.

"Nothing. Probably mice," I said. "Bound to be in a place like this."

"Or rats? I hate rats," he said.

I could see the fear in his face. There was a dull thud and a crash as something hit the floor.

"Big rat," I said, more bravely than I felt. "Perhaps something else."
One of us had to go. Mice I thought I could cope with; rats would freak me out, but even worse was the thought of playing scaredy-cat girl to a wimp of a man obviously even more scared than I was. I got up out of my seat and switched on the lights to the bottom of the shed, slipped past the lobster tank and stood outside the closed door to the model shed. He was right behind me, breathing a waft of garlic breath over my shoulder. I turned. He held a piece of wood about three feet long, the varnish a dull gold in the poor light.

"Dinghy tiller," he said. "Found it on the shelf."
He hefted it like a base ball bat. I stared at him.

"Soft ball," he said. "Played for the county. Open the door, then."
I could even forgive the bad breath as I clocked a manic gleam in his eyes. I'd made another wrong assumption.

"Go on, then. Open it."
I turned the handle and pushed open the door with my foot. The light from the fluorescent tube in the shed flickered on the interior with its shelves and models lined up nose to tail. I found a light switch on the door jamb and flicked it on. The wreck of a model ship lay on the floor. A figure huddled in the far corner under one of the shelves, much larger than a rat and much less scary, his knees up to his chest and his arms covering his head. He wore a grey hoody, patched jeans and trainers covered in blackened wood ash. He lifted his head and squinted against the light. He was painfully thin, high cheekbones

standing out in a grubby face and stubble that wasn't quite a beard. It was the hands I noticed above all else but nothing I could connect with, just a deep feeling that was as familiar as hunger pangs.

I knew those hands. How could I know those hands?

I stood speechless as the little man behind me pushed in front, tapping the length of wood meaningfully against his right palm, his head jutted forward. He didn't need to speak. His actions were enough, but maybe he didn't trust his voice. The figure on the floor drew his knees up higher and buried his head again in his arms. Nobody spoke. I stared at his fingers splayed over his forearms: long, elegant and filthy, nails bitten to the quick, the patches of eczema on the back of his hands dry and scaly where the sleeves had ridden up.

I ran my tongue over my lips, my mouth dry and found my voice. What was his name?

"Jason?"

CHAPTER 13

Tucked up in one of the chairs with the dirty plaid rug over his knees, he stopped shivering and cradled the mug of hot tea I'd given him. Hugh Phillips put the dinghy tiller back on the shelf. He seemed slightly abashed at his own bravery and reverted to the shy little man I'd only just met.

"You obviously know this young man. I'll come back in a bit to sort out details as to when you want me to start and how to catalogue stuff," he said. "Were you serious about the deal with the caravan?"

Oh yes, that was a definite. I'd got plans already. He backed out quietly to look at his boat.

"What are *you* doing here?" I asked, scarcely believing my eyes. He shook his head.

"What are *you* doing here?" he returned. "And I can't remember your name...sorry."

"Cassie. Just Cassie."

It took a while to explain.

"JJ's dead and you own all this?"

"Apparently. How, for God's sake did you get in, Jason? The fireman said there was no sign of a break-in. I checked the doors as well."

"Tomas showed me years ago. I used to knock around with him in the yard when dad and the twins were messing next door with the skidoos. We got up to all sorts of kid's stuff JJ knew nothing about."

"He was younger than you though," I said, thinking it was a strange relationship.

"Yeah but he didn't act young, like. My dad said he had an old head on his shoulders. He knew about fishing and the history of the yard. He was dead clued up for a little kid. That's why we couldn't understand how he drowned. JJ said he could swim like a fish and climb like a goat."

"I remember," I said, seeing my uncle's disbelieving face over the counter when he was told the awful news.

"I've missed him. Holidays haven't been the same since. He was a good laugh. JJ dead as well, then?"

We sat in silence for a moment.

"So how did you get in?" I asked.

"There's a loose piece of tin sheeting at the back of the shed where the models are. Tomas levered it open and stuck some false nail-heads in. He used to hide in there when Gareth was on a bender and he didn't want to go home. That's how he knew so much about the rigging. He went to the museum to watch the videos and learn about knots and things and how the old sailing ships worked and they let him in for free."

He was surprised when I said I'd trained as a journalist since then and wasn't just a serving girl at the snack-bar. It thawed him out a bit.

"Not much journalists haven't seen," he said. "Accidents and stuff."

"I'm only just qualified," I said. "Seen a bit though and written a few stories. Now I've got all this to think about."

He sat quietly. His thin wrists drooped over his knees.

"What am I going to do now? I only came here 'cos I thought JJ might help me. I can't stay here now, can I?" looking round at the dirt and clutter.

His eyes welled up again and I gave him a tissue.

"I'm sorry about the fire. I didn't mean it to happen like that. It was just a small one in the chippings when I got here. Never thought about it only it was warm and I was freezing. I poked it and it sort of spread under the door. I'm gutted. Sorry. And you gave me a veggie breakfast back then and it was brilliant, I remember. You were dead kind. Do you really own all this now?"

I nodded.

"Wow," he said.

I remembered back to that day his dad came for the lobster, as well as his mother's indifference to Tomas's death and the badly behaved elder brothers.

"So what are you doing here, on your own in the depth of winter freezing to death? You had a perfectly good family last time I saw you: Range Rover, jet-skis and a dad with plenty of money."

"I'm eighteen," he said. "I can do what I want, can't I?"

"Course you can," I said, ignoring the sharp retort, "except that I'd got you down for a student. You know, following your own path."

"I am a student," he said, still on the defence. "Dad wasn't going to tell me what to do with my life. I went to college. I've done nearly two years of an NVQ in social care. I can cook as well."

"Social care, you mean like nursing? That's a bit different to being a scrap-dealer like your dad."

I remembered what my uncle had said about him escaping from his brothers during our only fruitful conversations. He'd said Jason wasn't destined to be a scrappy; too sensitive and too bright by half.

"So what happened?"

"I had to leave home and I didn't know where else to go. Been in

Pwllheli for a few weeks with some mates I'd met during the holidays but it got a bit messy."

"Messy?" I said, my antennae on alert, trying to see his forearms but they were covered up. I said a small prayer and held my breath.

"Yeah, you know. They were into coke and stuff. It's not my scene. Then these guys from Manchester turned up and moved in. They brought loads of gear with them to sell and gave my mate freebies to use his flat. He was smashed out of his head. I couldn't talk to him. There was nowhere to sleep 'cos they took over the room I was in. So I just left a few days ago. They can find someone else to do their dirty work."

"What dirty work?"

"Pushing the stuff on the streets. I told them I didn't do drugs but they kept going on, like. So I packed my gear. Then they got nasty 'cos I knew they were dealing from the flat and I knew where it was. I said I wouldn't tell nobody and couldn't care less but they said they'd find me if the word got out. I was dead scared, so I ran."

I didn't want to doubt him. I just hoped he was telling the truth, unlike the homeless guy I'd met on the streets who had lied through his teeth about his habit and hoped I wouldn't notice. I changed the subject.

"You haven't told me why you had to leave home," I said.

He drew the blanket tight round his skinny thighs and held out his mug.

"Can I have some more please?" he said, like a child.

I brewed more tea, thinking he must be hungry as well. I stopped in mid-pour. What the hell was I going to do with him? What am I, Mother Teresa or what? First my bald-headed hero who wielded a baton like a pro and now a starving fugitive from a drugs den. Not to mention a property that needed fixing, a business to run and how to feel less than angry about having to give up a career. I poured his tea and handed it to him. It was almost laughable.

"Do your mum and dad know you're okay?" thinking of the big man

Arnie with the tattoos and his sharp-tongued wife.

He nodded.

"I texted them but they don't know where I am."

"So what was so bad at home you had to run away?"

He tucked his feet up under him and talked hesitantly at first, stumbling over words as though he were ashamed of telling me.

The twin brothers had been flogging parts from their dad's scrap cars on the QT, he told me, a lucrative business with profits that went nowhere near the company's books, and all under their dad's nose. Jason knew what was going on but was too frightened of them to say anything. They spent the cash on drugs at weekends.

"I saw them buying on the street one Saturday night outside a night club," he said. "I don't know what made me do it but I was suddenly sick of the way they'd treated me since I was a little kid. It was almost like a fuse blowing inside my head. I told Dad what they were up to. It was bad enough stealing from the firm but using the money for drugs was more than dad could take."

"So what did he say?"

"He went berserk when I told him on the Monday morning when he opened up. He waited 'till they arrived for work and shut the door behind them. Trashed the office. Tipped the desk over and roared like a lion. Scared the shit out of all of us. Eventually when he'd calmed down he said the twins could keep their jobs but they had to give up the drugs and find somewhere else to live. He wouldn't have them in the house anymore. Mum said they'd done wrong but she wouldn't see them homeless so she put them in one of the flats they own just down the road. They turned up for work alright but they were mental about me grassing on them."

"That was brave of you to tell your dad," I said. I remembered Arnie Blackwell's size and the huge biceps and imagined him in a temper.

"Dad might be a tough guy and he likes a drink," said Jason, "but he never did drugs. Lost a mate to drugs he told me once. Good boxer who fell on bad times, got depressed and hit whatever he could get hold of. You know like Tyson Fury? Only this guy couldn't get it together. Dad did everything he could, even paid for detox.

'He gave him a job at the yard and somewhere to live after his wife up and left. Then he got him work as a trainer at the local boxing club but he couldn't hack it. Dad found his body in the yard.Well dead. He'd O.D.'d on some hard stuff. He hates drugs, does dad."

"Is that why you left home? Threats from your brothers, I guess?"

He sniffed and blew his nose on the soggy tissue.

"They'll kill me if they find me."

I gave him the tissue box.

"So," I said. "You're hiding from your brothers and now you've got some nasty pieces of work from Pwllheli on the look-out for you? Jesus, Jason, what a mess."

"That's why I was looking for JJ," he said. "I thought he could help me, like. Get a job or something. He'd have known what to do. But he's dead. I can't go home. Dad doesn't know where I am and I've walked away from college. I'm scared."

I sensed a presence behind the counter, a shadow blocking the light and a cold draught on the back of my neck. I looked up at the wide shoulders and weather-beaten face of the Harbour Master.

"The door was open," he said, his voice deep and gruff with no hint of apology."Scared of what?"

Jason leapt from the chair and flung the rug on the floor, his face animated for the first time.

"Mr Roberts?"

How many more surprises, I thought wearily, but then of course they would know each other; the twin brothers in constant trouble on the water with their jet-skis and the threats of bans. It all came back to me just as my uncle told me about the Blackwell boys.

"Jason. You've grown a bit, young man. Didn't see you around last summer," he said. "So what the hell are you doing here in the middle of winter, boy?" proffering his hand to Jason over the counter.

The pleasure on Jason's face said it all. What I felt was the shame and embarrassment I'd felt the previous day after I'd learned why this burly man with his taciturn ways tried not to work Saturdays, caring for his dying wife whilst others were in the pub or watching football on the box. I wanted to say sorry. Would he have guessed what I was thinking? It was not the time now, if ever. He put an envelope on the counter.

"I've brought you the code for the marina gate, Miss Jones. The boat's on one of the yacht club's pontoons for the present. You can sort out payments with the secretary but it'll have to be moved to another berth or back on the wall at the end of March to make space for the permanent berth holders."

I thanked him. "I have to drive back home this afternoon.Would you like a pannad?" It seemed the only thing to do.

He came round the counter and I offered him the chair opposite Jason.

"Scared of what, boy? In a bit of bother, are you?"

"I think you'd better tell Mr Roberts everything you've told me," I said, brewing the tea. He took the mug from me but his eyes never left Jason's face. This was a conversation I felt I had no right to listen to, backing out quietly into the deserted yard. Hugh Phillips and his bike had gone but there was a note stuck in the letter box with a phone number and an email address.

'You were busy. Please ring or email to sort details for access to the shed. Will start next weekend. Hugh.'

I checked my watch. I needed to be on the road for two o'clock. I considered all the possibilities concerning the skinny kid sitting in my shed with nowhere to go. I couldn't take him home with me and I couldn't ask Helen's Nain to look after someone so vulnerable especially with dealers looking for him. I couldn't bear the thought of him out on the streets in the cold and he couldn't, or wouldn't, go home to his mum and dad. How easy it was for lives to go pear-shaped, I thought, thinking of the homeless addict in Pwllheli.

It was quiet back in the shed when I returned, Jason staring at the bar of the electric fire and the Harbour Master staring at Jason. I stood behind the counter, looking down on Will Roberts's broad shoulders and peaked cap, the work-reddened hands and the wedding ring on his left hand cutting into the flesh of his finger.

"Jason..." I said. Something had to happen. "I have to go back home this afternoon. I can't leave you here."

"Why not? I can clear up, tidy up the mess from the fire and look after the place. Nobody'll find me here."

"There's no food and nowhere to sleep," I said. "It's going to be freezing cold with this gale on its way and you don't look well. I could take you home to Dudley, make a detour this afternoon and talk to your dad maybe?" His face paled to a deathly white.

"No. No way." His eyes stared wide at the suggestion.

I was at a loss now.

Will Roberts raised his hand. I shut up.

"Cook, can you?" he said.

Jason lifted his head and nodded.

"Done a bit of caring, you said?"

"A year in homes for the elderly, yeah. Part of the NVQ."

"Right, here's a suggestion. You can come home with me until things settle down. You can earn your keep doing a bit of light cooking for the wife and some cleaning. You can cope with illness, can't you? Means I can get on with the job of looking after young ladies who want their boats moved on Saturdays. The wife'd like that, having a young face around. The carers are wonderful but they can't be there every minute. She likes being read to when she's tired or uncomfortable. You can do all that, can't you? Alright, Miss Jones?"

Speechless, overwhelmed, rooted to the spot, I swallowed and nodded.

"And when things settle down and this boy's off the radar with the dealers you can offer him a job in the yard in the summer. God knows you'll need as much help as you can get."

"But what about the guys I ran away from?"

I knew what Jason was thinking.

"It's a small-holding out near Blaenau Ffestiniog. It'd be unlucky if anyone came looking for you there. It's off the beaten track. Like chickens, do you? We've got free-range chickens we sell to the local butchers, eggs as well and a small flock of sheep ready for lambing. I could do with a hand."

"But I'm veg..." he started.

I shook my head. Just eat the eggs, I thought, hardly believing my ears. Jason caught my eye and just nodded. He was shaky on his feet when he stood up. I followed them out to the blue pick-up, watched Jason as he fumbled with the seat-belt and started to shiver. I went back inside and pulled the old plaid blanket off the chair and tucked it over his knees. He was too blitzed to object. I put the rucksack he'd brought with him by his feet and went round to the driver's side. Mr Roberts wound the window down.

"I don't know what to say," I said. "He's going to need some TLC for a few days. He's not fit to look after a dog at the moment. I think he's starving," I said quietly, "and will you let his dad know he's okay?"

"He'll be right as rain by next weekend. Call in when you're up next. I'll be in the office most days. I've put my details on the piece of paper in the envelope."

"Why are you doing all this?" I said, as humbled as I'd ever been, "and I was such a bitchy know-it-all at the wake. I'm so sorry."

He put the key in the ignition and started up, turning the heater on full blast and leaning his elbow on the window ledge.

"I was fond of your great-uncle, Miss Jones. He was a miserable bastard most of the time but he built this business from nothing after his children were drowned. He could have given up, hit the bottle, been a waster but he wasn't. He was a clever man who knew his boats, a real professional. You deserve the same chance. I'll look after the boy for a while and he'll look after you. Don't forget to lock the door," and drove off.

Jason waved a thin hand, his head leaning against the head rest. He looked exhausted.

I must have stood for ten minutes in the yard, scarcely believing how much could happen in the space of two hours, basking in the wonder of the generosity of a man I'd taken for an autocratic pig and relieved that Jason was safe. He'd tugged at my emotions as strongly as he had when I'd first met him, taunted and bullied by his brothers and ignored by his mother. I pulled my coat round me and wished there was someone to talk to.

But I hadn't finished with the day yet. I walked round the side of the shed and felt along the back wall for Tomas's secret entrance through the panelling. The galvanised sheets over lapped each other but one came loose when I pulled it, the nails were cut off to show the heads and the tin sheet sprang back into place easily. No-one would have noticed it had been loose, especially an old man who would be unlikely to venture into the narrow space between the cliff face, the over-grown vegetation and the back wall of the shed. I went back inside and found a hammer and nails in a toolbox and nailed the sheet tight to the wooden upright. The

sound of the hammer reverberated round the cliff-face
behind me. When I stopped, the only sound was the eery rustling of dead grass and nettles, a private, shut-in place that gave me the creeps.

I squeezed out of the passageway and stood in the area occupied by Hugh Phillip's sad caravan next to the Toyota pickup, the bonnet half hidden under a tarpaulin blown into folds to one side and flapping in the gusts of wind. One tyre was flat and the seagulls had splattered the silver paintwork on the roof. I could fix all of this on the phone, I decided. Let someone else sort it out and I'll pay the bills. The Toyota was too good to leave to the elements and I had a feeling it would serve me better than the Corsa. It had a tow-bar, not that I'd towed anything in my life but thought I probably would in the future, moving trailers around in the yard. It wasn't a prerogative of the male species as the old crows at the funeral seemed to suggest. I could learn. The new cheque book and bank card were burning a hole in my pocket and I knew David would advise on costs from a reputable garage. I covered it back up and doubled the tarpaulin over the bonnet, tying lengths of frayed rope to the bumper and hoping there was anti-freeze in the engine.

The sounds of tyres on gravel cut through the silence, my eagerness at the thought of a human voice, probably David arriving to feed the lobster, was suddenly tempered by the possibility of Jason's unwanted acquaintances knowing his whereabouts. No reason why they could know, I reasoned. How could they know unless they'd followed him? But he'd been gone a day at least. Unsettling thoughts chased through my head. I made the connections, then and wished I hadn't. Of course Jason would have talked to his mate in Pwllheli of his day visits to the yard over the years when he was on holiday, the one who'd been cuckooed by the new dealers in town and got stoned on freebies. I waited uneasily, summoning up courage. It was my yard now, after all. My problem.

A car door slammed and I heard footsteps, then a voice cursing quite clearly through the tin walls of the shed.

"Hey, Mick. Come and look at this. There's a fucking creature in here."

I hid behind the end wall, listening to footsteps and things being moved around, knowing I was right. I wanted to stay where I was and hope they'd go away but my handbag was on the floor behind the counter and I'd left one bar of the fire on. I had to face it. I walked out into the open space, my throat tight and the hammer I'd used dangling limply in my left hand, scarily conscious that my mobile was behind the counter in the shed tucked away in my handbag.

A man appeared from inside the shed, standing in the open doorway and gesturing to another man getting out of the passenger seat of an old BMW parked up tight against the step. The one on the step was thin and pale with a face like a weasel. His mate stood up, taller and built like a wrestler. I swallowed and found a voice and a brave face from somewhere.

"Hi.Were you looking for me? The business is closed for the winter.. We'll be open in April if you're looking for chandlery."

They stood by the open doors to the car like stuffed dummies dressed alike in track suits and trainers, hoodies pulled up over baseball caps. Their clothes looked thin and the wind began to gust bitterly cold over the harbour wall and sweep through the yard. I hoped they were freezing. All I could do was play the game and hope they'd go away.

"Looking for the old man runs this place," the skinny one said, "and a tall kid who helps him," added the other, scouse accents.

I shook my head. "No old men here," I said. "No kids either, tall or otherwise. Can't help you there."

They looked at each other. The tall one leaned into the car and pulled out a bomber jacket, shrugging his broad shoulders into one arm with difficulty. The wind tugged at it and blew the other empty arm behind his back. The one on the driver's side flipped his hoody down. Maybe it was the angle of his head, maybe the way he lifted his arm. I had a sudden déjà vu moment. Where had I seen this guy before or someone so similar, and only recently? The bigger man wrestled with the zip of his jacket.

"We'll look around, right?" and slammed the door shut.

My sense of property and possession was suddenly overwhelming. Being angry helped. I squared my shoulders and looked him straight in the eye. Cheeky bastard, I thought, taking a deep breath and raising my voice over the wind. I didn't have to pretend indignation.

"No, it's not alright. If you want to discuss booking a space to keep a boat in the summer you're welcome to come back in the spring when the yard's open."

The skinny one shrugged his shoulders. "We're just looking for a mate, that's all. Is the owner around ? An old man we were told," he said, shutting his car door and sidling down the side of the bonnet towards me.

"I'm the owner," I said, the brave words hiding my fear. I knew this man now, the shadowy figure waiting for my homeless addict, Pete, outside the cafe in Pwllheli, the one under the lamp-post, the same posture, the same clothes, "and if you've come to discuss business I suggest you come back in a couple of month, as I said before. If not, the gate's over there. This is private property."

I pointed towards the yard entrance aware of the incongruous sight of the hammer in my other hand, my knees threatening to buckle under me. He walked towards me, his voice thin and shrill over the gusts of wind.

"You the owner? We weren't told that, were we, Mick? This your yard then? On your own, are you love?"

"Not quite," said a voice from behind the BMW.

I'd never been so glad to see a solicitor in my life. David's gangly frame dressed warmly in winter trousers and walking boots appeared like a rabbit out of a hat, talking and gesticulating back towards the gate.

"Morning, Cassie. I tried to ring you but there was no answer and it was short notice. Ben and the lads from the zoo will be here in a minute. They're coming for the lobster and bringing a tank with them."

He rounded the car and stood in front of the bonnet, his voice pleasant but purposeful.

"Sorry to interrupt you, boys, only there's a wagon due any minute and he needs the space to turn round. If you wouldn't mind moving your car...is there anything we can help you with? Only the yard's closed for the winter, you see," he said, looking quizzically from one to the other. The two guys looked at each other as bemused as I was.

"No, we're good," said the driver, the one with the weasel face, giving me a cold hard look.

He wrenched the car door open and started up the engine in one fluid movement as his mate joined him. The tyres spun in a flurry of gravel, flinging up mud and stones and narrowly missing David's Audi parked in the entrance. I looked at him helplessly watching them disappear round the corner and out of sight.

"I am so, so pleased to see you," I said, trying not to cry, my breath catching in my throat."You have no idea. He was in the shed nosing around. I didn't know what they were going to do. Are the zoo guys really coming?"

The words tumbled out, the wind blowing my hair into my mouth. He took one look at the hammer in my hand, his face tight.

"Just a ruse. I didn't like the look of them. Going to fend them off with that, were you? What on earth were you doing with that and who the hell were they anyway?"

He was as angry as I was scared. I wiped my face on my sleeve and pulled myself together. I'd got some explaining to do.

"There was a loose panel in the wall of the shed. I was just hammering in nails and mending it when I heard the car," I said, clocking the scepticism on his face. "I'm not entirely useless, you know. I think they were looking for Jason."

I'd under-estimated this mild-mannered man. He didn't give me a chance to explain. He rounded on me, his face flushed.

"Jason? Who's Jason? I think you'd better explain what's going on. First the fire last night and now two ugly looking characters up to no good. I'm still responsible for this place and I could do without the extra worry. I've just passed Will Roberts coming from here with a young man in the car. Is that the Jason you're talking about?"

I was cold and shaky and angry now. We stood in the grey yard while the wind whipped up white horses on the water and the rigging on Hugh's boat clacked against the wooden mast.

"I can't help it if things happen," I said, on the defence now. "Look, can we go inside? My feet are frozen. I'll explain everything. I've got to get on the road soon. Please?"

He marched into the shed, throwing some food into the lobster's tank while the kettle boiled.

I told him Jason's story and my research into drug-trafficking.

"It's only practice," I said. "In case all this goes wrong and I have to go back to journalism. I didn't ask for all this, did I?" waving my arm around the shed. I put the mug down hard and the tea slopped over into the dust. I was angry now, the adrenalin wearing off.

"Look, my dad was murdered three years ago by a coke-head in London. Now Jason seems to have got his fingers burned by these dealers. Do you spend all your time in a nice cosy office just sorting out divorces and invoicing clients? Have you any idea the pressure these local kids are under from dealers? It wrecks lives."

I could hear my voice echoing shrill in the cold shed. The lobster had disappeared behind a rock. My hands were shaking. I hadn't meant to lose my cool.

"I didn't know that about your father. I'm very sorry," he said, "and you're right up to a point. It's a pretty sheltered part of the universe here and if there's drug dealing going on we don't hear much about it."

"Going on? Of course it's going on."

I was on a roll now. All the pent-up fear from the last few minutes burst out.

"Trouble is, round here there seems to be a conspiracy of silence when I ask questions. Nobody I spoke to wants the upset of being involved or divulging suspicions. They know it means dealing with dangerous people. I get the impression round here that if you can't see it, and it doesn't affect you directly, it doesn't exist. Everybody seems to know drugs can be smuggled in by sea. There are posters up even on the front in Criccieth to tell people to keep an eye out."

I drew breath, my chest tight. He didn't interrupt.

"The addict who murdered my father was a paranoid schizophrenic. He happened to pick up a deal of some extra strength crack, was off his meds and off his head. He could have stabbed anyone I guess, but it just happened to be my father."

We sat in silence. The tin sheets on the roof rattled in the wind and spider-webs at the window stirred in the gaps.

"I'm so sorry," he said again. "I didn't know. And the two men who were here?"

"Not connected to my father directly, of course not. But kids like Jason and his mate are vulnerable. Things go wrong sometimes even in the best of homes. Kids have arguments with their parents get kicked out or run away in the heat of the moment. They're just ripe for these bastards."

I knew I was getting spiky but I couldn't help it.

"I bet it was pretty cosy round here when you were a teenager. Try doing a few years in the sleazy parts of London and smell the bodies fished out of the Thames like the river police do. It's nearly always drugs and gang related."

I took a deep breath. "So those guys might have been looking for Jason if they were the same guys who'd taken over his mate's flat and started using it as a base for dealing. Jason told them he wouldn't tell anyone where it was. As if they'd believe that. I think they'd come to find him with an extra reminder. I hate to think how. Mr Roberts saved the day and took him home. They won't know that. Do you think he'll be safer there?"

He shrugged. "Will Roberts? He lives in a pretty remote spot. Good as anywhere tucked away in the hills. You don't want that boy here at the moment. Sounds like trouble."

He drained his mug and looked hard at me.

"You know, for a journalist you're not being very clever. I understand about your father and your concerns with the drugs issue but it seems to me you've got two choices. You're either going to build a successful business here with your inheritance or go back to reporting on a newspaper. If you start writing articles about local people and putting your head above the parapet with these new dealers you could find yourself in a position where you're seriously unwelcome on all counts. Leave it to the police and report anything you find to them."

I stood up, hardly believing what I was hearing. We stared at each other across the dirt and cobwebs. It felt like a repetition of the black crows and the closed clique at the funeral. Either fit in or go away. Don't upset the status quo. He was no different to the rest of them after all.

I was still digesting the unassailable fact that he was the one person I'd felt I could trust to give me good advice. Was it good advice or was I being unreasonable, obsessive, naive even? Maybe he was right. Jason could go home and face his hateful brothers and none of this would exist.

"Look," he said, his voice placatory. "You've had a hell of a weekend. Go back to work. I'll get some prices for some decent yard gates this week and you're going to need Broadband for email and a landline. I'll ring the sea zoo as well and see if they'll take the lobster away, although feeding the creature gives me an excuse to check on things every day. It's only for a few more weeks, isn't it, now?"

"And you'll invoice me for your efforts?" I said managing a wry smile, worn out with it all.

"Naturally," he said. "I'll add it to the ever-growing bill." He returned the smile. "See you next week," holding out his hand. It was warm and strong. I didn't want to dislike him. Not for anything.

"By the way," he said as I locked the door. "Where are you going to live?"

I shrugged. "Don't know yet. It'll come to me."

I went back to Joan's and packed my bags, reluctant to leave the warm kitchen and the safety-net of a proper home. The thought of my cold flat and the phone calls I needed to make and work first thing on Monday morning glued me to the kitchen chair longer than I intended. It was late afternoon before I set out.

"Your friend Mr Phillips has been in touch. He says he'll start the inventory next weekend and I'll start setting up the data base."

Her eyes were bright with anticipation. It occurred to me that involving other people made it frighteningly real. I gave her a hug, but she wasn't 'Joan' no matter how hard I tried.

"Can I go back to calling you Helen's Nain?" I said, "Don't ask me why. It just feels right."

She laughed and walked to my car with me.

"I'll be taking bookings for the season soon, cariad. I won't have room for you, as you know, and Helen will be coming to stay for a holiday in the summer. 'Tai Pilots' isn't fit to stay in until you've had a chance to do some work or sell it. So when you finish your job and move up here, where are you going to live?"

CHAPTER 14

It was Monday morning and only two weeks of work to go.

"So where are you going to live?" Tim asked, poking his head round the computer in a brief lull between phone calls, "and are you still going to investigate this drugs story? Even if it's just for yourself, you're not going to get yourself into trouble are you? Could get a bit sticky nosing around in the area you're going to live and you haven't got the paper to back you up."

His curiosity and his concern unsettled me as I didn't have half the answers. It also annoyed me.

"I'm not stupid."

"Sorry, just asking. You're not Lara Croft you know, if they come looking for you."

I remembered my weak knees and the fear I'd felt when the creeps had turned up at the yard and the hard stare from the one with a face like a weasel as they left.

"Sorry back," I said, looking at his crestfallen face. "I didn't mean to snap. I'll be careful or I might not bother with it at all if the business takes over. It's just that I can't bear the thought of not writing anything, you know, and nosing around for information. It's what we do, isn't it? Or we wouldn't be journalists. I don't want to lose the skill of it, business or no business. The boatyard might all fall apart then I'd have nothing to go back to, see? I'll be careful."

Not that I wanted to be back here or anywhere else office bound, I thought, slightly taken aback with my changing thought processes. But I still wanted to write.

"Yeah, I get it." He looked relieved and grinned.

I'd managed the week at work, hating my dismal flat in the evening more by the minute and even finding the buzz of the office irritating but scrapped the idea of travelling to Wales the following weekend. I'd been busy on the phone organising an overhaul of the Toyota with the garage my great-uncle had used and formulating ideas for my brilliant new accommodation. It would meet with disapproval, I knew, but I thought it solved all my problems for the summer.

The weather closed in with snow and ice as predicted. The 'beast from the east' hit with a vengeance. Storm Emma crashed into high pressure over Europe and caused havoc for travellers. The thought of a journey to North Wales to work in the boatyard in the shed with a gale howling at the door did not appeal. It was a good reason to brave the train to London and stay in the lap of luxury in Felicity's town house and have a proper conversation with my mother and a gossip with Trish. There was so much to tell them and I prepared myself to be swamped with questions. I decided to leave out the visit from Jason, of whom they knew nothing anyway, and especially the two scary guys.

Mother had rented the whole of the upstairs of Felicity's house, self-contained and ideal for co-ordinating the business of 'Grace and Favour.' It was doing well with some wealthy clients from the Middle East buying new town apartments and needing interior expertise. They loved it.

Felicity had excelled herself in a celebration dinner for me, candles flickering and dancing shadows on the silver and crystal. The four of us sat round the table, plates empty and glasses full, mother's with sparkling Perrier. She showed no sign of the desperation I'd been so used to where she drank to the point of what I presumed was the numbness she'd needed to keep going. I could only assume she was happy but I didn't ask; we were never that close. I was just relieved.

We focused our chats on their business and the practicalities of my inheritance, full of smoked salmon, fillet steak, champagne and two bottles of an expensive burgundy, a delightful change to my regular Tesco's £5 a bottle Malbec and ready meals for one.

"Glad it wasn't lobster," I said, relishing the oaked smokiness of the salmon, thinking of Neifion alone in his tank and whether I could create this quality of smoked food if the smoke-house was up and running.

"I thought you hated the creature," Trish said, breaking into my day dreams. "Isn't it going to the sea zoo? Or you could eat it."

"My great-uncle once said he couldn't eat anything that had a name and the sea zoo hasn't got back to David yet."

"But you're not your great-uncle. And what's its name anyway?" she asked.

"Neifion. It's Welsh for Neptune. It's been there in that tank for three years. It's all it knows and it's quite old. Lobsters need a home of their own. They're not great mixers."

Felicity snorted. "You're not becoming emotional over a lobster, are you Cass? It's only a bloody fish. And you still haven't told us yet where you're going to live if this cottage you've been left is derelict."

"Uninhabitable at the moment but not derelict and it's a crustacean, not a fish," I said, irritated by her ignorance.

"Sell the cottage," said my mother. "Use the money as a deposit for something down here for when you come back."

"Come back?" My head was elsewhere. London and traffic and offices? A strange transition nibbled away at the edges of my brain. Her voice pierced the fog.

She persisted. "So where are you going to live?"

I left the table and fetched my phone from my bag, scrolled down and turned the screen so they could see the pictures. There was a stunned silence, then "No." The chorus was emphatic with underlying tones of disbelief.

The caravan stood in a line of others for sale, all white, all much the same. Two berth, end bathroom, fridge, heater, clean and tidy and only £5000. Old van to be removed in part exchange.

"Oh yes," I said. "It's a brilliant idea and lets me live on site. I might keep Neifion as a guard-dog."

"But caravans are for gypos." Trish was horrified.

"That's racist," I said.

"Darling, you simply can't. It's not safe and what will..."

"...the neighbours think? Oh," it dawned on me, "you mean your clients when you're mentioning family. They might even visit the yard on a trip to Wales. Heaven forbid."

Some reassurance was needed.

"It's only temporary," I said. "Besides, I'll be wearing overalls most of the time. They won't know who I am. I'm having security gates built as well so it'll be quite safe at night. Good idea, yes?"

The atmosphere was frosty for a few minutes. Another bottle of wine and positive chat about my plans for the smoke-house and the snack-bar soothed the ruffled feathers.

I left the luxury of Felicity's central heating, soft pile carpets and a full fridge and headed back to my flat on Sunday night. Two weeks to go. Then my pay cheque would stop. The thought drove me to hunt the half-bottle of wine lurking in the cupboard. Jason texted. I hadn't heard from him since he'd been spirited away to his mountain retreat and hoped he hadn't done a runner. It cheered me up no end.

'All good here. Loads of chickens. Doing some cooking. Mrs Roberts is very sick but likes my creamy scrambled eggs and homemade chicken broth. Decided if I was going to cook I had to get over the meat thing. No sign of any bad guys. Good luck with the move. See u soon.'

I had an email from David to say that Broadband and the gates were ordered, an email from Hugh Phillips who said he'd started the inventory and was seriously impressed by the model ships, and also an email from the sea zoo. Unfortunately they did not have the capacity at the present time to take Neifion but would gladly advise me on his care. That was that, then, just me and the lobster. I picked up Jordan Peterson's book on the Twelve Rules of Life and re-read the first chapter on human and lobster behaviour. Perhaps Neifion and I could see claw to claw after all.

There was an office party to end my brief relationship with the paper, a party full of questions and a mixed bag of well-wishing and envy. Ed summoned me into his office before I left.

"Call me if you need advice, young lady. I'll be fishing in your neck of the woods in the summer. I'll pop in and see if you've learned your..."

"...fids from my baggywrinkles?"

He laughed and patted me on the arm. I was touched.

Tim said, "So can I come and see you? I've never been in a boatyard before."

"When it's tidy, yeah? Not before."

As I was leaving to a chorus of goodbyes and good lucks, he rushed over, peered at me seriously and said, "You be careful Cassie. Don't get into trouble. If you need anything..."

I looked at him, grateful for the sentiment and wondering how I could ever need anything from Tim. He was so young but he meant well. I kissed him and he put his hand up to his cheek.

I packed up my flat, paid the rent and booked the last two weeks at Helen's Nain's before the rooms were taken, the excitement practically choking me as I set off with the car jammed full, my precious laptop on the front seat. Broadband was in and connected, David had said. The gates he'd ordered on my instructions would not be ready for a month yet. I'd specified ones just like Doug Peterson's next door. I'd pushed the man to the back of my mind over the last few weeks but hadn't forgotten Mark had told me he went away for February and returned in March ready to open the yard properly in the spring. I would have to face him then. Cordial and distant, I thought, and avoid any conversation about the past.

"Let it lie," Trish said when I'd discussed it with her. "He's only going to be your neighbour. You don't have to go to bed with him, for God's sake."

On the Saturday morning I took final possession of my property. David brought the keys he'd been using and a bunch of flowers. He also brought extra rations of lobster food and two carrier bags from Tesco which he placed on the dirty counter, our uncomfortable conversation seemingly forgotten.

"The deeds will be ready for you to collect on Monday. Here are the rest of the keys. I expect you'd like to get your hands legally on the place now. I thought these might help."

From one bag he tipped out aerosols, liquids of various colours in plastic bottles, J-cloths, steel wool and three pairs of yellow Marigolds, a bottle of champagne in the other one. He stood in the open doorway and gazed out at the yard with its rusty junk and clutter.

"Where on earth are you going to start?" he said shaking his head.

"Right in here," I said, drawing a swirl in the dust on the counter top round the bottle. "Shall we open it?"

Then Hugh Phillips arrived on his bike, bounced into the shed wearing the same socks and his Beanie firmly planted on his head, handed me a carrier bag he'd slung from his handle bars, his rucksack on his shoulder with ledgers and pens and reference books.

"Welcome home, Miss Jones. I purchased a few supplies. I do hope they're acceptable," he said, lifting out milk, tea and coffee and biscuits. "Is the kettle on, by any chance?"

I stood behind the counter with the champagne in one hand and the kettle in the other absorbing the sense of belonging to the place. Making tea seemed as natural as breathing as I realised Hugh and David had never met and to mind my manners. I introduced them to each other.

"Internet set up? Oh joy," Hugh Phillips said when I nodded. "Paper's all very well but there are some items on these shelves even I haven't a clue about. And I can carry only so many reference books you know. I'll crack on, if you don't mind."

He nodded politely to David and disappeared into the recesses of the shed. David pulled out his phone and sat down, his face serious.

"I was keeping track of expenses so far. The gates will cost about £3000, and there will be a bill for the phone line and a full service for the Toyota. You'll need to keep an eye on your budget especially when you start to clear the yard of all this scrap, especially that old caravan and the old cars and trailers. Paying for labour can eat away a fortune in no time and you still haven't said where you're going to live. The renovation of Tai Pilots is going to be costly. Are you going to rent somewhere?"

"In a way," I said. "But it won't cost me anything." I checked my watch. "In fact, it should be here any minute. And I've booked a towing course."

I got up hearing the sound of voices out in the yard, opening the door to a small boy.

"Dad says he's come for the van."

A truck with two burly guys towing a flat-bed trailer rolled up, turned and reversed up to Hugh's old caravan. I left them to it.

"Come on. This is my best idea," I said pulling him down the yard where a Land Rover towing my gleaming white, two-berth home blocked the gateway. "Brilliant or what? Mr Robinson, I presume?" addressing the open driver's window.

"How much?" David said, horrified, after they'd all gone. "And what about security? Here on your own all night? The gates won't be ready for ages. It's not safe, Cassie. What if those guys come back?"

"I'll get a dog," I said, sick of all this protective stuff. I'd had enough from my mother in London. I didn't like dogs much, but it seemed the right thing to say. "And I've got a phone."

"Yes and the police don't monitor this area all the time. It's not exactly rapid response here. We're not used to trouble that much."

Here we go again, I thought. Let's not upset the apple-cart.

"There won't be any trouble. Who's going to know I'm here on my own, anyway? I won't go looking for it, that's for sure."

He left, tight-lipped, striding down the yard to recover the rest of the weekend. I hadn't expected him to be so unreasonable. I stood and watched him, uncertain for the first time and sorry again that he was upset and I hadn't shared my ideas with him. I didn't want to lose him.

A quiet voice behind me broke into my unease.

"He's only worried about you, Miss Jones. He's a nice man. He'll still be feeling responsible if anything goes wrong."

Hugh Phillips had materialised from the shed. I stared at him, an unlikely mentor peering at me through his rimless glasses, concern on his face, his black Beanie scrunched up over his ears and his trousers tucked into his sports socks with the yellow stripe. I ran down the yard and caught up with David as he turned the corner. Breathless, I ran up behind him and called his name. He stopped and turned round.

"I'm sorry I didn't tell you," I said. "Only I knew you'd make a fuss. I'll be alright. I thought it was a good idea. It'll save money and I want to be here all the time, otherwise I'll worry about what's going on if I'm away from it. It's the best thing, really and it won't be forever. Please don't be cross. I'll borrow a dog if it makes you feel better but I don't really like them that much."

A blackbird's song from the cliff above pierced the silence, a reminder of spring. I couldn't help my enthusiasm. He nodded and smiled briefly and opened the car door.

"Me neither," he said. "You'll have to make do with the lobster," and drove off. It was okay.

My responsibility now; feeding it, cleaning the tank, checking the pump, as if I hadn't got enough to think about. It felt as though my great-uncle had his wish after all. I walked back up the yard, inspecting the potholes and wondering how much it would cost for new gravel when all the junk had gone. Hugh was outside wandering round his boat, mug in hand on a coffee break, inspecting the hull of his boat. I had the shed all to myself.

I pulled the old stool from under the counter, carried it over to the tank and sat down with my face to the glass. Neifion lay on the stony bottom and waved his antennae in the bubbles from the pump, the one remaining claw resting above the head, black beady eyes staring at nothing.

"You're the ugliest creature I've ever seen," I said, "but I've been reading about you. Seems like you lot are a pretty good replica of human society. Top dog, would you be, before you lost that claw? Never get it back though, that dominance, would you, in the same way? I suppose I'll just have to hang on to you, being as you're so old. Sheltered

accommodation, right?"
I lifted the lid and measured out some food as David had said. It sank to the bottom of the tank, little flakes landing on the rocks and trapped in the weed. He waved his claw graciously.

"Can you bark?" I asked.

I sat back upright on the stool, shut my eyes for a minute, tried to still my mind and close it to the whirl of thoughts clouding my new identity. So much had happened so quickly, so many new people to meet, so many things I knew fuck all about, so much fear lurking under my belt tucked away under the bravado of appearing to know what I was doing under the confident exterior I was determined to present.

I knew I'd walked into a world of conventional gender splits where men were men and went to sea in boats and women would stay at home and weep. Or not. There were skills I could learn and ones I couldn't and I was going to have to compromise and use my wits rather than bash my head against a wall of derision and scepticism and then fail. I was going to have to earn my colours the clever way.

The pump hummed, a seagull perched on the shed roof and clattered its way to the gutter, taking off in a swoop of white wing past the window as I opened my eyes. The heavy richness of tar and wax and oiled wood permeated the air and mingled with waves of paraffin and diesel, thinners and paints, freshly brewed coffee and the lingering smell of cigarette smoke. The old man's spirit was embedded in this shed and it was about as far removed from my previous world of office and computers, meetings and takeaways, hair-dos and nails, as I could imagine. I felt it, absorbed it. It was mine now.

I got up with new resolve, picked up the stool and stashed it back under the counter. I needed a clean space to set up the laptop. I washed and polished the counter until I'd burnished the oak top to a rich brown, stuck David's flowers in an old paint tin and plugged the computer into the new sockets, the Wi-Fi glowing comfortingly blue as I booted it up.

I'd picked up two new plaid rugs from the Edinburgh Wool Shop to cover the easy chairs behind the counter. The wood burner winked at me but I needed the chimney swept and some advice. I'd had enough of fires for a while. I scrubbed the sink and polished the kettle, cleaned the cobwebs from the window and wiped the dead spiders from the corners of the shelves. It wasn't much, but it was a start. Just in case I had clients. A cosy sitting area I could chat or discuss business in, pretty with flowers and warm rugs. I was a girl, after all, I thought wryly, moving Henry Hughes' 'Immortal Sails' from the chair, sitting down with a coffee to read the leaflet for the towing course I was booked on.

A knock on the open door broke the silence.

CHAPTER 15

A girl with a fountain of blonde hair swept up on the top of her head shuffled uncertainly on the doorstep, heavy blue eye makeup and red-painted mouth in a tentative smile.

"I'm Denise, Doug's secretary. Well, you know, receptionist, dog's body, whatever. I just came to say hello. We haven't met and I know you've only just arrived but I've got a problem and I'm on my own. The boss isn't back until next week. Hey, this is nice," she said, looking around

"Thanks. I'm working on it," I said, shaking her hand over the counter. "I'm Cassie. Can I get you a coffee?"

She shook her head. "Another time would be cool but I've got this wagon needs to turn round. I wasn't expecting a delivery and the guys are getting cross. They can't make the turn in the yard for the new load of jet-skis that arrived yesterday and Gareth hasn't shifted them yet. Can they turn round in the yard here? Would you mind?"

Of course not, I thought, glad to make a friendly acquaintance. We walked back down to open the gates for the wagon, followed it back as it reversed into Doug's yard and stood back as the driver lifted the canvas and started to unload, just nattering generally, a proper everyday chat about the yards and the weather and Porthmadog and pubs. It was easy and felt wonderfully normal.

"Hey," she said to the driver. "They're not my boxes. I only had a delivery of those a couple of weeks ago. I haven't ordered anything else."

I turned to go but couldn't help listen to the raised voices. She wasn't giving any quarter.

"I didn't order this stuff," she said. "You can take it back. I've got fittings and pumps forever. And what's this? We had a new load of batteries only two weeks ago."

"It says here on the order form and it's signed for."

"Who's signed it? The boss is away and I certainly didn't."

A man emerged from behind a powerboat, head and shoulders stooped and body propelled as though on a mission, dark hair and moustache and a way of looking from side to side. I'd seen him before. I recognised the walk.

"I ordered them," he said, butting in. "You can stack them over there."

"No, you won't," she said. "What the hell are you playing at, Gareth? You're not authorised to order stock without my say so. You can't have used all that stock already."

"Yeah, well I have. Boss left loads of work. Can't fix boats without spare parts, can I?" glaring at her.

No love lost between those two, I thought.

"Well you can take responsibility when Doug sees the bill. I can't believe you've gone through all that stock already. You'll get me into trouble."

The driver and Gareth ignored her and carried on unloading. I could see the tears starting. She didn't need to be seen crying in front of these two.

"Come and have that coffee," I said. "The office can wait. There aren't any customers around," and steered her out of the yard.

"Bastard. I hate that man. Why Doug employs him God only knows but they're thick as thieves when they're in the yard and office together. Makes me feel like a piece of shit."

"Why do you work for him then?" I said, handing her a mug of coffee.

"He pays well and it's a job. I used to work in the marina office and chandlery in Conwy so I know what I'm doing. Boyfriend lives here so I've moved to be with him. Haven't been here long but I know about ordering stock and controlling it. The boss knew that and said I was in charge while he was gone. It's all admin this time of year, anyway."

I wish, I thought, looking around the shed at hours of physical work ahead of me.

"So what exactly does he do in the yard, this Gareth? Is he Angela's ex? I thought I saw him in Pwllheli a few weeks ago meeting a pretty shifty looking character outside a cafe. He's got a funny walk, like somebody walking into a gale."

She nodded.

"He calls himself a mechanic but he's a jumped up little prick. He does all the shitty bits on boats," she went on, "like toilet pumps and sea-cocks for sinks and showers, you know, general boat maintenance, replacing batteries, just generally fixing things. He doesn't do engines though. He's not a marine engineer, hasn't got the brains for that. Doug does all that. Works for whichever yard wants him, here or in Pwllheli and does a fair bit for Doug in the winter. Don't know about the summer yet."

"It must be tough having him around if you're on your own. When's your boss back?" I asked.

"In about two weeks. He's charm itself when he's on his own, is Doug, especially when clients are around. He likes women. Leaves me alone, though 'cos he knows I've got a boyfriend."

She finished her coffee but seemed reluctant to go.

"Tell you what, though, I don't reckon I'll stay much longer if I can find another job. There are things I don't get about this place."

I waited. She wanted to talk. I was happy to listen. In some ways it was pleasant sitting with coffee and female company. I opened the tin of biscuits Hugh had brought and she took a chocolate one absently, nibbling around the edges, her face thoughtful as though she was mulling over what to say.

"There's this white van," she said, out of the blue. "It's turned up in the yard a couple of times now. The driver parks his van by whichever boat Gareth is working on and stays ages. I can't see everything from the window and I haven't been here long so I've thought nothing of it. It's none of my business if it's to do with Gareth working. He's been here longer than me. I don't yet know what's normal, you know?"

I nodded.

"And then this thing about orders and deliveries. It seemed to be regular before Doug went on holiday but I can't seem to keep track of the stock at the moment, like just now with all this stuff coming into the yard and Gareth says he's using it. I can't know what he's doing all the time and if I ask him he'll be really arsy about it. It's my responsibility the ordering and everything so if it's gone pear-shaped I'll get the blame. And the sack."

"So have you checked in the stores?" I said. "Is there stock piling up?"

She shook her head. "He must be using it. It's just that... I can't explain. He's a shifty sod. I don't trust him.What could he be doing?"

"Is that a rhetorical question?"

She looked at me blankly.

"Sorry. I mean what do you think he's doing?"

She bowed her head and cradled the empty mug. Some of the blonde hair caught up in the pony tail on top of her head had escaped from its band and hung down her face in untidy wisps, framing a pale face. She looked up, large blue eyes almost pleading for an answer.

"If I say anything to Doug, he'd never believe me. I told you, they're best mates."

"Yes, but if Gareth was ripping his boss off, wouldn't he want to know?"

She bit her lip

"I think there's more to it. There's something else going on, phone calls and people calling and he shuts himself in the office and then goes away for weeks at a time. It's not normal, like out in the open, you know? If I told Doug what I thought about these orders, he'd deal with Gareth in his own way but he'd sack me as well. He's a scary man, Cassie. He wouldn't want any outside interference, like nosy secretaries who keep an eye on the books."

"What's wrong with the books?"

I thought I'd overstepped the mark there. I could feel her debating whether to talk or not. Then she did.

"I think he's broke," she said.

"No," I said. "No. I can't believe that. He looks pretty well set up to me."

"Yeah, that's what it looks like but creditors will be banging at the door if he doesn't pay his bills soon, not to mention the business rate to the council. I think Gareth's covering his back in case the business goes under and he's making a bit while he can, selling off the good stuff on the quiet and using cheap parts on the boats bought from the guy in the van."

"Isn't that dangerous, using cheap parts?"

"Could be. I don't know much about it but gear on boats takes a real pounding so yeah, I suppose it's risky. Thing is, if Gareth is doing some dodgy dealing and Doug finds out he'll have to tackle it carefully. If Gareth blabs about the other shady dealings I reckon they're both up to and Gareth goes down he'll take Doug with him."

"Shady dealings?"

She shook her head and stuck her nose in the coffee cup.

From what little I'd seen of him, Doug Peterson wore the trappings of wealth like a tiger wears its stripes: his designer clothes and the Rolex watch, the silver Mercedes convertible and the Range Rover parked in the yard, the yacht in Pwllheli I hadn't yet seen and the social life David had told me about with lavish parties to celebrate his numerous racing successes.

I sat back and stared at her, trying to work out the contradictions in my head.

"But he offered to buy me out," I said. "You must know that. He'd been trying to buy my great-uncle out for years. He must have money. This yard's worth half a million, my solicitor said."

"Yes, I'm sure it is, but when did he make you that offer?"

"He didn't exactly make an offer. He just said if I was going to sell in the future to give him the option of buying. He didn't know the terms of my inheritance and I didn't tell him but I do know what this place is worth now. How could he afford that if he's on the verge of bankruptcy? Then or now?"

"Things seem to have changed. I don't know what or when but I do know his accountant was visiting regularly before he went away. There were other guys visiting as well but he told me to go home early when they came so I haven't a clue as to who they were. Unless he comes up with a money miracle, I'll be out of a job anyway."

She checked her watch, glanced at me nervously.

"I have to go. I've spoken out of turn, haven't I? Will I be able to trust you? It's just that I felt I could talk to you somehow and I needed to tell someone. What will you do now I've told you? They said you were a journalist as well. I shouldn't have said anything, should I?"

Her eyes were bright. I thought she was going to cry and I handed her a tissue. I felt the same way for her as I had for Jason. My weakness for vulnerability seemed to be winning.

I leaned over and took her hands. They were cold and shaky.

"I'm not a journalist anymore," I said, "and I certainly won't gossip. But it does help to know. It's none of my business what his financial situation is and I'm not intending to cause trouble. This is my job and my yard now and I want to make a success of it. But if anything illegal is going to affect me or I discover stuff going on that shouldn't be, I'll do something about it in a proper manner, I promise you. I'm not going to stand back while someone shits on my doorstep. Alright?"

She smiled weakly and walked off down the yard. I needed another coffee and some digestion time. Then I cleaned and swept, the Marigolds saving the remnants of my worn nails devoid of varnish, Radio 6 keeping me company while I mulled over Doug Peterson. The more I heard, the less I liked which compromised my new resolve to meet him on his return with equanimity as a business neighbour. I wished in some ways she hadn't told me anything. It swayed my opinions, the niggling suspicions I'd swept under the carpet rearing their heads. It eluded me as I emptied the dust pan and washed the lipstick off Denise's mug.

My neat caravan home, tucked into the cliff behind the shed winked at me when I went outside to collect wellies and overalls from the car. It would have to wait for a week and then I would move out of Helen's Nain's for good. The cost of it weighed heavily on me after David's reaction and the warning that the money left would not re-grow on trees or anywhere else when it ran out. I needed to think ahead, to replace it.

The chandlery wasn't going to feed me, despite my uncle's wishes. He'd diversified over the years in a small way and so would I. That was beginning to take priority in the ideas piling up in my head.

I mopped the floor in the cubicle that served as a toilet, cleaned the basin and replaced the unmentionable toilet seat with a new white one. It seemed that the dirtier the jobs became, so my mind ran further amok into darker places. If, I asked myself, Doug Peterson was seriously in financial difficulties, and if he needed money desperately to save the business and still consider buying me out, whatever he did would have to be lucrative. If, I asked myself, he couldn't raise the money and his business collapsed, where would his customers go to park their boats and jet-skis? My mind ran riot.

I put down the mop and bucket, peeled off the gloves and washed my hands. If I'd been a smoker, now would be the time to roll some tobacco, just like my great-uncle, and savour the ritual, a thinking space between acts. But I wasn't, so I opened up the Internet and Googled heavy-duty electric winches. Then I emailed a couple of rock and soil survey companies.

It was a cold March but already the promise of spring echoed in the bird song in the cliffs behind the yard, the sweet call of blackbirds mixing with the cries of black-headed and herring gulls as they swooped over the yard. I was beginning to recognise the moods of the estuary, my favourite time when low tide coincided with the early evening. The harbour seemed to settle into a quiet lull, the river ebbing to a lazy trickle through the sand banks, the air permeated with the tang of drying salt-marsh as the gulls skimmed the water and made their way to roosting places for the night.

I fed Neifion and shut the yard gates behind me that night, my mind a confused medley of satisfaction in the day's work mingled with uneasy reflections on the day's events and Denise's revelations about her boss.

Then there were a myriad of minor anxieties, like how to repair my nails before Saturday night and a visit to the pub. I pressed my nose to the chicken wire holding the gates together and listened to the stillness. Peace won. The rest could wait.

Helen's Nain was waiting for me at the gate, her usual smile of greeting replaced by one of uncertainty. "There's a man waiting for you in the house," she said. "He knows all about you."

I laughed, uncertainly.

"It's not funny, Cassie. He's huge, but Will Roberts phoned me and said he was okay. He wanted to see you and Will said you'd want to see him. You'd better come in quick before he eats all my cake."

The man's hair was still tied back in a ponytail as I remembered from three years ago but grey now, the black moustache still framing his mouth with hints of white against the tanned skin. He stood up. I'd only ever seen him outside waiting by the snack-bar with a babe in his arms and only that once, but in Helen's Nain's kitchen he dwarfed the room. I remembered how distressed he was about Tomas and how gently he'd handled the baby. I was glad to see him.

"Mr Blackwell?" I held out my hand. It disappeared into his fist. We sat down and Helen's Nain poured tea. "You've found Jason?"

He nodded.

"He finally told me where he was. What a set-up eh? Will Roberts' small-holding? Never seen my lad so happy and well. I came to thank you. Nobody else knows where he is, not even his mother."

"And the twins?" I was concerned now.

"No. They find out where he is and touch a hair of his head it's more than their lives are worth. They know that. They won't be coming back to Doug's yard. Still got their jet-skis up here somewhere on the coast but they don't come to the van and we don't see them. Got their own lives, for what they're worth. Jason told you the tale?"

I nodded. There was a bitter edge to his voice.

"Seems like I've lost all my boys one way or the other, except for the little one of course. He starts school in September. I'm not going to lose him. Do things differently this time. Not letting his mother rule the roost and make excuses for him. She did that with the twins. Spoilt them rotten. Turned out bad, they have."

Helen's Nain topped up his mug. He shifted uncomfortably, the kitchen chair creaking in protest.

"I wanted to ask you..." He faltered, took a gulp of tea and put the mug carefully onto the cloth. "I mean, could you keep an eye on Jason? He's blown it with his college placement back home. Can't expect Mr Roberts to carry on, you know, baby-sitting him. I know he's got skills, he's kind, he cooks and knows how to keep things nice."

He faltered and slurped his tea. I waited.

"But let loose in town I worry he'll get into bother. He told me about the mate in Pwllheli. I believe him about the drugs. I don't want him getting like his brothers. Dealing, you know? I reckon they're still at it. I've washed my hands of them. There's nothing I can do about it now. Too late."

He ran out of breath. My brain went into overdrive with more pieces of the jigsaw falling into place, more ideas for the business. I could use Jason but not at the risk of any more threats from drug dealers. I needed to find out.

"I've got an idea," I said. "Can you come to the yard tomorrow and we'll talk about it again?"

I walked him to the gate, recognising the same white Range Rover parked up the road.

"I'm glad you came. I like Jason. I know he's not that much younger than me but he feels like a little brother somehow. I'll do my best to make sure he's safe but I can't promise what I can't control."

He lifted his hand as he passed me at the gate, a big man in a big car with a weight of sadness on his shoulders. Big men don't cry, they say, but he was very near to it in the warmth of Helen's Nain's kitchen with her bright eyes fixed on him in total understanding. I went back inside.

"I have to go out," I said. "Can you put my tea in the oven?" and shot upstairs to change.

I parked the car on the promenade in Pwllheli, paid for a couple of hours and started walking. It was late in the afternoon and the sun had disappeared. I didn't think I'd find my homeless addict, Pete, sitting on the pavement so I wandered through the streets remembering where I'd been cold-shouldered by the youth leader I'd interviewed only a month ago. The Youth Service door was locked.

I tried a couple of cafes, two pubs, just a quick look inside and I knew not to start asking questions. It would have been too obvious to check out the local police but then I thought, why not? The door to the police station was closed and a large poster itemised opening hours during the day and an emergency number to ring.

I checked out the bus-shelters and then the railway station. There he was, curled up in a corner outside the waiting room. The lights were on inside, a 'cleaning in progress' sign on the platform. He was rummaging around in a carrier bag and pulled out a can of lager, caught my eye as I sat down on one of the benches. He stared at me for a moment. I didn't think he'd recognise me but it was worth a try.

"Hair's still purple," he said and took a long pull at the can.

I couldn't help it. I laughed out loud.

"What's so funny?"

"Seems to be the greeting of my life," I said. "People seem to comment on my hair before they've even said hello."

He took another pull. "So what do you want this time, purple head?"

"Information, and it's damson, not purple. Supper and a bit of extra cash for your breakfast?"

"Maybe. Waiting for a friend," he said, tipping his head towards the open door. A girl appeared in a checked overall with a bucket and mop in one hand.

"Her too?"

I nodded.

I followed them to a chippy. We sat in the steamy warmth and I watched them cram fish and chips and bread and butter and two bottles of Coke each.

"Going to get it together, we are, Amy and me," he said. "Found a room and she's working. Fed up with the streets, now."

I'd heard that one before.

"I've told him," Amy said. "He's got to stick to it now. Come off the drugs, like. All that money wasted. Bloody stupid. He's on methadone now."

"Good for you," I said, meaning it. "Look, I need to know stuff. It's not for a paper this time, more for a friend. He's had a bad time and it got a bit nasty with these new dealers coming in, the County Lines thing? Threats and stuff if he doesn't do some work for them."

"Don't do violence," said Amy, shaking her head. "That's bad. What do you want to know?"

"There were two scousers in the area. Are they still around? That's all. Just to let my mate know if he can sleep easy for a bit. One's a small guy with a face like a weasel and his sidekick's a big guy. Drives an old black BMW."

There was a silence as Amy mopped the ketchup off the plate with her last chip. He said nothing, but his knee was jerking under the table.

"Pete?" she said. "Go on, it can't hurt."

"Yeah, alright. Those guys went," he said. "Not enough trade. Back to the usual now. Stuff still gets into town but it's the same dealers who've been here for years. Costs more, though."

"How do you know?" Amy's head snapped up from her plate. "You're not supposed to be around this stuff anymore?" She'd coloured up and was angry now.

"Yeah well, people talk. I'm not buying, I told you."

"But they've gone," I persisted. "Are you sure about that?"

"Yeah, I reckon. There's more to be made in the posh places where the second homers have got statics and chalets. But different class of dealers. There's not enough money round here for those two. They've moved on. Probably up to Rhyl or somewhere."

"There'll be others," Amy said, "but you'll stay away from them, won't you, Pete?" looking at him meaningfully.

I put two twenties on the table. I couldn't afford it and they'd more than likely buy vodka or a hit of something but it was worth it.

The following morning, Arnie Blackwell turned up at the yard as promised, took one look around at the rusting cars and remains of old trailers and made a phone call. Seemed as though scrappies had a far-reaching network and he was calling in a favour. I told him I'd find Jason some work in the yard in the summer and he could stay in the house in Borth-y-Gest and make parts of it habitable enough for him, at least.

"I'll be up most weekends," he said. " Anything you need or don't know how to handle you let me know, right? Looks as though you're doing just fine, but you never know. Phone me. It's the least I can do for keeping an eye on the lad."

He handed me a business card and I watched the gleaming white Range Rover with the personalised number plate disappear out of the yard, leaving me with a warm glow of comfort and protection.

I needed to talk to Jason, having blithely organised his life without his consent. It never occurred to me he'd say no. I locked up and decided to take the Toyota, the biggest car I'd ever driven, reversing it out of the space by the caravan and playing around with the knobs and levers until I could at least guarantee that turning right didn't mean left.

I stopped at the gate, checked the gears and started the turn then stopped. A silver Mercedes filled the narrow lane ahead, the soft top down and the bronzed face of the man I dreaded meeting again inched level with me. He nodded his head in greeting, locked steely eyes onto mine and drove into the yard. I couldn't help it. He was just as intense, I thought, as I missed the gears and lurched off in second, my resolutions about pleasant equanimity on shaky ground and my palms sticky on the wheel.

March morphed into April. I moved into the caravan and became owner, caretaker and night watchman. If T.S. Eliot thought April was the cruellest month, he must have been in a bad place, which I wasn't, apart from the confused stirrings in seeing my neighbour going about his normal business and cordial greetings when we did meet and that wasn't cruel, it was just interesting, workable and manageable. I was too busy creating my own little world to dwell on what now seemed like a fantasy world of gossip and suspicion. Drug-trafficking seemed somehow unreal and my enthusiasm for feature-writing had ebbed away with the tide.

May slipped into June with the weather heating up to a tropical heatwave. I'd shelved the thought of extending the slipway out into the channel until I could afford it but bought a three ton electric winch to enable small boats, or jet-skis, to be recovered up the steep concrete slope at the press of a button. My cordiality with Douglas Peterson, boss of Madoc Marine, did not extend to bypassing the possibility of under-cutting his business. I checked with David about the terms of the will. It specifically mentioned the renovation of the boatyard to its former use but didn't specify how much of it. I needed to make money to supplement my inheritance and the lump sum was fast running out.

I took a good hard look one evening at the old snack-bar, once Angela's pride and joy with its red and white striped awning rolled away, locked up and languishing away at the end of the Boat Shed near to the gate. I remembered the courtyard she'd created under the cliff-face with the tables and chairs and parasols, the spotless stainless-steel counter and the board with the menu for the day chalked up in her elegant handwriting. My great-uncle had diversified, she'd said. So could I.

I found her in Tesco behind a till, her hair a shabby, mousy brown scraped back off her forehead, tied in a stringy ponytail and eyes dull behind cheap glasses. I'd avoided her until now, picking another till when I saw she was on shift, Tomas's death still real enough to fuel my own inability to face her grief. I couldn't put it off any more. It brewed until it slapped me in the face.

"Will you come and have coffee with me?" I said. "I need some advice."

She carried on pushing the shopping through. I waited and packed the stuff into bags.

"I'm off on Saturday," she said. "I know where to find you."

Of course she did, back in the yard where her son died. I didn't think she'd come.

Hugh finished the inventory, his eyes still bright behind the rimless glasses despite the hours staring into the laptop, Helen's Nain catalogued it all and turned her energies to summer guests and the website sprang into being and went global. I hadn't thought through the practicalities of responding to a client. I didn't think it would happen.

"What are you going to do when the stocks run low, Miss Jones? They won't replace themselves you know. Shouldn't you be looking for specialist timbers to buy in? I can do some research if you like."

He'd kept the Beanie on even in the heat to keep the sun off his bald head and appeared every weekend to work on his boat and was as polite and old-fashioned as ever. The sandals and socks remained but with variations in the stripe and the winter trousers were replaced by baggy shorts.

Jason moved into Tai Pilots and camped out in one room and I turned my mind to the snack-bar. He and Angela held meetings in the shed, their head bent together over the counter as they plotted ideas and plans to renovate and upgrade it. Angela couldn't afford to give up her job in Tesco but offered to manage and train Jason. Her eyes had brightened and she had her hair cut into a short boyish bob. Jason said she was brilliant to work for. She even gave him her tips for prawn sandwiches.
I applied for the renewal of a food licence.
Jason worked in the yard and on the snack-bar and disappeared to the pub at weekends to make friends. I worried about his re-emergence onto the social scene and his obvious whereabouts, but nothing bad happened.
Then it did.

CHAPTER 16

"You got a tent I can borrow, Cass?"

Jason faced me in a pair of paint-stained jeans with a paint brush in one hand.

"As it happens yes, but it's old."

He shrugged. "Tent's a tent. It's only for one night."

Memories flooded back as I rooted out dad's tent from the shed at Helen's Nain's and left it in the Boat Shed for him to pick up. Shadows of memories good and bad flitted through my dreams that night, of festivals and fires, tired feet and dark forests, hedges and golden cornfields and the strange comfort of complete isolation. The tent had become my home for those few short months, the countryside I slept in surprisingly simple and undemanding. I'd never been afraid on my own.

I woke in the morning to the sound of Jason's voice in the yard talking to his mate sitting in a car parked outside. He knocked on the caravan door, buzzing with the details, the tent swinging in one hand.

"So where's the site then?" I asked.

"In Llanbedrog, just down from Abersoch."

"I know it," I said. "From way back."

"Loads of music. My mate's just outside. There's a gang of us going. Back on Sunday."

He bounced down the yard to the waiting car. I watched him go from the open door with a mixture of envy and anxiety. I called after him.

"Jason..."

He turned and looked up. I didn't need to say it.

"Yeah, yeah."

They drove off, music booming loud through the windows.

I spent all day in the yard, working the frustration out of my tangled thoughts by moving trailers into a tidy straight line and practising my reversing. Arnie's mate had taken away all the rubbish and left a space above the harbour wall, a good parking area I thought. I took a sneaky look at Doug's yard to gauge how much space was needed for how many small boats. Or jet-skis. I checked the newly installed winch at the top of the slipway, the electric motor whirring smoothly as I pressed the button and watched the steel cable turn in the drum. All it needed was a customer.

For the first time, I studied my uncle's wooden rowing skiff, upside down and chocked up on blocks, the pine planks dull and dusty. I drew a line in the dust with my finger as Jason flitted in and out of my mind, off to enjoy his nineteen year old life as he should. I could have gone to the festival, I brooded crossly, had I not been the owner of a fucking boatyard. What had happened to my life with shopping and fun and parties? And relationships? I'd almost forgotten what they were like. The Saturday night crowds in the pub hadn't thrown up one single likely candidate I thought was worth a second look. My frustration seethed. I couldn't leave the yard and it was too early for a drink and there was no one to talk to or yell at. Stay busy, I said to a passing gull. Stay busy, as the harmony and enthusiasm of the last few weeks faded away. It'll pass.

I fetched a cloth and wiped the dust off the planks, then fetched the sander from the shed, the cable coiled up like a dead snake on a shelf where my uncle had left it. I found an extension cable and plugged it in, Googled tips for sanding and occupied myself with the soothing long strokes, the fine grade paper kicking up little balls of wood dust, acutely aware I was repeating history and not caring a fig. It seemed right. As I sat on an old baulk of wood for a break and looked across the hull of the boat, I could swear I saw my seventeen year-old self with the ragged haircut standing and waiting for the old man to acknowledge my presence.

David's Audi broke the spell, coming to a halt in front of me. He hadn't visited for a while and I wasn't sure he'd wanted to. Keeping an eye on the accounts seemed to be his main commitment. I stood up, sander in hand. He had a way of unfolding himself from the car, lithe and sinuous like an athlete. I'd forgotten how tall he was and what an easy, relaxed face he had. I'd also forgotten how much I liked him despite his obvious disapproval at some of my decisions. He looked around at the tidy yard, the newly cleared spaces for parking boats and the new winch bolted into the cliff wall.

"Plotting a takeover, are you?"

"I might be," I said. "It's good to see you. What do you think?"
He was in-between jobs and couldn't stay but voiced his approval on the progress in the yard and handed me an envelope.

"If you would like to join us, we would love to have you on board. You did say you'd never raced in a yacht before."
I opened it: a date for a race to Ireland in July, a party in the sailing club in Howth and a dinner in Pwllheli on the return.

"I've never been in a yacht, never mind raced in one," I said. "I wouldn't know what to do but yes I'd love to and you've just saved my life. Thank you. That's brilliant." The child in me bubbled over in gratitude but he was already on his way.

The evening ritual beckoned me at eight o'clock, a ham salad with two glasses of white wine under my belt and a third glass to carry out my last inspection of the yard before locking the gates. The 'poor me' syndrome had evaporated to nothing after David's invitation and I sat with my legs dangling over the harbour wall watching the tide flood in. The sun set in a welter of heat with the promise of more to come and the last rays had tinged the pebble beach at the end of Ballast Island a deep peach, the spikes of wooden piles from the old wharf silhouetted black and stark against the sky. Bird-song faded and a lone gull swooped low over the water. I drained my glass in a glow as rosy as the sunset and locked the gates.

Three o'clock in the morning. The phone rang, Jason's name on the screen and a wave of nausea in my gut before I'd even answered.

"Jason? Are you alright?"

There was a pause. Then a girl's voice.

"Is that Jason's friend? It's Amy. From the cafe, remember, yeah? The chippy? You bought me and Pete fish and chips?"

Christ. I sat up and put the light on. I didn't need to ask if Jason was alright. I just knew he wasn't.

"You have to come and get him. Something really bad has happened."

I calculated how much wine I'd drunk and how many hours since. On the edge but I didn't care. I leaped up, dressed, downed a glass of water for all the good it would do and jumped in the car, mindful of the speed limits in the pitch dark all the way to Llanbedrog.

Pete was waiting, tall and gaunt like a wraith in the shadows at the gate to the field. I followed him in the car through a sea of tents, the track littered with cans and chip boxes, the occasional shape flitting between tents. He stopped outside a circle of small tents at the edge of the field backing onto the beach. I looked beyond to the black nothingness that was the open sea and remembered sitting there with Trish. Amy appeared with a torch and led me to dad's old tent. She crouched down and shone the light in. Nobody spoke for a minute.

"We found him over by the trees. Pete carried him here. You gotta do something." She was sobbing now, the words catching in her throat.

"There's blood on him. Pete's got it on his jeans."

Jason was huddled on his sleeping bag in the corner. I couldn't see his face.

"Jason?"

He turned his head, arms cradling his chest, mud and blood streaked over his face and hands, his jeans torn and filthy and blood oozing through the denim on his left knee. I crawled in to the tent and knelt down by his side. There wasn't much room and the light was dim. He opened his eyes.

"For God's sake what happened? Can you talk? Where are you hurt? Can you move? I'll call an ambulance."

"No. I can move. No, don't, Cassie," as I reached for my phone.

"We couldn't call the police 'cos..." Amy burst into tears.

"Shut up," said Pete on his knees in the tent flap. "She'll understand. He's had a bit of a beating. We heard him shouting down the field. Some guys ran off as we got there but couldn't see who it was. He just needs to get home that's all. Stop blubbing, Amy. She'll look after him. You take him home, miss, before any one comes back. He'll be alright. Clean him up a bit, that's all. You'll know what to do."

Really? I wished I shared his confidence.

I backed out of the tent. Jason rolled over and managed to crawl on his knees out of the tent, cradling his chest as Pete helped him into the passenger seat. Amy stood like a scared rabbit, her face streaked with tears and a smear of blood. Pete stuck his head through the window.

"Scary shit going down here tonight. There were some bad guys around blabbing their mouths off, trying to muscle in on the local dealers, like. We're gonna keep our mouths shut and get the hell out of it in the morning. Catch the bus back to town early."

"Bring my tent when you leave," I said, nearly speechless with fear for Jason's injuries and anger at the situation he'd got into. "I'll come and find you in the morning. Ten o'clock. Wait in the bus-shelter on the promenade." I couldn't thank them. Not then.

I drove carefully, aware of the risk of drink-driving and transporting a mauled and bloody teenager in my car. I was lucky. The roads were deserted, the first streaks of dawn appearing over the sea. Jason snuffled and was silent. Talking could wait.

I bundled him into the Boat Shed and turned on the lights.

"Sit down before you fall down," I said. "Let's have a look at the damage." I turned the fire on and filled the kettle, putting off the moment when I would have to deal with this. I'd never dealt with scrapes, fights or injuries and I didn't like blood any more than I liked dogs, I thought irrelevantly.

"You'd better tell me what happened, Jason. Now, before I clean you up."

I handed him a tissue. He blew his nose and leaned forward into the light. His face was scratched and there was a gash above his right eye, the blood dried now but had trickled down his cheek onto his neck. His arms and hands were caked in mud and wisps of dried grass and the tear in his jeans had opened up to a bloody knee.

"It was Jem and Zac." I could hardly hear him above the kettle. It turned itself off.

"Your brothers? My God. Go on."

"It was while the bands were on. There were loads of people watching, we all were and then I noticed Jem at the edge of the group by some trees. I was hoping he wouldn't be there but I knew they still came up for the summer. Dad told me. So I kept my head down so he wouldn't see me but I watched him. A guy would break away from the crowd and go over and they'd disappear for a few minutes and then come out back into the crowd. Then someone else would go. They'd got to be dealing. Pete said they were big shots up here trying to muscle in on the local scene."

"So how do you know Pete and Amy? Seems a bit of a coincidence they were the same two I was talking to in Pwllheli."

"Not really. Pete used to come to my mate's house for stuff when I was staying. He was alright. Used to get his fix and crash out in a corner. He's harmless enough but he knows what's going on. That Amy's getting him straight. Scared the shit out of them tonight, though."

I poured hot water into a bowl and hunted for something to clean him up with, tearing up a clean tea-towel. He'd stopped shaking and his voice was stronger.

"So what went wrong?" I said squeezing out the cloth and starting to clean his face. It was mostly scratches. I could cope with that.

"Some guys in the crowd went over and started a bit of pushing around. The music had stopped and people were crowding round. I thought there was going to be a fight. Then Jem started mouthing off. He got one of the guys by his shirt and started shouting at him about how he didn't know nothing about dealing; he was just a little shit and he'd never make the big time. Putting him down grand style, he was.

'Then Zac appeared out of nowhere. He was all over the place, smashed out of his head, leaping around and shouting about pissy little wraps. Then he shouted to Jem and everybody could hear, he said, 'we've got the big bucks coming, ain't we bro?'He started singing, dancing around in this space in the middle of a circle of people like a fucking banshee."

"What do you want me to do with this gash on your head?" I said. "You're the one with the first-aid certificate." I couldn't believe how calmly I was dealing with all this, soaking up his adrenaline-fuelled talk.

"Just cut a plaster up and tape it across, like stitches."

He waved his hand impatiently, wanting to crack on. I didn't want to stop him.

"Then Zac saw me. He shouted, 'Hey, there's our small bro, the one who grassed us up.' It went dead quiet then. People started to disappear. I reckon they knew this was a family thing. I wanted to be friends. They're my brothers after all. I thought it might be okay after all this time."

He hung his head down, using it as an excuse to study his bloody knee but I could see his eyes were wet.

"You'll need to take your jeans off to deal with that knee," I said. "What happened then?"

"Jem said I'd never had that beating he'd promised me. He said I couldn't hide behind dad any more 'cos he wasn't here. Then they started towards me. I ran across the field but it was pitch dark and I couldn't see where I was going. Then the ground sort of gave way and I was standing on the edge of a slope down to a boggy bit at the edge of the wood with dead trees and water below me."

The words tumbled out of him.

"They came up and started pushing me in the chest, tossing me from one to the other and laughing. I couldn't go anywhere. They were saying bad things about dad and the business, calling me a little shit and I needed to keep out of their way. Then I could feel them getting serious, like they were bouncing off each other, then the pushing got harder. I yelled for them to stop. Then Jem punched me hard in the chest and I lost my balance and fell down the slope. There was stinking water and brambles and twigs."

He stifled a sob, upset now after re-living the action, his face pale.

I reached into the shelf behind me, the bottle of Scotch replaced following my uncle's tradition. It had seemed a good idea. I poured two shots into the coffee mugs. He gulped his down.

"I scrambled up the slope but my chest hurt so I just lay there. Then Pete came with Amy. He'd heard me shouting."

We sat in silence and I topped up the Scotch. A blackbird trilled outside and daylight filtered through the window. He put his head back against the chair and closed his eyes. I covered him up with one of the new tartan rugs and decided the knee could wait. I wasn't sure about his chest but he'd stopped hugging it. He needed some down time. I needed time to think.

I tucked him up on the bunk in the caravan after breakfast, his face a mess and his eyebrow a neat lattice of plaster stitches.

"You'll have to deal with the knee yourself," I said and handed him the first-aid kit. I left him with instructions not to move until I came back and not to phone anyone with tales of bravado. I was serious and he knew I meant it. I shut the gates behind me and put the 'CLOSED' notice up.

I drove to Pwllheli, eyes gritty from lack of sleep and found Pete and Amy in the bus-shelter on the front. The tent was propped up against the bench.

"Those guys who beat him up..." Pete started.

"Yeah, the blond ones," Amy said. "Are they his brothers?"

I nodded. The back story was no business of theirs.

"What's going on? I mean, more than usual. You two seem to know what's what," I said, hoping a little flattery would help. "Seems to me poor Jason got something he didn't deserve."

"Well he wouldn't play ball with the County Lines would he?" Pete said. "His mate from the flat told everyone he was a grass 'cos he got busted after Jason ran off. Reckon his brothers think the same thing."

"Why would it bother them, I mean, more than usual?"
Pete shuffled his feet. The sole of his right trainer flapped loose against the tarmac.

"Tell her Pete, I'm sick of all this," Amy said turning away and gazing out towards the marina.
The tide was out and the smells from the black mud wafted rank in the morning sun, flooded the bus-shelter and mingled with the stink of chip papers and stale beer.

"Those brothers, they've bought a boat," he said, "big inflatable job with massive engines. Seen it in the marina. Word is, they're going to be using it for bringing stuff in by sea. The mouthy one kept saying there's more where this came from. Stoned out of his head last night, he was, going on about big deals and the like. Most from outside took no notice but there's a few of us been around here a long time. Reckon there's something big planned but that one couldn't keep his big mouth shut, could he? Boasting he was, about the big time."

"That's why they beat Jason up," Amy said. "In case he knew something. He's not like them. He doesn't do drugs, does he? He's sweet. I like him."

"Gotta go," said Pete. "That's all. Hope he's okay. Just tell him to keep his head down and stay away from up here."
He got up. I needed more. I put my hand on his arm. "Look, any idea when there's going to be a delivery or what or how? Can't just be them involved, can it?" Got to be a story in it, I thought desperately, my buried interest in stories surging to the surface.
He caught the urgency in my voice, but he pushed Amy out of the shelter and away. He'd said enough.

CHAPTER 17

The door to the Harbour Office was open. Will Roberts was in the back office talking to Mark. I stood by the counter and waited, unsure whether I was doing the right thing or not and David's warning about letting the authorities deal with any suspicions ringing in my ears. I studied the wall chart with the moorings for the season and a diagram of the buoys in the channel for the summer months. The sandbanks and the channel shifted every year with the weather and the flow of the rivers and I'd seen Will Roberts out on the harbour launch checking the depths, the hot weather and the long period without rain to sluice the channel, worrying for those with deeper keels.

"Can I talk to you for a minute?" I called over the counter. He came through to the reception. "Outside? Do you mind?"

We leant on the rail watching the gulls. I asked him how his wife was but he didn't want to talk. He asked after Jason, praising his care and kindness for such a young lad.

"That's why I need to tell you, because of what's happened to him. I didn't know what to do or who to talk to and then I thought you were the best person. But just you," I said meaningfully, nodding towards

Mark through the open door. "You'll know what to do."
He lowered his chin into his neck, listening carefully as I told him everything.

"I know it's only gossip but it seemed pretty real last night and the guys who told me were quite clear about what they'd heard."

"The lad alright, is he?"
I nodded. "Shaken up but he'll be okay. I think I'll lock him up for a few weeks." I was half-joking and half-serious.
He pushed himself back from the railings.

"Have you told his dad?"
I'd thought about phoning Arnie, then imagined him heading up the peninsula to Abersoch like a rampaging bull to sort out his two boys in some pub or other and being locked up for his efforts. But they were men now, not teenagers any more to be given a hiding by their dad. I'd seen the distress in his face when he thought he'd lost three of his children to bad times. I'd also thought of the damage that would ensue if his temper got the better of him and he confronted them. I'd also thought, and here I hesitated, if they were involved in something serious they wouldn't be on their own. Arnie Blackwell, despite his formidable strength and size, was not invincible.

"No," I said. "I think I need you to tell me what's best."
He caught the uncertainty in my voice.

"Keep out of it," he said without any hesitation. "I can't tell you why, I'm just telling you, Miss Jones, but thank you for all the information. I'll give it the attention it deserves. Now I suggest you get back to running your business. Not thinking of investigating it yourself, I hope? Making some money from a story perhaps? Leave it with me, if you please."

"Of course," I said, "if that's your advice." In your dreams, I thought.
He dismissed me as gruffly as he had when I first met him. This time I

didn't take offence. I trusted him to do whatever he needed to do. But it wasn't going to stop me being nosy.

Jason recovered from his scratches and bounced back as though nothing had happened. He occupied himself painting and polishing the snack-bar and I waited impatiently for the licence I needed to re-open it before the end of the season. It didn't much matter. There was so much else to do. Hugh Phillips had made a list of the names of the model ships in the room at the back of the shed and checked them against the details in his old copy of 'Porthmadog Ships.' The manager from the museum visited and helped. I dusted them carefully and put them back on the shelves, marvelling at the detail. Neifion seemed to be eating less. I phoned the sea zoo for advice.

"It's just age," the marine biologist said. "He'll probably turn up his claws one morning soon. He's very old."

Doug Peterson came and went out of the yard in his Mercedes, barely raising a hand in greeting if I passed him in the road. Sometimes he was away for a while and Denise popped in for cups of sugar which she didn't need.

"Still don't get it," she said one day. "You'd think he didn't own this place, he's away such a lot. It's as though he hasn't really got a proper interest in it. Not like you with all these new ideas and enthusiasm. He's paid all his bills and it all looks normal now. I checked with the Land Registry and it said the business was owned by a company called 'Tradewind, Inc.' Obviously that's what he trades under."

"Perhaps it's a consortium," I said. "Must have cost a lot to buy the property. Corporate money, perhaps, not just his."

"Yeah well, as long as it's all above board and they pay me at the end of the month..."

The weekend of the race with David to Ireland loomed. I left Jason in charge and packed a bag, my first time out since the beginning of the year. The yacht was moored against a pontoon in Pwllheli Marina and ready for sea when I arrived. David introduced me to Heidi, his co-owner, neat, agile, a short practical haircut and a tan that spoke of an outdoors life. I assumed she and David were partners they were so easy in each other's company. I'd never asked him or anyone else if he was married.

"He's not the sort of person you ask unless you're intending to make a play for him. How crude would that be?" I said on the phone to Trish, "and he's not my type really, although he's a lovely man. I just don't fancy him and he certainly doesn't approve of me half the time."

We slipped out of the marina at nine and headed for the race mark. It was flat calm and I couldn't see us sailing anywhere, never mind Ireland. I sat on the deck as instructed with my back against the cabin roof and soaked up the sun as we motored out to the start line in the bay, the other yachts jostling for places as best they could in a ghost of a breeze. Heidi joined me, pointing out the contenders.

"That's Doug Peterson in the Sigma. Your neighbour, isn't he? He'll be a hard one to beat. He wins a lot of races."

She talked about her job as a geologist with Bangor University. I asked her if she had known David long. It seemed an okay question. She laughed.

"Since he was born," she said. "Quite a long time, in fact. He's my little brother. Didn't he tell you?"

I digested this news as the first cat's paw rippled the surface of the water. If only I'd known. Or would it have made any difference? I liked him a lot, but he was my solicitor. He wasn't my type, as I'd told Trish. But then I didn't really know what my type was any more.

The wind picked up. I was sent into the cockpit and clipped on, tucked in a corner out of the way as the yacht heeled alarmingly and sails were sheeted in. The crew seemed to relish the work as they strained at the winches. Bardsey Sound appeared and disappeared in a misery of vomit as the waves picked up and tossed the boat through seas as confused as I was. Eight hours of this and I knew I would die.

"It'll get better in the open sea," Heidi reassured me, holding the bucket as I heaved. "This is just off the Tripods. It's always nasty here. Big waves and overfalls."

It was nasty all the way. I stopped throwing up in calm seas off the Irish coast in the shelter of Howth Head and had already employed my phone as soon the signal came back. I booked a ferry ticket back from Dublin to Holyhead the following day. Train and bus would do the rest back to Porthmadog as long as it was dry land. Never again, I swore to myself as we nosed into a berth in the marina.

I found the showers and luxuriated under the hot water, washing away the day. I dried my hair carefully, determined to put on a brave and well-groomed appearance after all the puke and misery. The bright lights in the shower room showed up the parting in the middle of my scalp, now nut-brown with the constant exposure to the sun, the purple hair colour fading into streaks with my natural black. I made an effort with the styling and felt better, blessing my hairdresser for the perfect cut, my one luxury in a world of dirt and overalls.

I swung open the shower room door and headed back to the boat, feeling altogether more human. Doug Peterson stood in front of me on the ramp leading back to the pontoons. He stopped and I stopped. There was no way round. We stood like a couple of sparring partners, his face tanned from the day's sailing and the eyes as piercing as ever. He hadn't spoken to me since I'd moved into the yard and even on brief eye contact through the car window he still made me feel like a schoolgirl.

"Sick?"

Something in his voice stopped me walking around him, the mocking, patronising tone I'd remembered softer, even quizzical. Or was it mocking?

"Very," I said. It was pointless saying anything else. He would have known during the post-race gossip that David's new protégé couldn't hack it.

He shrugged. "It wears off," he said and moved round me and up the ramp.

I joined the party in the Yacht Club that night, reluctant to face the hardened sailors of the day but persuaded by Heidi that I needed to shrug it off.

"They've all been seasick at one time or another. It's no disgrace. You'll get used to it."

"No I won't," I said. "No chance. Never again." But at least I'd showed my face, my pride still intact.

Doug Peterson celebrated his win as predicted, holding court and surrounded by his admiring crew. I slipped out early, feeling completely alienated from the scene and made my way back to the boat. I curled up in my sleeping bag and slept fitfully in the cramped bunk in the forecabin, my head full of monstrous waves and curling crests and the sound of the wind whining in the rigging. I thanked David and Heidi for the experience the following morning and ran for the train to Dublin, relishing the solid earth under my feet and the thought of my business waiting for me, my brief intimidating encounter with Doug Peterson receding in a rush of optimism.

Ed visited briefly, as promised, back from his annual fishing trip with the rude skipper from Pwllheli. Journalism seemed a million miles away with the stuffy office and the list of jobs cataloguing the detritus of other people's lives. That was how I remembered it, not favourably, used now to being my own boss and regulating my own life.

It was good to see him. He loved the yard and the shed and the model ships. "Amazing," he kept saying, "and this is all yours?" as he picked up old blocks from the shelves and ran his hand down the planks of timber.

"As long as the money lasts. It seems to be rushing out like the tide at the moment. I need to start earning soon, at least for next year. Then we'll see."

He sat comfortably outside the shed door with a pannad and a slice of Helen's Nain's cake. He was still overweight and the plastic legs of the chair splayed alarmingly when he moved. "You're not still chasing this drugs thing, surely with all this to look after?"

"I might be," I said, then decided to tell him, "in fact, yes, I am. I don't know what to do with it for the best though, if I'm around when something breaks. Pics and stuff. The money would be useful."

He drank his tea and finished the cake and only moved when the sun disappeared behind the cliff and shadows lengthened in the yard. It was August after all.

"Will you go back to work on a newspaper?" he asked.

A blackbird sang from the wisps of willow herb in the rocks above us. The tide had turned and slid in green and silent, changing the view in a way so familiar now I could judge the hour by the marks of the water on the posts on Ballast Island and the disappearing banks as the water darkened the sand and covered the rocky beach.

I felt his eyes on my face. What could I say?

"Perhaps not," he said. "It's very beautiful here." He fished in his pocket, and brought out an envelope.

"You'll find names and contact numbers of a few chosen news-desks up here. Might be useful if you just happen to be in the right place at the right time. Always take your camera and be careful," he said and looked at me meaningfully.

He levered himself out of the chair.

"Tim sends his regards. He's up here on holiday too. He'll be visiting you soon, no doubt. Good luck with the business."

I walked him to the car and shut the gates for the day, the air chilly in the shade. I wondered what winter would bring, my head already full of plans for the following summer. The air was still, the silence almost palpable.

The muffled sound of an engine filtered through the quiet. A late visitor heading for a mooring on the incoming tide and a pub meal after a day at sea, I thought, but not a sailing boat. These were heavy-duty diesels with a powerful purr. The white superstructure of a powerboat slid into view like a wedding cake against the grey water, navigated the harbour buoy and slowed to a standstill opposite me in the channel, angling in to the wall of Doug Peterson's yard. Bow-thrusters buzzed and the boat nosed in to the pontoon. I recognised Gareth who jumped off and tied mooring ropes to the cleats

It was bigger than any of the powerboats for sale next door and an unusual sight for the estuary, the name 'Pegasus' picked out in gold letters on the stern. Doug Peterson, standing on the fly-bridge stopped the engines and took off his baseball cap. He ran his hand over the cropped hair and pushed his sunglasses on top of his head. He surveyed the lie of the boat like a victorious gladiator, pointing and calling instructions to Gareth on the pontoon.

"Bloody hell," said Jason, creeping up on me.

"I thought you'd gone home," I said. "What do you think of that, then?"

He pondered a moment, staring at the powerboat. "Do you always wrinkle your nose when you don't like something?" he asked.

"Do I?"

"You did then. It was quite funny. You didn't know I was watching. Arrogant shit, isn't he, that Doug? Never speaks to me. Acts like God's gift, you know? And Gareth pretends he is. Saw him in the pub the other night flashing his new watch around like his boss does. He must be doing okay to afford an expensive Seiko."

We stood and watched as Gareth adjusted ropes and fenders.

"Haven't seen a boat that posh in here before," Jason said. "Must be worth a fortune. See you tomorrow."

Denise and I passed each other in Tesco the following morning. Curiosity about the 'Pegasus' got the better of me.

"You mean the 'Fairline' that came in last night? It belongs to a client wanting some new batteries installed. It's usually based in Pwllheli but the owner's away and all the mechanics are booked up. Doug's booked Gareth for the week to finish it by Friday then take it back to the marina."

"Everything going alright with the business, then? You were a bit worried a while back."

She shrugged. "Seems okay. They were dead snappy with each other this morning, Doug going on about Gareth doing a proper job 'cos it's an expensive boat. Gareth didn't like that. You could cut the air in the office with a knife. Mind you if he's still using dodgy parts, Doug won't know the difference as long as it all works. He's away again for a few days and back on Friday. Not my problem. See you later."

I heard the boat's engines start up on Friday evening as I was shutting the gates. Muted voices and footsteps on the planks rose up from the pontoon below the wall. I had a sudden urge to watch and listen, the memory of Tomas and his eavesdropping sharp in my mind. I opened the one gate and slid out through the narrow gap, pulling it to behind me and crawled into the overgrown patch of bramble and buddleia separating the two yards. I squirmed through the undergrowth until I was level with the top of the wall almost opposite and level with Doug Peterson now on the bridge of 'Pegasus' and Gareth below sorting out ropes.

He was talking on his phone sandwiched between his shoulder and ear, one hand on the wheel and the other pressing instruments on the console. I knew enough to guess it was a GPS Gareth cast the ropes off, jumped on board as the bow-thrusters whined and the boat edged out and turned in mid-channel. I couldn't help my reluctant respect in the manoeuvring, my only experience of moving boats in tight places limited to 'Annie', with her grimy ship's wheel and unreliable turning circle. I slid out of the prickly space, dusted off the dead leaves, let myself back into the yard and closed the gate behind me, watching the white hull disappear up the estuary towards the sea. I checked my watch; two hours to high tide. They would be in Pwllheli in thirty minutes.
So would I.

I couldn't explain to myself why I went, especially after Will Robert's warning. It wasn't a burning desire any more to catch a story, a feature for my own personal use but a combination of tenuous links that made me query my own sense of reason, a restlessness, a fear of Doug Peterson that prevented me from settling and a need for closure to the gossip and tales I'd heard, heightened by Jason's experience with his foul brothers. Whatever. I could always come back if nothing happened and laugh it off. But I hadn't forgotten Ed's advice.

Piling my camera, recorder and spare batteries, notebook and pens, a bottle of water, bread and cheese and apples into a carrier, I checked I'd got the envelope Ed had given me. The phone was ready to put on charge in the car, the Corsa less conspicuous than the Toyota. I phoned Jason before I set off to say I'd be staying with a friend for the night. I didn't want him involved.

I drove slowly down the lane leading to town, stopping in the lay-by at the bottom of Pen Cei steps to plug in the phone and took the road to Pwllheli, catching glimpses of the powerboat out at sea running parallel to the beach at Criccieth and Abererch and finally turned off the road over the river and railway line to the marina. The road to the breakwater passed the marina office, boat yards and yacht chandlers now closed for the night and ended in a small roundabout and a turning circle. The entrance to the harbour lay below the fence, the deep-water channel marked by beacons. I parked away from the fence, the grey Corsa blending into the landscape of dunes and scrub but I didn't think anyone negotiating the narrow channel below me in a boat would bother to look up. 'Pegasus' appeared like a white swan on the grey water, approached the Fairway buoy, slowed and headed for the entrance. I saw the dark outline of Doug Peterson clear on the bridge and Gareth on the deck.

I took some pictures, despite the failing light and shot off back to the marina in the car, scanning the sea of masts for the moving boat but everything was still. I walked along the top of the walkway outside the main reception for a better view of the entrance to the pontoons. The boat had turned just inside the entrance and was berthing on the diesel pontoon, the one I remembered passing as we left for the race to Ireland. I backed against the wall, glad I'd had the sense to wear a black wool hat pulled down over my ears. The purple streaks were fading but were still bright enough to identify me.

A member of staff walked down the pontoon to the boat to operate the diesel pump and I mentally squirmed as I imagined the invoice from the quantity of fuel. Which way would they go now? On to a pontoon or out towards the sea? I guessed out to sea and ran back to the car, drove back to the dead end by the roundabout with my camera round my neck and clicked the shutters as the boat swung into the ebb tide, motored along the channel past the beacon again and out into the bay. It turned to starboard and out past Gimlet Rock, out of my line of sight, the harbour lights now full on and winking as darkness fell. I stood there for a moment, feeling the chill of the night round my ankles, suddenly very lonely and wondering what to do next.

Headlights out of nowhere pierced the gloom and a dusty black VW with a sea kayak tied to the roof rack pulled in beside me, the driver's window wound down. I couldn't quite believe my eyes.

"Tim?"

"Hi Cassie." It was almost as though he'd been expected, but Ed did say he was on holiday and threatened a visit. He grinned. "Not much point in being a journalist if you can't do a bit of sleuthing. Passed you at the end of your road. You didn't see me so I just followed you. Thought you might be up to something. Ed mentioned you were onto a story. Are you?"

I took my hat off and ran my hand through my hair, disbelief mixed with pleasure. I didn't think I'd be glad to see anybody, especially Tim, but I was. He'd said if I ever needed help to let him know and I'd laughed. He'd been an annoying, immature geek in the office and it wasn't that long ago, but he'd also been quick, nosy and liked good stories.

"I think I might be," I said. "If you don't want to come, just go away and keep quiet, alright? It's just a hunch."

"I like hunches," he said. "If I can help, count me in."

He followed me out of the marina, along the promenade towards the sea and turned left down through the council estate, past a boatyard and the lifeboat station. We parked the cars and found the footpath up to Gimlet Rock, a jagged chunk of cliff standing above the beach. I'd seen it from the sea as we left the marina on my sailing trip to Ireland.

"I'll warn you now," I said, packing all my stuff into a rucksack and retrieving a warm jacket from the back seat. "I'm going to stay here as long as it takes. I'll tell you what's been happening and you can decide for yourself if you want to stay."

The geek image I had of him disappeared as he produced a hand-held radio and binoculars from the glove box.

“Marine radio. I use it when I go kayaking to tell the coastguard where I’m going. Tell me the story then.”

There was a lot to tell.

It was five in the morning when the first blackbird trilled, a yellow streak of dawn creeping into the grey sky above Harlech and outlining the Rhinnogs beyond. I pulled myself out of an uneasy doze, cold and stiff but not ready to give up yet. The radio had been quiet apart from the shipping forecasts. The weather was forecast to deteriorate with severe gales later that day. Tim got up and went for a pee, disappearing briefly behind a rock, the sea black and menacing below. Along the shingle beach to the west, breakers were beginning to curl and break white as the breeze picked up.

A clear voice on Channel 16 calling Holyhead Coastguard pierced the silence and shook me out of my stupor. Tim shot back into view, zipping up his trousers and snatching up the radio from the top of the rucksack. He flicked through to the requested channel. Fishing vessel ‘Viva’ was reporting black smoke billowing from a powerboat in the overfalls to the west of Porth Ceiriad, now heading towards it and standing by for instructions.

We waited for the next transmission staring futilely out to sea, the fire miles away and out of sight as the dawn light was shattered by headlights below the Rock, beams bouncing into the air as cars drove over the speed-bumps on the approach road to the lifeboat station. The grassy slope behind us gave a full view, car headlights picking out the hulls of boats in the yard below and figures running like black ants into the station. The lifeboat launched in a blaze of search-light and worked its way down the harbour to the beacon where it powered up in a welter of white water, the bows lifting to the swell off the Fairway Buoy, and turned west towards the Tudwal Islands lying like sleeping black tortoises in the distance. Channel 16 flashed on the radio screen.

"This is Holyhead Coastguard. Holyhead Coastguard. Any vessels in the vicinity of Porth Ceiriad to go to the assistance of a powerboat reported on fire in the region of Trwyn Cilan."

A warbling sound trilled from the radio.

"That's the lifeboat alert. It goes to Channel 0. We can't get Channel 0," Tim said, staring out to sea, screwing up his eyes in frustration behind the specs. "We'll just have to wait."

We ran down to the path and drove through the sleeping holiday chalets to the point by the harbour entrance.

"I want you to stay here," I said, "and call me when the lifeboat comes back in. I'm going back over to the marina."

I didn't need to ask him twice, the irritating junior reporter I remembered long gone and the professional kicking in.

"Thanks," I said, touching his arm, "I'm glad you came."

I let myself through the security gate into the marina, the code filed away in my head from the trip to Ireland and made my way to a pontoon near the marina entrance, tucked behind a yacht and sat on the cold planks with my back resting on an electricity bollard. The sockets were empty, the sailing season slowly coming to an end and the hustle and bustle I'd seen on the race day a distant memory. I sat for an hour. I shivered and my stomach rumbled as the early sun glazed over with high cloud and the breeze gusted and set the shrouds tapping against the masts around me.

Then like a war-zone where nothing happens for long periods of time and suddenly all hell breaks loose, cars started to arrive at the marina car park, the sound of engines cutting through the still of the morning air. Police and a mechanic in overalls clattered through the security gate and down the ramp. I hid behind the bollard and they marched past me to the end of the pontoon, their feet echoing in the still marina. My mobile buzzed.

Tim phoned. "You'd better be ready for this," he said. "I'll come back to the Marina office where I can see more."

I crouched down behind the hull of a yacht with the camera ready, clicking the shutter as the lifeboat appeared, towing the white hull of 'Pegasus', both boats lining up on the end of the hammerhead. A lifeboat man shouted instructions from the bridge of the powerboat as the hull came to rest. Gouts of black water pulsed into the marina from hoses in the cockpit. The lifeboat moored up, the engines throbbed quietly, the lifeboat crew released the tow-rope, lowered a gangplank and secured the boat to the pontoon.

The scene seemed to draw its own breath, a pause button in an action movie, a still-life of tall masts and sleek hulls like resting racehorses. The uniformed police figures waited whilst ropes were tied and fenders fixed. I held my breath and kept still, waiting for the inevitable sight of Doug Peterson and Gareth to appear on the lifeboat's ramp. My phone buzzed.

"Keep your head down," said Tim. "There's a gurney coming."

Two men pushed a stretcher down the pontoon, the wheels clattering on the wooden slats. I held my breath and crouched down as they stopped at the base of the lifeboat's ramp. A black body-bag on a stretcher was carried down the ramp and loaded onto the gurney. The men wheeled it back towards the marina reception. I sneaked a picture, my palms damp with sweat. Who was in the bag? Gareth or Doug Peterson? I was desperate to know.

The pumps continued to spout water from 'Pegasus.' The policemen climbed on board and disappeared down below.

I phoned Tim. "See if you can poach a WiFi signal from the marina office and wait there for me."

A few spatters of rain marked the dry planks of the pontoon and galvanised me into action. Throwing my camera over one shoulder I ran to the hammerhead where the lifeboat was moored. I held up my old press card to the lifeboat man left on the pontoon. "Press. Can I speak to the boss? The cox?"

"You didn't waste any time, did you?" he said. "Don't know as he'll tell you much, though. Hang on a minute."

I waited, the drops of rain dampening my hair. I tucked the camera into my jacket, notebook at the ready as the cox jumped down onto the pontoon.

"Press. Local," I lied. "Have you got a story for me? Anything please? The main papers'll be here soon and I won't get a look in."

I could see he was desperate to leave.

"Please? I was waiting for you to come back in. I've been up on the Rock all night. I know something's going on. I heard the call-out and saw you leave."

He scratched the back of his head and considered me for a moment. A gust of wind blew my hair over my face. I must have looked a wreck.

"We were called out to a powerboat with an engine fire," he said.

"Yes?"

"There was some activity involving the Border Patrol."

"And? Come on mate, it's going to hit the press later anyway. Who was on board? What was the Border Patrol investigating?"

"You'll get the full story on the press release later. The Border Patrol intercepted a significant drugs haul at Porth Meudwy and seized a sizeable amount of cocaine. Several arrests were made on land by police. That's all I can say."

"So what about the two guys in Pegasus'? I saw them go out on the tide last night. I know who they are. Where are they now, then? Who's in the body-bag?"

He drew a breath, impatient to get away, loath to say much more, I could tell.

"The Abersoch ILB is currently looking for one person reported missing overboard from the boat. It will continue to search unless the weather deteriorates. That's it, miss." He turned away and walked back up the ramp.

Pegasus tugged gently at her mooring ropes as the wind picked up. I watched as a head appeared out of the cockpit and the man in overalls climbed off.

"I'll be back when I'm told it's okay," he called to the policeman inside the cabin.

I tucked my camera well into my coat and hurried after him along the pontoon, my hat now firmly back on my head covering my hair completely.

"Excuse me. I was looking for Gareth the mechanic?" I said, a little breathless as he turned round. "I work for Doug Peterson. There are some messages for Gareth about work and he's not answering his phone. I just called in on my way to work to see if I could catch him. He said he'd be here. And then I saw all this." I waved my hand towards Pegasus. "What's going on?"

"Call out to the coastguard, love. Boat was on fire and they found a body in the cockpit. They're not saying much. Gareth's not around if you're looking for him. Whatever, he's a lazy good-for-nothing bastard. Did some work on Pegasus at your place in Porthmadog, didn't he? Lovely boat that was. Nearly burned her to bits, stupid bugger."

"No," I said, as wide-eyed as I could manage. "Not Gareth. Why? What did he do? Is he the one who's dead?"

The man glared at me.

"One thing he didn't do, whether it was him or not," he said, "was put his tools away. Looks as though the lazy sod left all his spanners loose. Stuff all over the engine compartment. Boat hit the race at Trwyn Cilan, I reckon, and bounced it around in the waves. A spanner or wrench or whatever hit the terminals and shorted the new batteries he'd put in. Sparks, love. Big sparks. Smouldering cables running next to fibreglass minus the insulation he couldn't be arsed to put back. Black smoke enough to scare the shit out of anyone. There's just about enough left in the mess to see what happened. Lucky it didn't sink. Have to wait until the forensic guys have been before I can get to it."

"Forensics? Why them? They only come after crimes, don't they?" I asked.

"Yeah, well if I know anything about your boss I can imagine he wouldn't be too pleased if he found out Gareth did a lousy job and caused the fire."

"So you think it's Gareth then, who's dead?" I asked, trying to look shocked. "A fight, or burned to death or something? That's terrible."
He shrugged. "Can't tell which of them's in the bag They won't say. They're out looking for the other one. But not for long," he said, looking at the sky. "If he couldn't swim well, he wouldn't stand a chance. That boat was a long way off-shore. It's going to blow like stink. You'd best get off the pontoon love, while you still can. Just have to hope for the best for whoever's out there. Rather him than me."

I looked with him up at the scudding clouds now billowing into a strange formation like folds of grey cotton wool, the predicted change in the weather gathering on the horizon. The wind would whip the sea into a maelstrom outside the safety of the harbour, a grey, heaving terror of peaks and troughs and tumbling white water. I fought with mixed feelings of dislike for both men, but would never wish for a death in such terrifying circumstances even though my fear of Doug Peterson surviving clawed at my stomach. If it was him out there and not Gareth and he was rescued and sent to prison, he'd find out it was me who was responsible for alerting the authorities. I thought of his hard eyes and that compelling way of looking through you. He'd never let it go. He'd never forgive.

I glanced back at the lifeboat now motoring back to its moorings and 'Pegasus' bucking like the white horse of its namesake as small waves broke against its bows and the pontoon started to flex under my feet.

I left. There was nothing I could do except meet up with Tim, send my pictures over to the news-desks Ed had given me, hope they'd be accepted from a mere civilian who happened to be in the right place at the right time and that my lies to the lifeboat man didn't catch up with me.

CHAPTER 18

We sat in the yard in the late sunshine that afternoon after the flash storm, short and sharp with violent winds and torrential rain, my phone busy from newspapers calling, eyes gritty from lack of sleep. The heavy rain had spattered the cars, tables and chairs with gravel dust and run in rusty torrents off the roof of the shed. Jason wiped the chairs dry and made tea. I fetched the Scotch. Denise came over; she didn't need sugar, just comfort, her eyes smudged blue with tears and disbelief and the reality of a yard with no news of her boss or Gareth.

"Can't see how he would have survived," Tim said, as he fiddled with his marine radio for Channel 16, "whoever it was."

The Welsh news that afternoon had been saturated with the seizing of a major consignment of cocaine from a yacht and a local powerboat, a collaborative effort between North Wales Police and the Border Force. Twin brothers, they said, known to be drug dealers had been arrested along with members of a new County Lines gang supplying the area. One body had been recovered from the powerboat which had been reported on fire out in Tremadoc Bay. The Pwllheli and Abersoch lifeboats had now resumed their search for another person reported to be on board. A yacht suspected of carrying illegal drugs from the West

Indies into the country and transferring them to the powerboat had been escorted into Holyhead by the Border Patrol boat. The skipper and crew were arrested.

We'd been sitting there, it seemed forever, a gathering of shocked souls drinking tea and supping whisky as the hours wore on, waiting for news of the identity of both men that would affect each one of us in different ways. Will Roberts arrived in his Harbour Master's uniform, a brief nod to me signalling he'd already known a plan was in place to intercept the boat but the timing of my information was essential. I'd done the right thing then even though I'd disobeyed him. He didn't mention my involvement. He had no news of either person on board. Jason poured him tea.

Then his phone rang. His face was solemn as he left his seat and walked over to the harbour wall to take the call. He returned to the table slowly.

"They've identified the body recovered from the 'Pegasus'," he said, looking at Angela. "I'm afraid it's Gareth."

Angela turned to him with a mixed expression on her face, her ex-partner Gareth, the man she hated and blamed for the death of her child. I could only guess how she was feeling.

"But that means... How did he die?"

"To be blunt, Angie, and you'll find out details soon enough, anyway, they're treating it as a murder enquiry. They found his wallet with his cards in it. It's not been released officially to the press just yet."

"That means that Doug is still missing. Did he kill Gareth and then jump overboard to escape? He must have been mad. It must be two miles to the land and then there was the storm. Could he still be alive?" Angie asked.

"Yes, it's possible," he said.

"Good God," Denise said, her face ashen against the bright lipstick.

"What will happen if he comes back here? He'll guess..." She turned to me.

The silence cut through the evening birdsong. My queasiness turned to nausea.

"The police will be out looking for him on land as well as the lifeboats at sea. It might be best, Cassie, to take their advice on where to stay tonight unless we hear any different," Will Roberts said.

Then Arnie Blackwell's white Range Rover crunched in over the gravel. He got out and went round to the back door, letting a small child slide to the ground. He walked across holding the child's hand in his big paw, his eyes resting on Jason and a warm smile of acknowledgement.

"You've heard about the twins being arrested?" Lines were etched deep round his eyes, his voice faltering as Jason got up and moved to stand by his father.

"Where's mum?" he asked, glancing over to the car.

Arnie shook his head.

"Gone," he said.

They needed to talk. What was there to say to a private family tragedy? I crouched down to the level of the child's brown eyes.

"Hello," I said. "I'm Cassie. You must be Ben."

He looked solemnly at me, an ice-cream cone dripping in one hand.

"You've got purple hair," he said.

"And you've got ice-cream on your nose. Would you like to meet my lobster?"

I stayed in Helen's room at her Nain's for the week. It seemed strange but safe with no news of washed-up bodies and no arrests. The sea search for Doug Peterson had been called off. I lived in a bubble of uncertainty even though I was assured he was unlikely to be alive. He could have reached land, I kept saying, on any one of the remote beaches and coves and just disappeared. His hard eyes pierced my dreams and I tossed and turned in bed, sitting up by the window in the small hours looking for shadows in the street lights.

"You've lost weight, cariad," Helen's Nain said over the morning pannad, pushing a plate of brownies towards me.

I shook my head. "Sorry. I'm not hungry. I can't eat, can't sleep, can't work. What am I going to do, Helen's Nain, if they never find him? I just know he'll come for me. He's got the hardest, most unforgiving eyes I've ever seen." I could feel the tears starting. "I can't do anything about it, can I?"

"Well then, you'd better take your mind off it and let time take its course. These stock sheets need checking and you're running out of hard wood. Hugh says you need to source some suppliers soon."

It would be another few days before news came.

CHAPTER 19

Abersoch, just down the coast, the beach crowded with holiday makers. The child near the rocks wore a pink sunhat with a floppy brim. It was the hat people on the beach saw first, before they heard the screams shrilling along the soft sand, a high-pitched, relentless sound over the gentle breaking of the waves. The mother ran, others scrambled to their feet and followed her towards the source, a primeval curiosity drawing them unwillingly down the beach to a rocky outcrop thickly laced with seaweed. The mother snatched up the child and the group gathered around. A pink plastic bucket and spade lay abandoned on the tide-line.

A hand emerged from the weed like Excalibur, pale and wrinkled from the sea, six inches of wrist twined with brown ribbons of weed like wet snakes. A wave broke on the rocks, lifted the weed and the mass shifted, the white wrist and hand swayed gently as the water surged and bubbled. A flash of silver caught the sunlight. A man bent down to look.

"Christ, do you reckon that's the guy who went missing from the powerboat, you know, during that drugs bust, a couple of weeks ago?" he said to his mate who bent down, unperturbed, to look closer at the remains of the bloated face.

"I know him," his mate said, "at least, I recognise that watch. It's Doug Peterson. My lad keeps his jet-ski in his yard. That's his Rolex. Arrogant sod."

"Shouldn't speak ill of the dead," said a woman. The crowd drew back in horrified silence.

An incoming wave picked up the weed, separating the tendrils and outlining a human form, the head jammed between two rocks and the face turned towards the sky. Small green crabs scuttled out of the eye sockets and down the bridge of the nose.

The man punched a number into his phone.

I was varnishing the oars belonging to my great-uncle's rowing skiff when the Harbour Master's pickup drew up by the Boat Shed door. Will Roberts climbed out. I could tell by the relieved look on his face there was news.

"Bit of closure for you now, Miss Jones. You'll stay and make a go of the business now, I hope?" he said, glancing at the oars. "You'll need five coats on those, by the way."

After he'd gone, I sat on the upturned hull of the skiff and contemplated my new life as the gulls wheeled past and the tides transformed the world at my feet every six hours. Would I go back to London, as my mother wished, look for another job on a newspaper and leave all this behind? Not a chance.